River of Sins

A Bradecote
and Catchpoll Mystery

SARAH HAWKSWOOD

Allison & Busby Limited
11 Wardour Mews
London W1F 8AN
allisonandbusby.com

First published in Great Britain by Allison & Busby in 2020.

Copyright © 2020 by SARAH HAWKSWOOD

A CIP catalogue record for this book is available from
the British Library.

First Edition

ISBN 978-0-7490-2619-6

Typeset in 11/16 pt Adobe Garamond Pro by
Allison & Busby Ltd.

The paper used for this Allison & Busby publication
has been produced from trees that have been legally sourced
from well-managed and credibly certified forests.

Printed and bound by
CPI Group (UK) Ltd, Croydon, CR0 4YY

For H. J. B.

Chapter One

The Feast of St Mary Magdalene, July 1144

The woman moaned, very softly, as consciousness returned. Her head ached. She was moving, and in a boat, for she could hear the soft sound of water parting and closing as the paddles dipped. She was gagged and bound, and wrapped in some cloth which she felt she knew. Yes, it was the feel of the coverlet of her bed. She did not struggle, and part of her wondered why. For a moment she questioned whether this had been some form of kidnapping, to sell her to a foreign trader. It made no sense, but then none of it did. The boat seemed to glide through the water as though the world had no cares in it and was at peace. Her captor spoke not a word, beyond the occasional grunting breath as he rowed.

They did not go very far, she thought. She wished they had, for then she would have had more precious time. There was a scraping of wood, a splash and a muttered oath as a line failed to catch at the first attempt, then the rope tightened, and the boat juddered and stilled. She was more dragged than lifted onto dry land, and her aching head was bumped again. She was rolled out of the cloth onto dewy grass and found herself gazing up into a softly lit sky, just past the sun's full rise over the horizon. A skylark was singing.

The gag was removed from her mouth, and she was pulled into a sitting position, but her hands were kept bound behind her. She looked at him, and at the axe in his hand. She ought to be afraid. She was not, and she thought that unsettled him. He wanted her to plead? Well, she would not, because she had seen men look like that before. They wanted to hear the pleading, and then do what they wanted anyway. Even at the last she would not give a man that satisfaction, whatever other satisfaction she had given men over the years.

'Why? And why here? Where is here?' she mumbled, her mouth still dry, and looked about her. They were on some small islet in the river, and it was familiar, but from long ago. She frowned as she dragged the memory from the depths.

'Do you not recognise it?' The voice was hard. 'No, perhaps you were too young. You do not know why either, but I will tell you that. Your mother was found floating down the Severn, but that was just the end of it. This is where it happened, where he discovered her whoring. The other man escaped by diving into the water, but she did not. He had the right to punish her for her faithlessness, and you are as bad. It must be in the blood from her. He dragged her to the water, down one of the slopes, and held her under till she stopped struggling. Then he let her float away. Why do you think we left? Grief?'

The headache was replaced by spinning – but spinning of thoughts. It was impossible, surely it was impossible? And if it was not . . . She felt sick then. There were some deeds too repellent.

'No.' She refuted the thought with the word.

'Yes. I did not recognise you either, otherwise I would not . . .' His face contorted.

'But you have lived in Worcester all these past years and . . .' She shook her head. Her memories were hazy, of a boy teetering upon the edge of manhood, about to change but still gangly of limb and indeterminate of voice.

'Why should I link The Whore of Worcester with a little girl I last saw when she was a snivelling brat of five summers.'

She ignored the question. 'When did he die?' She wanted to know that at least, how many years the man she recalled as big and brutish, and always angry, had lived with a taken life upon his soul.

'A year after we left. Some inflammation of the lungs took him. He had me apprenticed in a good craft, so I was secure. I worked hard, hard enough to earn the hand of my master's daughter, and when he died, well, I had my own business.'

'So he sort of drowned too.' She was glad. 'Fitting, I would say.'

He struck her across the face. It hurt, but what did it matter. Soon there would be no more hurt.

'If I am like my mother, then you are like him, a bully who blames others for his own failings. You will kill me to take the "taint" of our sinning together from you, blame me, but it was you who came to my door, you who paid the coin.'

9

Yes, as always, the man blamed the woman. It was the woman's fault for tempting, the wife's fault for not tempting enough. They thought themselves better, but they were simply bigger and more powerful. He was a *nithing*, a bully's whelp, for all he held the axe.

She did the last thing she could do to show he did not have command of her; she laughed. Her laughter was a little ragged, and in her head were a jumble of urgent thoughts: she would be alone, without comfort, but she had always been alone all her life; better this sudden end beneath the blue heavens and with a skylark's song in her ears than old and raddled and cold in the dark. Then there was the desperate rush of thought. She did not want to die, not yet. She prayed silently as he grabbed her by her dark chestnut hair, and the laugh grew shrill. *Holy Mary, pray for us sinners . . .* She was still laughing as the axe struck home.

The lad bringing the swine to the water's edge had not seen much, thanks be to God, thought Heribert, the manor reeve of Bevere. It was enough to turn a grown man's stomach, and his had turned as soon as he realised that crows were pecking at human remains. As he had rowed across the narrow channel where the Severn parted about the islet, he had been telling himself that it was some beast that had swum across to Bevere Island and died there, but no natural death would have left the raw and bloodied mess, and he could still see clothing. He coughed, swallowed hard and returned to shore, grim-faced. He strode with purpose to the manor, took the pony from the stable and rode with urgency into Worcester. Although it was but a few miles, the lord sheriff would expect to hear of this immediately, and four feet were much faster than two. He would have to tell Father Prior also, since the land was in the priory's holding.

It was a solemn man, slightly out of breath and still with a sickly pallor, who presented himself in the castle. He was out of luck in seeking the lord sheriff, since William de Beauchamp was gone three days past to one of his outlying manors. He did, however, find the undersheriff, the lord Bradecote, who had come into Worcester to order new boots, since his lady told him that his complaints at the leaking of his old and very comfortable pair were as regular as the priest saying the offices, and that they were indeed beyond repair. He had spent a half-hour with the man recommended by Serjeant Catchpoll as the best in Worcester and was now back at the castle enjoying an exchange of news before departing for home.

'The swine boy saw it first, my lord, crows fighting over something large on the island. Praise be he is not older and more curious. I took the boat across and' – Heribert the Reeve shook his head – 'I never wants to see the like of it again. A soldier might have seen such a sight upon a battlefield, but no peaceable man would . . .' He wiped a hand, one that shook slightly, across his mouth. 'There was blood, so much blood, and the body hacked about so that it looked like something from a flesherman's block, and the face was . . . gone. I could not even tell you if it was man or woman, for I did not look close to try and find out. I came here, as fast as the pony would bring me, my lord. God in Heaven save us from whoever did this.' He crossed himself devoutly.

'You did the right thing, Master Reeve. You say there was much blood. Was it fresh, the corpse?'

'Must be, my lord, for my boys was down at the bank opposite last evening, larking about at the water's edge. It had been hot, and they had worked hard till an hour before sunset. What is on that island now would have been noticed.'

'Is your boat always tied to the bank?' Serjeant Catchpoll, who had been alerted by a guard that a man was come to report a body, had entered the chamber silently and was leaning against the wall by the doorway.

'Aye, it is, in the summer months. It is brought out of the water come October, afore the winter rains and rising waters swell the channel.'

'So, everyone in Bevere knows it is there?' Catchpoll wanted to be sure.

'In the manor and in Claines itself. There is no secret to it. I do as my father did before me and use it to take sheep across for the new grass in spring, though it does not take them long to crop it short, and I fish, when there is the time.'

'Do any others use it?' asked Bradecote.

'Well, I would say as a good many young couples have "borrowed" it so that they might watch the sunset together without fear of disturbance, if you get my—'

'Yes, we do.' Bradecote had no time to listen to local courting customs. 'We will come back with you to Bevere, and if we may borrow your boat, we will see what has happened for ourselves.'

'And do I have to . . .' It was clear that the reeve had no wish to return to the scene of bloodshed and gore.

'No, you need do nothing except lend us the boat and some sacking, or covering, for the corpse.'

'I can provide that, my lord.' Heribert the Reeve sounded very relieved.

'Then let us be on the move. Is Walkelin about, Catchpoll?'

'Last saw him by the priory gate being shouted at by Mistress Longstaff for not finding her cat.'

'We look for lost cats, Catchpoll?'

'No, my lord, assuredly we do not, but the old woman thinks we should.'

'Then I am sure he will be delighted to leave Worcester and come to help us.'

'Help us, my lord?'

'He can row.'

'Ah yes, now that is a very good use of an apprentice serjeant.' Catchpoll gave a fleeting grin, but then his face settled into its usual grim and wary lines. 'I am already thinking that whatever was used to hack the body is on the river bottom.'

'Unless it was something needed by the killer every day. Wash it clean in the river and walk away with it in clear view as any man might with an axe over his shoulder or a knife at his belt.'

The reeve, whose colour had gradually been returning to normal, went pale again.

'No. I will not believe it.'

'Believe what, Master Reeve?'

'Would not hurt a soul, not him.'

'Who?' cried undersheriff and serjeant in near unison.

'Edmund, son of Gyrth. Bit slow he is, but gentle with

13

things. I saw him with an axe over his shoulder this morning, and he said as he was taking off a branch of the elm that was lightning struck last week and looks like to fall.'

'Which he might well have done. We are not saying any man with an axe is the killer.' Catchpoll often wondered how his fellow men could jump to conclusions. 'As the lord Bradecote said, let us be on our way.' He ushered the reeve out, and, as Bradecote came abreast of him, muttered, 'If he saw two frogs in a puddle, he would be one to think it had rained frogs.'

It did not take long, at the easy canter of a horse, to reach the river by Bevere Island. The manor, little more than a cluster of dwellings about a wooden palisaded enclosure, was in view but not so close that anyone by the river would be distinguished. They left the horses there, collected some sacking and went the last part on foot, with the reeve showing every sign of being a reluctant member of the party.

'My lord, my boat is for your use but . . . You are sure I do not have to . . . ?' The reeve still wanted assurance.

'No. We will not need you upon the island, but would speak with you again, so remain here.'

'Yes, my lord, of course.' The man's relief was audible, and he stood upon the bank, looking downstream rather than at the islet and the dark shape upon it.

The crows, in attendance like hungry mourners, flapped away with caws of annoyance as the little craft nudged into the bank, and Bradecote, rather more nimble than Catchpoll, jumped ashore. He tied the end of the painter to a sprawling willow bough, and they climbed the bank, noting the bare earth which had been long trampled into shallow steps. The smell assailed their noses as they drew close, the smell of butchered meat, but no animal carcase ever wore clothes. The ground was dark where the blood had pooled, and the flies were not so easily disturbed as the birds of carrion. What lay before them was obviously human, but beyond that not instantly identifiable. The head was nigh severed from the torso, and where there had been a face there was a face no more. The body had been hacked, more in a frenzy than an attempt to dismember, and with such force that the broad, pale curve of a pelvic bone, visible through the gore, was split in two.

'Sweet Jesu, he was right. You can't even say if it was a man or a woman,' Walkelin muttered and crossed himself, swallowing hard.

'A woman,' responded Catchpoll, without hesitation.

'But how, just glancing at that . . . mess?'

'You do not need to look at the obvious to tell you man or woman, Walkelin. Look at the ankle, the foot. The lower legs are untouched. That is a female's leg most like, and the feet are small too. Not final proof, but it pushes you one way. I imagine the hands are under the corpse and tied behind the back, for there are no parts of a hand you can see, and if a person has their hands free they naturally raise them to protect themselves against a blow, even if it will not save them. My guess is the hands will be small too. See also what is visible of the gown cloth looks as if it is a long gown, not a youth's tunic, and the hair . . .' Catchpoll's frown became intense, and he crouched to lift the end of a hank of dark chestnut hair that had not lain in the pooled blood.

'God forfend,' he whispered, almost to himself.

'The body has been hacked about to prevent us knowing her identity. I mean, you could not recognise the face even if you were blood kin.' Bradecote's features contorted in distaste.

'I think that was not the first purpose, though, my lord.' Catchpoll was still crouched beside the body, drawing knowledge from it even in its mangled silence. 'This was an odd killing, because there was planning to its start, bringing her here, but then the killer gave vent to hate, to a rage like some bloodlust of battle. I have never seen the two together. Most killing is in hot blood, some in cold. This . . .' Catchpoll sucked his teeth.

'Well, we may not be able to give her a name, but we can take her to the priest in Claines for a decent burial and—' Bradecote halted, as Catchpoll shook his head, his mouth set in a grim line. 'Why not?'

'Because I think she may well be out of Worcester, my lord, if my instinct is true, and Father Anselm will give her ground in which to lie.'

'You mean because a local woman would have been missed already, in such a small place as the manor of Bevere or Claines?' Walkelin was working things through, methodically.

'Well, that is good thinking, young Walkelin, but takes us only so far. I think I may yet give a name to her, though it does not cheer me to say it. However, until I am sure . . .' Catchpoll was almost talking to himself.

'Then we wrap the corpse as best we can, and we get the reeve to lend us a cart to get it . . . her . . . back to Worcester.' Bradecote spoke decisively. 'Is there anything more here? Walkelin, search about and see if the killer left any trace of his

16

presence. It is unlikely but . . . the axe, and it was surely that, is most likely out in the depths of the river, and lost to us, as Catchpoll feared.'

'Very true if it was one he stole, but if it was his own, and for his trade, he could have washed it in the water and gone back with it, my lord. You had the right of it. A good axe is worth keeping, and besides, it would be noticed if he had "lost" it. We have to keep that in our thoughts too.' Catchpoll was still staring at the remains, though neither of his companions chose to do so.

'True enough, Catchpoll. So, we are looking for a man, a man who can be calm enough to bring his victim here and set about a killing almost as an execution, but then gives in to rage. If he is coming from Worcester then he must also have had a cart, since he could not conceal a bound woman over a horse.'

'Unless she came willingly, my lord' – Walkelin looked up from peering among the long grasses fringing the islet that had dried to barley gold – 'and willing or not, why was she killed here, not in Worcester, if that is where she lived? And there is nothing here, except some animal fed upon another, recently, for there are little tugs of fur. Buzzard, I would say, with a coney perhaps. Less likely to be disturbed if it ate here. There's nothing the killer could have left.'

'You mean she could have had a meeting arranged here and met her killer rather than being brought here? I suppose that is possible . . .' Bradecote, ignoring the natural history, frowned.

'I do not see a woman walking out of Worcester at the hint of dawn, as soon as the gates were opened, and if she did, she would be noted. And especially not barefoot, not with those

17

feet.' Catchpoll was dismissive, but then frowned and looked more closely at the pale feet. 'Those are feet that do not go barefoot, for the skin is soft except for . . . Now, that is odd.'

'What is, Catchpoll?'

'Look here, my lord. Them's scars. Very old, mark you, like burn scars upon the soles of the feet. I never heard of a child as walked across a red-hot hearth.'

'You mean it was not an accident, Serjeant?' Walkelin looked horrified.

'You, lad, do not know just how nasty people can be. Not only would she not have walked barefoot, I would swear she could not.' Catchpoll pulled a thinking face. 'But you are right to ask why the killing was here. It must have some meaning to the killer.'

'But it is just a small islet in the Severn, Catchpoll.'

'Aye, my lord, but big enough for the folk of Worcester to seek shelter here once, when the Danish king sought vengeance for their not paying him dues. That was before even our oldfathers drew breath, I should think, but the reeve talked about it as a place for young couples – and coupling too no doubt. What if this was where they first met and exchanged kisses, if nothing more? If she was an unfaithful wife . . . ?' Catchpoll sounded unconvinced by his own words and shook his head.

'You do not think that? Why, Catchpoll?'

'If my guess is right, she was no man's wife, my lord.'

'So, if she did not leave Worcester at first light, then perhaps she left yesterday.' Walkelin still liked the idea the woman came at her own wish. 'What if she had arranged to meet the man, spend the night with him and then . . . he did this?'

18

'It is sense enough, Walkelin, but you see I do not think she would ever leave Worcester like that.'

'Come on, Catchpoll. However reluctant you are to give us your guess, you need to tell us who you think this might be.' Bradecote watched his serjeant closely, and for all that Catchpoll was the lord sheriff's serjeant by title, Bradecote felt that he was his by bond now. The man was unusually grim, as if actually saddened, and Catchpoll disapproved of sympathy for victims. It got in the way of finding them justice.

Walkelin, his search proving fruitless, also looked to his senior.

'I hope I am wrong, my lord, but I feel it, deep in the gut instinct. I think this is Ricolde.'

'Ricolde? Should I know her?'

'Not as a happily married man, my lord. Ricolde is, was, the finest whore in Worcester.'

Chapter Two

If he had thought his answer would surprise his companions, Catchpoll was not disappointed.

'"The Whore of Worcester",' murmured Walkelin, in a voice of awe, and crossed himself again.

'Well, whatever her fame, and you both sound as though it was great, I have never heard of her,' Bradecote remarked, almost petulantly. 'You say "finest", Catchpoll, which sounds an odd description of a whore.'

'She was not like the others, my lord, not any man's for a fumble in the alleyway in exchange for a halfpenny. She was . . . a lady among her sisterhood, if you see what I mean?'

'I cannot say that I do, Catchpoll.' Bradecote had no good opinion of whores.

'She has been plying her trade best part of twenty years in Worcester. I do not know how she started, other than she was not born or raised within the walls, but from when I first knew her, and that has never been in the "know her" sense, my lord, she has had a little place of her own, kept neat as any proud housewife's, not some greasy hovel, and she had her price, a high price. She dressed well, aye, and seemly too of the daytime, and the man who could afford her had her to himself for the night, or as much of it as he dared be absent from his own bed, if he was married. She was not just for a rushed hour of flattering lies and soft caresses. I suppose she was more like a leman, except not kept by one man.'

'So, it is likely that the man who killed her was wealthy enough to have afforded her.' Bradecote was caught between relief at this narrowing of suspects from every man in Worcester and the realisation that wealthy men could pay for good oathswearers.

'Unless a man who wanted her, and could not afford her, gave in to lust and took her by force.' Walkelin blushed scarlet. 'I mean took her from Worcester by force.'

Catchpoll heaved a sigh and shook his head.

'You dismiss this, Catchpoll?' the undersheriff queried.

'She was careful, my lord. A whore who is not careful does not live to see thirty summers, and she must have been that. It is a life with risk to it, from disease, of course, but also from them that buy the flesh. She would not let a man into her chamber who was drunk, for example, which is always a wise start.'

'And how do you know all this, Catchpoll?' Bradecote could not resist lifting an eyebrow.

'Because she treated the law with respect, and I, being the law in person on the streets of Worcester, treated her likewise. Never threw me a chancy look, but always a polite acknowledgement, and we had an agreement.'

'An agreement?' This sounded intriguing.

'Began years back, when first I had cause to ask her things. There had been a falling-out among guildsmen and a death. I had a pretty fair idea one of the suspects used to go to her. She swore he had indeed been with her the night of the killing and said The Whore of Worcester's word was good. She said it was a bit like a priest and the confessional. What passed between her and a man was kept close, but she would not lie for one, however often she lay with one, and if I asked her a simple "Was he with you such a night?", she would answer God's truth.'

'Which begs the question why any man who spent the night with her would bring her to this, and how did he get her here? She has not been here since darkness fell last night, so how was she brought out of Worcester as soon as the Foregate was opened without the man with a cart being noted?' Bradecote shook out the sacking in which they could wrap the remains.

'We might find he was, my lord,' suggested Walkelin, hopefully. His seniors gave him a look that suggested such good fortune was the stuff of dreams, but Walkelin was not crushed, and offered another thought. 'And if it was that he brought her here, he cannot be a married man, else he would worry about his wife revealing his absence through the night.'

'More likely to be widowed or single, but there are wives in Worcester, for all they would play shocked virtue, know their husbands stray, but say nought because they have the position and power of a wife, which is a thing of worth.' Catchpoll looked thoughtful.

He took a sack and eased it as best he could over the head and down the torso to keep the body together, and another up the legs a way above the knee. They slit open two sacks down the sides and laid them out, one on top of the other beside the body, so that they could roll it, cautiously, onto them. It was then proved that Catchpoll had been right; the hands were bound at the wrist and were not hands that saw heavy labour.

'See, them's woman's hands, and kept nice too.' Catchpoll peered closer. 'There's even a silver ring upon a finger.' He leant to study it upon the hand, sticky with congealing gore. 'It is wrought, so any silversmith in Worcester should know if it is his and might just recall who bought it. That will be your task when we get to Worcester, Walkelin. Safest left on the finger till we get her back.'

'Yes, Serjeant.'

They placed the other sacks over the body and lifted it, carefully, to place in the boat. She was not heavy, for which they were thankful, and with Bradecote lifting the corners near the head end, Walkelin foot end, and Catchpoll, whose hands were already the most bloodied, supporting the middle, they made their way to the bank, where they stopped, adjusted their holds and descended with care – and some swearing. It was as they reached the narrow strand, no more than two feet wide, that Walkelin, watching where he put his feet, gave a cry.

'That's not a footmark from us, is it, Serjeant?'

Catchpoll looked down. It was toe towards the water, and a blade of darkened grass that had stuck to the sole had been left pressed into the mud. It was also partially obscured by a larger footprint.

'Not ours, lad. Well spotted. I ought to have seen that when we arrived, but I am thinking you, my lord, were on that spot.'

'You mean me and my big feet, Catchpoll.'

'Would not put it that way, my lord, but yes. Means the man was of middling height, not as tall as you, but then, that does not limit us much, for you are one of the taller men I know.'

They set the body in the boat, and then realised that fitting all three of them in it as well would not be possible.

'Looks like the reeve will have to give us a hand on the other side, my lord, and then I will send Walkelin back for you while a cart is fetched.'

'Fair enough, Catchpoll. He won't like that.'

'And do we care?' The serjeant shrugged.

'No. Just remember to send Walkelin back and not leave me to try and wade across. I may be tall, but it looks far too deep to me, and I am no swimmer.' Bradecote looked at his hands, which were stained and sticky, and at the marks on his clothing. He could wash his hands easily enough in the flow, but would the bloodstains not give cause for remark? He watched the reeve take the rope and tie up the boat as it reached the bank, and could have smiled at the way he tried not to look at what lay in it. His reaction when told to assist in the removal of the body made Bradecote think he might simply bolt for the manor and hide within the palisade, not that Catchpoll would have let him. When Walkelin returned in the boat, he was grinning.

'I am not sure the reeve will not have this for firewood by evening. He acts as if it is cursed and is telling Serjeant Catchpoll the lord Sheriff ought to give him money for a new boat.'

'I can imagine Catchpoll's response.'

'Indeed, my lord. Now, if you dare step into this "haunted" craft, I will row us back and we can leave the man to his imaginings.' Walkelin grinned.

'Not until we have spoken to Edmund the Branch-feller.'

'I had forgot him, my lord.'

'I have little doubt we shall all do so very soon, especially since we need to get the body back to Worcester, but it seems wasteful of time not to at least speak with him, if he is close by.'

When they reached the bank, it was evident that Catchpoll had been of the same opinion, and he reported that Edmund, son of Gyrth, was being sent to them, with the cart.

'And would you care to toss a coin over whether this man is any brighter than the limb he felled, Serjeant Catchpoll?'

'I would not, my lord. If he can show us the tree, and is little brighter, we will leave him be for sure.'

So it proved. Edmund was a huge ox of a young man, slow-witted but clearly benign, who showed Serjeant Catchpoll the struck tree and the new cut where but recently had been a branch. He even offered to show him the branch.

'I did not steal it,' he repeated, over and over, being sure that the office of sheriff's serjeant went to a man who took up thieves and thieves alone.

Catchpoll rejoined his companions entirely convinced that Edmund was not a killer with an axe.

They were not grinning as they entered Worcester, with Walkelin driving the Bevere manor cart and Bradecote and Catchpoll riding behind, like a respectful escort for the dead, and leading Walkelin's mount. The man at the gate had just come on watch and could say nothing of what was seen that morning, but promised to send his predecessor to the castle within the hour to tell the lord undersheriff all he knew. With this they had to be content. At the castle they placed the body in the cool of an empty cell, and Catchpoll set a man-at-arms to take the cart back to Bevere, since Walkelin was needed to take the silver ring about the silversmiths of Worcester. It was Catchpoll who removed it from the now-stiffening finger and rubbed it to remove the blood, which then remained only in the etched marks. Bradecote took it from him and peered closely at them.

'This is not a pattern. It is words, an inscription. It says "*Ic beo min*".'

'Ricolde had no letters, I would swear that,' declared Catchpoll.

'And what does "I am mine" mean?' asked Walkelin.

'There is no reason she needed to have been able to read them to ask for the words to be inscribed, and as for meaning . . .' Bradecote paused, pondering.

'Of course it might be a ring a man gave her in payment instead of coin,' suggested Walkelin, 'but he did not have it made as a gift for her, to impress, because it would have said "You are mine". "I am mine" has no sense to it.'

'It does if the woman wanted something to remind her that however much her body was used, she was her own soul.' Bradecote was thinking of his Christina and how she had survived her years of mistreatment. Only by keeping her inner self separate had she done so and perhaps a whore . . . He scowled, for it felt all wrong to find a similarity between his beloved wife and a woman who sold her body for money, and yet in some cases, might it not exist? The girl Nerys Ford, God rest her soul, had not taken to selling herself from choice but from need. Had she not died, she would have grown to full womanhood, and would he have felt pity for her then? In truth, he would not, and it was his failing.

'You might have it aright there, my lord,' Catchpoll nodded, 'which gives us a good chance of discovering the man who made it, and who could tell us who paid for it. Such a ring would linger in the memory. Walkelin, take it and show it to every silversmith. Meet us at Ricolde's dwelling when you have your answer.' He turned to his superior. 'If she greets us at the door, my lord, we will have to start again as to our victim, but I will be the happier for it. If not, we asks all about when she was seen last.'

'Agreed.' Time was when Hugh Bradecote would have resented the serjeant taking charge of decisions, but there was no proving of superiority in this, just common sense. Catchpoll knew the heartbeat of Worcester, to the point where Bradecote had even dreamt that the cobbles told him things through the soles of his feet. Walkelin departed.

'I must send a man to Bradecote, to tell my lady I am detained by a death. I do not see we will end this today, do you, Catchpoll?'

'No, my lord, not unless we is very lucky, and the gate watch recognised a man and cart at dawn with a woman-sized bundle upon it.'

'I should perhaps wait here for the watchman.'

'I doubt we will be long, my lord, and, though I hates to say it, and would not in front of young Walkelin, when it comes to

27

hunting in dark corners, my eyes ain't what they were a while back, and a second, younger pair, might be of service.'

'You want my eyes, but the rest is useless, Serjeant?'

'Not my words, my lord, not my words.' Catchpoll gave his death's head grin.

Serjeant Catchpoll led the way through the streets down towards the wharfage. All Saints Church loomed with benign height over the generally squalid homes about it.

'A lot of the flesh trade, and I don't mean meat for eating, is done the south side of the church, along Shipmonneslone, so much so most people just call it Gropelone these days. Passing trade, so to speak, from the shipmen running up and down the river, keeps 'em busy. Ricolde, well she might have had a regular captain or two who would "stop by", but she was a bit further along and away from the rest, on Brodestrete.' Catchpoll walked on. 'Here we are, and respectable tradesmen either side. You should have heard the complaints from their womenfolk, until it was realised guilty men buy trinkets for neglected wives.'

It was a very unassuming house, single storey but with a tall and steeply angled roof. The door looked new wood, or at least nearly new. Catchpoll knocked upon it and put an ear to the planking. The shutters were shut, but that meant little. There was a keyhole, which implied the door could keep things in and people out. He lifted the latch. The door was not locked, and he glanced at Bradecote. If you had a good lock and left the premises, why not use it?

Within it was one chamber, with a partition to chest height that divided the back half from the front. It was not lavishly furnished, but what there was was well made, and the front part was neat and tidy, excepting for the disorder of the rushes on the floor. There was a hearthstone, which Catchpoll touched.

'Not even warm, my lord.'

There was a bench with a back to it, a stool, and against one wall a grain ark, with upon it two bowls, beakers and spoons, an earthenware cook pot, a pitcher, a ladle and a large paddle-shaped spoon.

'She cooked for two,' noted Bradecote.

'I gets the feeling that a night with Ricolde could include a decent meal, if wanted. Think on it, my lord. If some of her men were wifeless and reliant upon a poor cookmaid, a good pottage, and soft words, would be a good start to a night that would end in a warm bed. For some it might even have been the food and company as was most important. Old Alfric the Potter, he used to come here, though he has been in the earth three years now. He was an old man, and if Ricolde had worked her wiles upon him in the bed, I doubt he would have lasted till then. He never hid that he visited her, even boasted of it, and I always thought he came to her to pretend he was still man enough to mount her, and in fact was happy to have a good meal and a cuddle 'neath the covers. He was just a lonely old bastard.' Catchpoll spoke with gentle pity.

'I doubt any such men would have killed her, so we discount those in their last years.'

Strings of onions, garlic and leeks hung from a beam, and herbs also. It was much like any house where a goodwife spent her days. It was the rear part of the place that was different. There was a coffer, in which Catchpoll found a small casket containing a silver torque, headbands of silver interlaced with ribbons and three brooches. There were three good gowns, neatly folded, two girdles, one of polished copper panels with cabochon turquoises, coifs, linen shifts, braidings, two pairs of shoes, lined with moleskin, and a fine cloak with its hood lined with a thick chestnut fox fur. Catchpoll held it and a gown up, and Bradecote blinked.

'I love my wife, but I could not afford to dress her like that.'

'Nor could half the lords in the shire, I would think. She never dressed cheap and untidy. Only the best for the best, I would say.'

Bradecote looked at the large and sturdy cot, which clearly had a well-stuffed palliasse and a crumpled sheet of linen upon it.

'Her clothes were not untidy, the hearth is swept, but the bed, Catchpoll, has not been made, and either her lover was extremely energetic or there was some form of struggle here. Also, it may be midsummer, but there is no blanket of any sort on the bed or in the chest. I think we assume he rendered her unconscious and wrapped her in it.'

They looked at the bed and the story it told, and both were, for a moment, embarrassed as they thought of the woman they had found on Bevere Island, but in other circumstances. Bradecote coloured, but Catchpoll gave a slow smile. Then Bradecote leant to finger strands of dark chestnut hair, more like a lock pulled from the head. The palliasse was clean, but for a small, dark smear of blood at the head end.

'We'll see him dangle for you, Ricolde,' whispered Catchpoll, as if giving her a promise. Neither man had any doubt that it was she who had met a gruesome end that dawning.

'We could look upon the floor, among the rushes, in case he lost something of his own here or forgot to put it back on, if he harmed her after . . . But surely, if he had knocked her from her senses and carried her away, they would have been seen even if he took the bedcovering, rolled her in that and got her into some cart?' Bradecote shook his head and went upon his knees to look beside the bed. 'But that seems so planned it means he intended to kill her from the very start. I do not understand.' He looked up and across the bed at Catchpoll.

'Well, my lord, first thing we need to find out is when Ricolde was last seen hereabouts. The neighbours might say they have nothing to do with her, but I would guess the women watch and gossip when they can, and summer evenings are light.'

Bradecote pulled something from under the bed. It was not something discarded by a lover, but a stout box, and it was heavy to drag. Within it was silver coin, and more than Bradecote might see at once from one season to the next, and a cloth bag, embroidered with a crudely formed flower, which bulged and was found to contain forty silver pennies.

'Well, she really did not sell herself cheaply, did she,' commented Bradecote. 'I wonder at the portion set aside in the bag. Perhaps it was saving for some new expensive thing.'

At this point Walkelin entered, cautiously, as if he might be leapt upon by some dangerous beast, and then relaxed as he saw only his superiors.

'The ring is hers. I spoke with three silversmiths, and all had made things for her, but it was Reginald Ash as made the ring. What all of them said, very firmly, was that she paid in coin, never by . . .' he blushed, 'you know. Now, Reginald Ash has no woman, so he need not say that for any reason other than truth.'

'That fits with what I know of her,' agreed Catchpoll. 'If Ash came to her bed, it was not for payment, but him doing the paying. She had a sort of . . . independence to her.'

'And there can be no doubt now as to the identity of the body, so we make it known and we listen closely,' Bradecote spoke half to himself.

'You really are starting to sound like me, my lord,' said Catchpoll, but he was not smiling.

Walkelin was recruited to look for any lingering sign of the man, but not as much as a thread was discovered.

Chapter Three

The first thing was to decide what should be done with Ricolde's possessions, because, as Catchpoll said, they would disappear quickly once it was known she was dead, and everyone knew that she had no kin. They left Walkelin to guard the place and went to the castle, where Catchpoll looked as best he could at the body to see if there was a key at her girdle, or where her girdle ought to be. He found none. He then sent a man-at-arms with a handcart and instructions to Walkelin to place anything that could be moved in the cart to bring to the castle, and to leave the man-at-arms at the door, at least for the day. Nobody other than the sheriff's men was to be admitted.

As the handcart was wheeled away, the early guardian of the Foregate appeared, looking wary, as if fearing he was in trouble. At first he babbled about never sleeping on watch and not taking coin to look the other way, but once Catchpoll had told him not to be an idiot and had explained the reason for his summons, he settled a little.

'We want to know about the first people to leave Worcester this morning, especially anyone with a cart and something covered in the back of it.' Bradecote tried not to intimidate, but the man was beginning to breathe fast again.

'There was Huw the dong farmer, but what was in the back of his cart was what there is from a man who gathers middens. Nothing was covered, except in the first flies of the day.' He frowned. 'Then there was the empty salt cart with the two men from Wich as bring the priory salt every few months. I have seen 'em before, and there was nothing in the cart but empty salt barrels. There were no other carts, just the lads who work at the tanner's, on foot, and . . . Now him I did not know.' The man looked thoughtful.

'Who?' The undersheriff tried not to look too eager.

'I do not know, my lord, as I said.'

'Describe him,' growled Catchpoll.

'Horseman, and the sort I would say was paid for his sword. He had a packhorse with him, so I would imagine that was all his worldly goods wrapped up upon it.'

'And would any of these "worldly goods" have been draped over the animal like a large bedroll or a woman rolled in a blanket?' suggested Catchpoll.

'A woman in a . . . Well, there was a big cloak about his bedroll. It was good and thick, and long enough I suppose, if she was not too tall.'

'Describe the man, in size and looks.' Bradecote thought it sounded all very unlikely, but they could not afford to ignore it.

'He was a man with broad shoulders and as square a jaw as ever I sees, my lord, taller than me as I would judge, but it is hard when a man is on horseback. He had greying in the growth upon his chin, which was not yet a beard proper, and he had a dark red cap upon his head.'

'His horse?' asked Catchpoll.

'A brown horse, and I do not recall any white upon its face.' The man looked back to the undersheriff. 'He glanced at me, my lord, as I gave him a good morrow, and it was as if he looked through me.'

'And there was nobody else, early?'

'None, my lord. Most folk are those coming into Worcester, and we checks for any as need to pay toll as the lord Sheriff commands.' The man was eager to avoid censure.

'No doubt. Thank you. If we find this man, and have cause to keep him, I will send for you to confirm it is who you saw. And if you should see him again, you come here and tell of it, straight away.'

'Yes, my lord. Of course, my lord.' The man was already making his obeisance and drawing back. Important people were trouble to the lowly, and he knew his place.

Catchpoll jerked his head towards the door, but laid a hand upon his arm as he passed and asked for his abode, so that he might be found if needed.

'How far would a man on horseback get if he was not trying to look like a fleeing murderer, and could a sword have been the weapon rather than an axe?' wondered Bradecote, when they were alone.

'You can make a mess of a body with a sword, but, in truth,

my lord, I would still say it was an axe that did for her. As for how far, the more important question is not distance but direction. I grant you if he took the north road it is more like he would go up through Wich, unless he was heading for a local manor, but after that,' he shook his head, 'we would be hard-pressed to find him. I think his only use to us would be as the answer if all else fails.'

'What do you mean, Catchpoll?' Bradecote frowned.

'Well, my lord, if it all goes quiet, and we gets nowhere, however hard we tries, then the answer to give out is that it has been discovered that the man who did it was this man, now long gone into the north. That would keep everyone from trembling in their beds that a killer was still at large.'

'It would not be true.'

'Of course not, my lord, but sometimes there is no neat finish, and untidiness upsets folk.'

'So, you are saying we lie, Serjeant.' Bradecote did not sound as if this agreed with him.

'If we must. I don't like it either, my lord, but we has to keep the confidence of the people. If those who think to break the law feel we would always find them, fewer do more than think, and if the law-abiding have faith in us they are more willing to tell us things.' Catchpoll could see the undersheriff was still not convinced. 'Lies, like life, are not black and white, my lord. This would be a soft, grey lie which would help keep the peace in the future, and—'

'Keep us from the lord Sheriff's displeasure?' Bradecote's forehead wrinkled, questioningly.

'That might be an added good outcome, my lord,' declared Catchpoll, as though the idea had not occurred to him.

'You are a devious bastard, Catchpoll.'

'Thank you, my lord. Now, do you want us to strike north in the hope of finding this missing swordsman?' He sounded as though an answer in the affirmative would be the wrong answer.

'It would be thorough, and we have no other trail to follow, but it sounds unlikely that he is connected, and we have little chance of finding him. No, Catchpoll, we look in Worcester for the killer of Ricolde. After all, how would a man passing through know of Bevere Island? He has to be local, and for all the violence of his hacking, he is no madman.'

'Very true, my lord. And how about we go to see Father Anselm at All Saints? She was of his parish, and priests knows more than you might think about what exactly goes on.'

'He will not break the confessional.'

'No, my lord, but there is a lot that is known that does not come by that path.'

Father Anselm, the priest of All Saints parish, was an approachable man, who long ago decided that he was best able to guide his parishioners if they did not fear him. He was short, rather round, and possessed of great patience. Bradecote and Catchpoll, now joined by Walkelin, whom they met returning from Ricolde's home, found him 'paying' a girl to sweep the church, even though it had been swept that very morning. She set about her task very thoroughly as he winked at Serjeant Catchpoll and came towards them, smiling.

'Will not take charity,' he whispered, 'but her father has broken his arm and cannot work, the mother is dead, God's

37

mercy upon her, and she is struggling to feed four little brothers and sisters.'

'You know your parish well, Father.' Bradecote's smile was as genuine as the priest's.

'I would be a bad servant of Christ if I did not, my lord. Now, when I am visited by so many of the lord Sheriff's men, I wonder what it is you seek, assuming it is not moral guidance.'

'Good Father, I am afraid we come with news that you have one parishioner the less, and by evil intent.' Bradecote's smile twisted.

'Oh dear.' He crossed himself.

'Father Anselm, you might not have seen much of her in this place, but you will know of her well enough,' said Catchpoll. 'We found a woman's body, hacked to death on Bevere Island this morning, and it is proved to be Ricolde, who was—'

'"The Whore of Worcester". God have mercy upon her soul. Poor, poor woman, and today of all days.' The priest sounded genuinely grieved. He shook his head and sighed. 'Her deeds will be judged.'

Bradecote thought the man's eyes misted with tears. He himself had not thought of the irony of the date and wondered if it had any significance.

'We all of us sin, Father.'

'We do. And you will think her sins great and obvious. I do not say that is not so, but beneath all that was a soul who tried her best.'

'She did?' Walkelin could not keep silent, and his face showed his astonishment.

38

'She did, my son. "By their fruits shall ye know them" and many of her "fruits" were good. You look amazed, because she was "The Whore of Worcester". I knew her title, but I also knew so much more of Ricolde. She came rarely into church for services, and if she did, crept in late and left swiftly. I met her first one night, upon the feast of St Mary Magdalene, yes, upon this very day. I was awake, or rather I think God woke me, and came to the church upon impulsion. I found her prostrate before the altar, weeping and praying. She shrank from me and apologised for her presence. I told her that God's house is open to all, and asked why she wept. She told me she wept for her sins and prayed that the blessèd saint would intercede for her, because she would understand. We talked, and God taught me much through her. He taught me not to assume a soul was like the outer person.' He paused for a moment.

'I said that she could cease the sin of her way of life, though I see it was easy to say and hard to do. She smiled. You know, her smile, her true smile, was very beautiful, but very sad.' The priest sighed. 'She said that she could go to a nunnery in another shire, claiming to be a widow and with her "dower" for her admittance, but how could she face the sisters every day with her life among them based upon a lie? If she told the truth, what House of Nuns would want her? I told her that I heard it said the leman of King Harold, as came after the Sainted Confessor, ended her days in a nunnery, and she laughed and said a king's favourite was not the same as a woman who plied her trade with different men and took coin after each meeting. She said, and there was bitterness in her voice, that a man might sin and it would be forgiven, heads shaken over it perhaps, but if it was a woman and she "fell", by foolish choice or mischance, there was no going back.' Father Anselm shook his head at that. 'There is much truth in what she said.' He stopped, lost briefly in contemplation of the failings of man. 'She told me her tale without tears and without anger, though she had a right to both.'

'And what was her tale, Father? If it was not a confession, then you are not bound to keep it close, and there might just be something . . .' Bradecote did not demand but requested.

'It will not help you, my lord Bradecote, but I can speak it. She said her mother died when she was very young, drowned in the Severn, and her father and older brother left the village and she was given to her father's sister, a woman whose husband took advantage as no man ought. When she was about twelve her aunt discovered them together and threw her out. She came into Worcester, where she was not known, and took work in a tavern, where men looked at her the way her uncle had looked. It was a natural progression, and the extra halfpennies she kept, rather than spent, so that she could pay the rent of a small house of her own. If she had to be a whore, she said, she would not creep about alleys. She thrust up her chin, as I remember, and said that she would not be the victim of men, whatever they thought. They would have to pay a high price for her. Then she told me I was one of only three men who neither looked at her in lust or disgust, and one of the others was you, Serjeant Catchpoll, and asked if I would accept charity from one who earned her pence by sin. I said I would pray for her sinning, but yes, and then her smile was radiant, triumphant. Ever since, and that has been for nigh on ten years, she has brought me a scrip of coin every feast of St Mary Magdalene, and at the Nativity, a goodly sum, and I have used it for girls who have none to take them in when left fatherless and motherless. The nuns at Wroxall to the north of Stratford take them and teach them godliness, and also to bake and stitch, so that they might be employed in some lord's manor if they do not take the veil. Four girls have been "saved" from having to take her path, though she never knew that I ensure that they say prayers for their unknown benefactress. I must send to the prioress and tell her the sad news. You say she was killed brutally?'

'Yes, Father. Her body was scarcely recognisable, but for the colour of her hair and a silver ring upon a finger.' Catchpoll kept his voice even.

The priest grimaced as if in pain.

'Father Anselm, we do not know if she was killed because of her . . . way of life or because she was Ricolde, and that may have bearing upon the safety of other women in Worcester. When you spoke with her, was there ever indication that she felt threatened by any man who . . . paid her?' Bradecote still felt embarrassed, discussing what she did with the priest, however familiar he was with the details.

'No, but then we only spoke of how the girls progressed, and then she would make her confession. She had no cause to like men, and I think she despised them, us. Women such as Ricolde are "used", but she had made it so that it was almost she "used" them, their weakness, to buy her bread and keep her warm. Pride is a sin, and I told her so, when she said that she was proud to be the best in Worcester, and yet . . . if you have to follow a path, there is a sense to being the best you can.

41

Knowing her has made me a better priest. She will be long in my prayers.' Father Anselm sagged a little.

'There is one thing more that Ricolde may do of which the Church would approve, Father,' murmured Catchpoll. 'She died without kin, but with possessions, fine possessions. If we leave them, they will be a . . . temptation to others. The thought is that she would not mind them being given to the Church to sell or dispense as charity, and from what you have said, that seems sure. May we bring her things to you?'

'You may. Any that can raise coin for the poor will be sold and any day-to-day things go to those in need. She would indeed approve. Thank you.'

'We also found a box of silver and within it a bag of coin,' added the undersheriff. 'From what you say, it must have been the bag ready to leave for you this night. It, and the other silver in the box, I will have Walkelin bring to you, that Ricolde may aid good works even after she has left this life and for masses for her soul.'

'I would pray for her without any such, but again, I thank you.'

They left Father Anselm to pray for Ricolde and began to walk back to the castle, all three in contemplative mood. They were nearly at the cathedral before Bradecote spoke.

'He may light candles for her, but is there anything at all in what Father Anselm told us that can light our way?'

'Not much, my lord. If her mother drowned in the river, then we must assume she was living near the river, which might just be the link to Bevere Island, but the place must have been of the man's choosing, not hers so . . .'

'Could it be the uncle?' asked Walkelin. 'If he came to Worcester and saw her and—'

'The name is not a common one, I grant, but—'

'Why do we assume it was her childhood name, Catchpoll?' interjected Bradecote.

'Very true, my lord, but that means it would be even less likely a man would see her after twenty years, and grown to womanhood, not a girl, and recognise her, and even if he did, why take her to Bevere Island and kill her? It makes no sense, no sense at all.'

'There is a sense in it, somewhere, from some point. We just have to find out what and from where.' Bradecote rubbed the bridge of his nose. 'I think we have to knock on doors and find out what gossip is abroad about who visited Ricolde these last few weeks. Whatever set this "rock" rushing down a hillside to crush her must have been recent. A man would not plan what we saw on Bevere Island for months.'

'Then we have three ways to do it, my lord. Walkelin suggests, I asks and you stamps your lordly boot and demands.'

'This lordly boot is worn to holes.' He raised a foot and showed the leather splitting.

'Still bigger and better than most.'

'At this rate I will still be in Worcester when the corviser has made my new ones, Catchpoll.'

'We shall see, my lord.'

As expected, the inhabitants at the lower end of Brodestrete at first claimed to know nothing of the wickedness that went on in 'that place', as the women called Ricolde's home. Whilst

Ricolde's dwelling was tainted by what went on within it, every frontage spoke of respectability and quiet prosperity. Walkelin was reduced to listening only, after the very first encounter when the woman boxed his ears and said she would tell his mother he was a bad boy. Catchpoll had to disguise his amusement with a coughing fit. The men were reticent, either thinking that in other circumstances it might be them being named or because they felt a man's pleasures, if not illegal, were private. As Catchpoll said, grimly, hacking a woman to death was very illegal. The women, once they got past feigning ignorance, were more forthcoming. Some knew Catchpoll and decided there was nothing he had not heard before. They might start haltingly and with a trace of blush, but once in full flow they warmed to their theme. Most was salacious 'detail' that they had woven upon bare fact and it did not really expand the list of names, though, as Catchpoll murmured afterwards, if half of it was true, Ricolde would never have had the energy to as much as go out to buy bread.

There were also several women in the street who disliked Catchpoll because they thought themselves above him and withdrew into haughty silence or sharp words. It was upon them that Bradecote was let loose, and he could do hauteur to a level way above theirs. The master weaver's wife was the worst and made the mistake of letting her temper show, as she kept them upon her doorstep in the softening western sunshine of evening. Admittedly, she had not taken well to Catchpoll reminding her that he recalled her as a scrubby girl playing chase along the riverside. When Bradecote joined in she turned on him, taking no note of his garb, and rudely asked what business it might be of his.

'Entirely my business, for I am Undersheriff of Worcestershire and thus representative of the lord King's Grace.' He held himself very erect and looked down his long nose at her. They had been knocking upon doors for well over an hour, and his stomach was reminding him it was many hours since he had broken his fast in his own hall. He was not in the best humour.

'The lord Bradecote,' added Catchpoll, for good measure.

'Whatever you may know about who visited Ricolde, the murdered woman, you will tell me or I will have Serjeant Catchpoll tie your hands and lead you through the streets to the castle, and you can sit in a cell until your tongue loosens. Try explaining that to your own neighbours, mistress. What gossip would that start?' Bradecote sounded cold-hearted to the point of enjoying cruelty, and Catchpoll's thin lips were clamped together in so hard a line they went white, just to stop him laughing.

'But, my lord, what would a decent woman know of a common—'

'Whore? Well, you have eyes and ears, and show me a woman, decent or whore, who does not use them.' Bradecote did not soften and intentionally linked all women together. 'You will have seen an axe cleave a log in two. Think upon how it is when used upon a woman's face. That was her fate, and I will see the man that did it hang.' There was cold anger in his tone, and it was not feigned. The weaver's wife turned pallid, and her hand went to her cheek.

'I . . . I did never pry, but I have seen Morcar Grimson leave her door just before cock crow, and him with a sickly wife.'

'In the last few months?'

45

'Aye, my lord, but ten days past or so. And before that, in the last month, Roger the Healer came to her door at dusk, and entered, and what he ministered to her I cannot say, but I know of no draught that would keep him until after I went to our bed.' She could not resist a slight smirk. The other names she gave were those they had heard from others. Bradecote thanked her for her help, without a smile, and when the three men left her, Mistress Weaver had to sit down and send the servant wench to fetch her a beaker of cider.

Bradecote's expression did not lighten as they walked. Catchpoll glanced sideways at him.

'You know, if you wasn't a lord and the undersheriff, I would say you have the makings of a good serjeant, my lord.'

'And no higher praise can you give, eh, Catchpoll?' Hugh Bradecote smiled then, wryly. 'Thank you. I am overwhelmed.' His stomach gurgled.

'Well, you may be so, my lord, but your gut is shouting that it is underfed. We eat, yes, and then do we pay our visits this evening or on the morrow?'

'Unless a name strikes you as obvious, Catchpoll, we sleep upon our knowledge, little as it is. It has been a long day, and we will need our wits, confronting men with wives. We want no shocked spouse committing murder with the cooking knife.'

Worcester saw plenty of deaths not from the passing of years but by accident or intent, and regularly enough not to get excited, but the news of the death of 'The Whore of Worcester' spread like licking flames and was greeted with shock, though a few of the pious, and certain wives, also muttered about 'the wages of sin' and shook their heads. The morning saw Ricolde's earthly remains given solemn burial, and Father Anselm made it perfectly clear that in death the Church accorded her the same respect as the most illustrious of Worcester's burgesses or indeed a beggar from the streets. Death levelled all, brought all to no man's judgement, but only to that of God, who was both just and merciful.

The three sheriff's men were present at her obsequies, which were well attended. This surprised the undersheriff, but Catchpoll had a good idea why.

'Curiosity, for the most part, and a little nastiness from some, come to gloat over her departing. You see, nearly all the people who came wanted to see who else would come, and, to be fair to her, Ricolde was one of the most prominent people in Worcester. Nobody on the streets has been saying "Who?".'

'So, there will be as big a turnout when your time comes, eh, Catchpoll?' Bradecote grinned.

'There had better be. In fact, just make sure young Walkelin notes everybody, because anyone who has even dreamt of breaking the law in Worcester will be there, mostly to check for certain that I am indeed dead and they buries me good and deep.' Catchpoll's eyes twinkled. 'So, he will have to be on his toes thereafter.'

'I am learning, Serjeant. Given time, and I hope your years are many, I will be as crafty, mean and knowing a bastard as you tell me I must be.' Walkelin achieved a look of innocent studiousness.

'Good lad.' Catchpoll chuckled, but then grew serious. 'Did you see anyone in the church who looked uncomfortable?'

'Besides Alnoth the Tailor, who pulled many faces, could not keep still and kept mumbling about his painful arse-hangers? Well, quite a lot of the wealthier men did, but that was because their wives were looking at them even more closely than we were, as I reckon. I think they saw it as a test to find out if their man had ever passed a night with Ricolde.'

'The trouble is that we need to know who did that too, and neither man nor wife is going to come forth and declare, willingly, that there was any connection,' grumbled Bradecote. 'What we have from her respectable neighbours is very far from being a full list. We have half a dozen names, and unless they paid an earl's ransom, Ricolde would have been living off thin pottage with only that many "admirers".' He remembered the heavy box of silver and looked pensive, but Catchpoll gave a grunt of amusement.

'"Admirers". Never heard 'em called that before. You know, I think a lot of 'em used her as a badge of wealth and position, and she used that to her advantage. If a man could afford her, he was a man of substance, and some did not mind that they were seen at her door, because it proved as much.'

'You admired her in the true sense though, Catchpoll?' Bradecote wondered, for he knew Catchpoll, who adopted a 'look but do not touch' policy with shapely women, still enjoyed the looking.

'I did, my lord.' The serjeant frowned. 'It was as though she was too decent to leer at, and you may laugh at that but . . . I can think good, healthy, lusty thoughts over a woman who shows herself off, wants men to think of her that way, but Ricolde never played the whore with me, nor as she went about the

48

streets day to day. In fact, she was as haughty as a fine lady. The silversmiths said she never offered to buy goods with her body in exchange, and that was at the heart of it. What she did by night was her "craft", and if there was a whore's guild she would have led it, and the rest of the time she had no interest in playing off tricks to attract custom. She did not need to, not for many a year.'

'But could she have had a man who did admire her?' asked Walkelin, thoughtfully. 'You have told me oft enough, Serjeant, with home killings, that the passions of love and hate lie close together, close as lovers. If a man who paid for his nights with her fell in love with her and wanted her to be his leman alone, then what if she said no? Could his love become hate, so that killing her would keep her from all others?'

'Now that, young Walkelin, is an interesting thought.' Catchpoll nodded his approbation. 'I doesn't say it is the answer, but it is one answer.'

'It is, but only works so far, surely.' Bradecote wanted to be persuaded but was cautious. 'It would account for a man killing her, yes, but does not explain Bevere Island.' His brow furrowed. 'Nobody would take a captive there to kill unless it had meaning, at least to the killer.'

'Then I go back to the uncle. If that was a place where he took her as a girl, it would be very meaningful.' Walkelin would not be budged from his thought.

'But if that were so, Walkelin, why now, so many years later? A man from close to Bevere, whichever side of the river, would have come into Worcester often enough over the years and must surely have seen her. Which means he would have recognised

her years ago. It seems impossible, but so does everything else.'
The undersheriff rubbed his chin. 'All of which means we have
two different places to hunt, in Worcester and outside it, and
each only seems to offer us half of the answer. Of the names we
have, Catchpoll, are any men you get your "serjeant's feeling"
about? Have any a past we might find important?'

'Not much, my lord. Roger the Healer looks such a pale
stick of a man I am surprised if he had the strength.'

'To kill her with an axe?'

'No, my lord, to use his other "weapon", in the bed. And if
he chose to kill her, then he would use a poison, surely, since
that is where his strength lies, in potions not muscles.'

'That is good sense, Catchpoll. So, he is low on our list. Next?'

'Morcar Grimson. His wife has a sickness of the bones that
pains her and twists her hands so she can barely lift a spoon.
He is as honest as any merchant, which is to say, he eases round
the law very cautious like, and I never heard of him having a
temper. I would not be surprised if Mistress Grimson knows of
his dealings with Ricolde and accepts it quietly. He sees she is
cared for and lacks nothing, and what he has lacked she cannot
provide, poor woman. If she felt she had the love of his heart,
she might not begrudge him an outlet for the needs of the body.'

'Not promising.' Bradecote halted and bent down, wincing.
A stone had got into his boot through the hole. 'Ow! Do not
tell me the corviser is our man, or at least not for another day or
two. I need him to finish my boots.'

'Robert Corviser is the best of his craft in Worcester, and I
would wager the shoes on Ricolde's feet were of his making. He
would also not cheat you, my lord, nor any of his customers,

but in dealings with the tanners I have heard grumblings that he is not so honest. He has threatened to play off one against the other, by saying he would not get his leather from such a man and lose him custom from others, or praise to God's Heaven another who let him have hide at a lesser rate. It ain't against the law, but it is a mark that he is not above pressuring folk. I like his work, but not the man.'

'But again, you could not see him taking Ricolde to Bevere Island and killing her like that.' It was not a question.

'No, my lord, that I could not. He is married and to a shrew of a wife, so he might need a bit of comfort, but would not kill the source of it.'

'Have we thought about a woman?' asked Walkelin, half to himself.

'Often,' grinned Catchpoll and enjoyed his 'serjeanting apprentice' turning scarlet of cheek.

'No, Serjeant, I mean what if a wife was angered at her husband going to Ricolde but knew lashing him with her tongue would get her no more than a black eye? Might not such a woman use his money to pay a man to kill Ricolde?'

'I hopes not, because that means going through all the bastards in Worcester who would kill their own mothers for a handful of pennies, and that is not a short list.'

'What Walkelin says is possible though,' admitted Bradecote, and Walkelin blushed further at the approval. 'When we look at these men, we must look at their wives also. Are the others married?'

'Odo Bylda is married, and with six children at his wife's skirts. If anything, I would think she would be glad of the rest. He's a big man, strong enough to wield an axe with ease, as you would expect in his line of work, and he would have good, sharp tools. He has been in a few fights over the years when in ale, but as I said before, Ricolde would not let a drunken man over her threshold, in either sense. What is more, I saw him but two days past, and his hand wrapped about with bandage and his temper foul. He has a broken hand and cannot do more than direct his journeymen.

'Gerald Bellworker is a widower, and a man who works hard and does long hours. If he saved his coin for a night of pleasure with "The Whore of Worcester", none but a priest would begrudge him. He's as honest as the bells he casts, and they ring true.'

'Which leaves us with Thurstan the Shippmann. So, what of him?'

'I cannot say much, my lord, for he is not known so well beyond face and name. He plies a craft up and down Severn with everything from iron ore to cloth and—'

'The river! Catchpoll, we are fools!' interjected Bradecote, striking the heel of his hand against his brow. 'That is how Ricolde was got out of Worcester unseen. She was taken to her death by boat!'

Catchpoll and Walkelin stared at Bradecote, and then Catchpoll closed his eyes and swore, long and hard.

'Should have seen that from the start. Fool, yes! I must have fewer brains than Edmund the Limb-lopper. I am sorry, my lord.' The serjeant looked genuinely upset.

'We are all of us as much to blame, Catchpoll. We are

landsmen, for all that such a river runs us close by, and we think of foot and horse long before we think of oar or sail. It makes good sense. Ricolde lived not far from the quayside, and we do not remark every craft that is tied up there. It would be small, a boat one man could row, or sail perhaps, if there was wind, though it has been still these last few days. If it was early enough, it might not even have belonged to the man that took it, and he returned it without the owner ever thinking it had gone.'

'If it was not his own boat, perhaps he knew that it would not be missed.' Walkelin chewed his lip, thoughtfully. 'That is, the man knew the owner was sick, or would not be upon the river yesterday.'

'So, we need to know who owns small boats, whether any were noticed as absent early and then reappeared and if any man had given out that they would be upon other business. I doubt there would be anything in a boat to prove it was used, but we ought to check as we go. I foresee a forenoon with the potential to fall in the river.' Bradecote looked at Walkelin. 'You look the best man for crawling inside boats to look for things that might prove a connection, or getting wet.'

'I agree,' nodded Catchpoll, and Walkelin sighed and muttered how serjeanting apprentices were much put upon.

The Worcester wharfage was always bustling, and Worcester was heartily glad of it, since it drew custom within its walls and brought goods to be sold and worked. The rivermen proper were a tough lot and did not mix much with the townsmen, since they came, drank and often whored, then passed on up or down the Severn. There were also the local boatmen, who carried folk and goods across the flow a little up- or downstream when it was quicker than walking and carrying, or fished with spear and net. Most of the men were not keen on talking to the sheriff's men, because they were busy, although they opened up a little when they were told the reason. The sheriff's toll master, checking that toll was paid on goods coming and going by river as well as by land, knew nothing of use, but told them Thurstan the Shippmann had gone upriver the morning before and pointed out the first of the local men who worked the river, though Catchpoll could have named him anyway.

Siward eyed Serjeant Catchpoll in the manner of a mouse who does not know if the cat has already fed. He had found himself under the gimlet eye of the serjeant once or twice and did not like it much.

'Mornin', Siward. We are here about Ricolde the Whore.' Catchpoll's face gave away nothing.

'A bad business and no mistaking, Serjeant. What cause could a man have to harm her?'

'That is what we seek to find out, Siward. The lord Bradecote is keen to know if any boat was not in its normal place yesterday morning or any man unusually early upon the river.' Catchpoll waved a hand in the direction of the undersheriff, but kept his eyes on Siward, who looked uncomfortable.

'I can't recall any boat out, except Walter's that I found loose below the ford a little after the priory bell rang for Prime, and he said he was late rising.'

'Walter? Walter who? Point him out to us.' Bradecote's tone did not brook refusal.

'He is mending a net, over there.' Siward indicated a tow-haired man in his late twenties, who was indeed mending a net, and with the expression of a man who had to concentrate upon any task. The sheriff's trio did not have to be looking at Siward to know he was very relieved to pass them on to somebody else. His sharp intake of breath and long exhalation gave the game away.

'What happened to your boat then, Walter?' enquired Catchpoll, conversationally, as they gathered about the net mender.

'Nothing. I say a swan loosed it. I saw a swan the day before and it stared and stared at me, something wicked. Some of the other boatmen have said a swan will hold the soul of a drowned man, and it must be true. That swan thinks like a man and wanted me to be without my boat. I have seen the swans pecking at the ropes that hold the boats often enough, trying to untie them.'

'Do you remember securing your boat the night before?' Catchpoll was patient.

'Oh yes, and the swan must have been good with knots, which proves it had the soul of a boatman in it, because it knew how to undo it. It even kept the rope, for it came back without one.' Walter looked triumphant.

Bradecote looked at Catchpoll, despairingly. Walter was not to be moved from his belief that supernatural forces had untied his boat, but was quite content to say that he had overslept the night before, having taken too much ale at a tavern.

'Since we do not believe in spirits inhabiting swans, do we think that boat was left insecure or was it taken, used and then left to float downstream so that if found it would seem mere mischance?' pondered Bradecote, as they walked on.

'It fits, and yet . . . Let us hear what others have to say, my lord, and then we can decide.'

'Very true, Catchpoll. Who next? I—'

'My lord Undersheriff,' a voice hailed Bradecote, and he turned to see who it was.

'Master Simeon.' Bradecote acknowledged the Jewish merchant's obeisance with a smile. Catchpoll touched Walkelin on the arm and moved away to speak with the other boatmen. Unconsciously, he regarded Simeon the Jew as one who would far prefer to offer news to the lord undersheriff rather than himself.

'My lord, I have heard about the death, the killing, of Mistress Ricolde, and I had dealings with her and may have something of use to you.' Simeon made an open gesture with his hands.

Bradecote was surprised at the man giving her so formal and respectful a title.

'"Dealings"? I cannot see her needing to borrow money.' He frowned.

Simeon the Jew laughed, which took the undersheriff aback, and his smile was broad and genuine.

'*Todah raba!* Thank you, my lord. There are few who would look to the innocent use of the word "dealings", especially with one they could not trust.'

'But you are a man devoted to his family, Master Simeon, I know that, and I do trust you.' Bradecote looked quite serious.

'Ah, again my thanks, my lord, and you are right not to laugh, forgive me, for it is not a time for laughter.'

'You knew her . . . business?'

'What man or woman in Worcester does not? I knew, but trade is trade, and she bought goods from me, fine goods. I would not refuse to sell things to her because she traded in what she possessed, though I would not introduce her to my wife. The thing is, the last time she came to the wharf and spoke with me – oh, and she never came to my house because she said she did not want to shame it – we talked a short while, beyond business.' Simeon's smile returned but as a sad echo of his previous delight. 'She was a very comely woman, and somehow, though I ought not to say it, she managed to make a man feel . . . a man.' His slightly swarthy cheek darkened with a blush. 'It was pleasant to talk for a while, even as a good husband. We spoke of nothing unseemly, the trade on the river, the season, and she mentioned she was aggrieved with her landlord, who was going to raise the rent come Michaelmas, when she said she rented from Lady Day to Lady Day, and he had no right.'

'Master Simeon,' Bradecote's eyes narrowed, 'you are not going to tell me she rented from Mercet, are you?' The man nodded. 'Well, from another I would say that was stirring trouble for trouble's sake, but as I said, I trust you, and trust you never to set me upon a trail for no reason, because you are a sensible man as well as honest and would prefer the law to look favourably upon you.'

'Of course, my lord.' Simeon this time brought his hands together. 'Keep always within the law and with its smile upon you.'

They looked each other in the eye, and although there was humour, there was also an acknowledgement from each of honesty between them.

57

'Can you tell me anything of Morcar Grimson, Master Simeon, since he is a fellow merchant?'

'Morcar?' Simeon frowned. 'You suspect Morcar?' He sounded amazed and a little wary.

'No, but yet all men who were seen at her door . . .' Bradecote left the sentence unfinished and saw Simeon relax.

'Ah.' He paused for a moment, choosing his words with care. 'His is not a happy house. He is a good man, at least a good merchant. He buys well and sells at good profit. He is also a loving husband and as good as circumstance permits, but circumstance is . . .' He shrugged. 'His wife ails, poor woman, though thankfully she has given him a son to follow in his business. Her bones pain her and her limbs twist. She can scarce direct her household, and pain is at her shoulder all the time. He has spared no sum, tried the services of every physician in Worcester, but none can do more than ease her with syrup of poppy and then her mind wanders. She cannot be a wife to him, and I doubt he would put her to such distress as to try. A man should keep unto his own wife, assuredly, and I am sure Morcar did for many years, but from what I have heard it was she who suggested Mistress Ricolde. You think that strange, my lord?'

'I . . . I suppose not, if she cares for him greatly.'

'Indeed. So Morcar has taken to visiting Mistress Ricolde and does his penance for it, but is eased and can be a good husband in all else. He would be the last man in Worcester to want the woman dead.'

'Thank you, Master Simeon. That means we need not upset Mistress Grimson with questions. I will look into Ricolde's lease and Mercet, though if he was involved in anything to do with her death you can be sure his hands were kept clean.'

'Of a surety, my lord. Mercet is a man whose hands are the dirtiest in Worcester and yet without stain. It is a clever trick, but perhaps one day it will not be enough. I hope you catch the man who killed Mistress Ricolde. We none of us know when our time will come, but there are many who set themselves up high in Worcester who will be judged more harshly and none more so than Master Mercet.'

With which Simeon bowed his head and passed upon his way, and Bradecote was left thinking that however unlikely it was that they would find Mercet implicated, Catchpoll would be delighted to have good reason to tread on Mercet's toes.

Chapter Four

Bradecote rejoined his men, who were talking of tides and eddies with an old man with snowy white hair, and did not pass on Simeon's information to Catchpoll until they had worked their way to the quayside end. Catchpoll grunted, not as pleased as his superior would have expected.

'Wouldn't put it past him, trying to raise a rent like that and pressuring an "easy" target such as a woman without kin at her back, but I would guess Ricolde was never late with that rent and Mercet, the greedy bastard, would not go as far as killing her to get a few pence more when she paid on time. Not that it will stop us going and annoying him, and finding out just what his own relations were with Ricolde.'

'You think he went to her?'

'A man that rich in Worcester? He would want to show he could pay for her, though I doubt he offered her coin. He would be trying to get his night for free, but I would have loved to have seen her giving him a blunt refusal.'

'If she did, might he not have set one of his bullies onto her?' suggested Walkelin.

'To "teach her respect" perhaps, but not kill her, no. By the way, my lord, it seems Siward was not as honest with us as he ought to be. The old man, Kenelm, he knows the river better than all, having been upon it nigh upon three score years, and he knows the men upon it also. He gave us the whisper that Siward has a tendency to be gone before any man else is about and returns with a good catch of fish. He says this is because he is about when they rise for the first flies, but everyone else thinks is because he is taking fish from the fishery that belongs to the manor of Whittington, it being nice and close, and adding them to his own meagre haul. One day, when we are not hunting murderers, I might find myself at the riverbank nigh unto Whittington very, very early . . .' Catchpoll gave a grim little smile. 'The thing is, old Kenelm says he was below the ford himself around Prime and saw Siward bringing the boat back from further down the river. I imagine the man lied to hide his fish tricks and because we was interested in men out early as possible killers.'

'Does that mean the boat got as far as the stretch above Whittington too early to have ferried Ricolde to her death about dawn, or did her killer row in the dark?' Bradecote did not sound as if expecting a good answer.

'Well, it would have been very dark, my lord, for we have had barely even a sliver of moon these last few nights, and I for one would not want to row in the black dark. The other thing is Bevere Island. That killing was never done in pitch-darkness, and even if he had the forethought to bring a candle, it would be as much use as a firefly. No, she must have died after dawn, and that loosed boat is down to Walter having the brain of a sparrow. It could not have floated down so far from above Worcester.'

'But it must be a boat, surely it must. And that means one of the men on the quay knows far more than he is telling us.' Bradecote was frustrated.

'My lord, a loosed boat drifts with the flow, and so the boat could not have got as far, but if the man rowed it back . . .' Walkelin offered.

'Then someone would have seen him, wool-brain,' chided Catchpoll.

'No, no, Serjeant, it would work if he rowed the boat back to just upstream, came to the bank and then pushed it into the current. That way it could have been Walter's boat, and remember he was very sure he had tied it well. The man who killed Ricolde would thus have come in through the Foregate, though he never left through it. Which means we ought to have been asking not who went out at all, but who came in. We never asked the gatekeeper about them and we should have.'

The look he got from his superiors indicated that however true this statement might be, they were not rejoicing that he had said it. Serjeant looked at undersheriff, and undersheriff at serjeant.

'What goes out, comes back in,' murmured Catchpoll and sucked his teeth.

Bradecote contented himself with closing his eyes in an expression very like pain.

'He told you where he lived, Catchpoll. Go and ask him about any townsmen entering early, any who had not also left. There might be some good reason why a man went and returned a short time after, and we now know, or think we know, that in this case they did not leave by the gate. Walkelin and I will go and speak with Robert Corviser and see what we learn from him and, hopefully, his wife.' He shook his head. 'I cannot bring the two things together, Catchpoll, the death being connected to Bevere Island, but also to something in Worcester.'

'My lord, should we ask the men we speak to if they have kin in Claines or Hallow? If a man has visited oft enough that link might yet be there?' Walkelin liked to be positive.

'Yes, it is worth the asking, though if they see the connection for themselves, they might be disinclined to be honest with us. However, we keep hunting. When you have as much as you can from the Foregate man, catch us up, Catchpoll. We head first to Corviser, to see how my boots progress, and thereafter to the Healer, who is upon the same street, yes?'

'He is, my lord, and I can speak with Gerald Bellworker, whose premises are close by to the gatekeeper.'

'Good. If we can gather all we can from inside Worcester, we can then go back to Claines and across to Hallow, and discover the past, for that must be a key in all this, somehow. Good luck.'

* * *

Robert Corviser was the best shoemaker in Worcester, and even his rivals grudgingly admitted his stitching was the neatest and his leathers the best quality, though if you did as good a trade as he did, buying the best leather was not a problem.

He looked up as Bradecote entered his premises and appeared not to register Walkelin, following him.

'My lord, you must be patient. I promised you your boots by the morrow, but good work cannot be rushed. I—'

'Master Corviser, I am not here about my boots, though I will be glad to have them, very glad. No, we are speaking with those who had connections to the dead woman, Ricolde.' He described her circumspectly, seeing a female form to the rear of the workshop. He saw Corviser stiffen.

'Connections, my lord? I had no—'

'We discovered two pairs of good shoes in her dwelling, and my serjeant saw them as of a quality that marked them as your work.'

'Ah yes, yes.' The man relaxed a fraction. 'I did sell her shoes, and she paid in silver, I swear to you.'

'Oh, we know she bought goods with coin, as opposed to bartering,' declared the undersheriff, as though this was so well known as to be irrelevant. There was an audible sniff from the woman, who was listening. 'Can you tell me when she last made a purchase from you?'

'In May, as I recall, my lord. There was awkwardness to fitting, her feet being not as most people's following a nasty accident in her childhood. The soles of her feet had been burned, and her toes curled from the way she grew once they healed. She had bought from me before, but she was not "heavy" on footwear, as some are.'

'Why should she be, if she spent most of her time on her back,' hissed the woman, and Bradecote turned to address her. 'Mistress Corviser? What do you know of this woman?' Bradecote gave the question no stress.

'Same as everyone else, my lord. She was a whore, and no decent woman would have speech with her.' Her tone was all moral outrage.

'So, you never spoke to her when she came here? It was always your husband?' asked Walkelin, stepping to the side so that the undersheriff's height did not leave him unseen.

'Never. I would have had him refuse to make her shoes, but he says as coin is coin, no matter how it is earned, and it buys bread.'

'With the quality of your husband's work, and his prices, I judge there is plenty more than bread at your board, Mistress Corviser,' responded Bradecote, smoothly, leaving Corviser unsure as to whether he ought to defend his prices or show pride at the appreciation of his skill. He then turned back to Corviser. 'When she came to you, you took a pattern of her foot as you did mine.' He gave just a hint of a knowing smile as he said it, subtly implying the shoemaker had been granted legitimate view of a shapely ankle. 'And when you delivered the shoes, was there any problem with them?'

'Problem? No, my lord.' Corviser sounded suitably affronted.

'Then why did you have to visit her so often?' Bradecote still sounded calm, almost bored.

'I did not, my lord. It is a lie!'

'You say three different people are lying when they say they saw you enter Ricolde's home on Brodestrete, on four different evenings this last month . . . and not come out?'

'They were mistaken.' Corviser almost ground his teeth and glanced, fearfully, Walkelin thought, at his wife. She was a spare-framed woman with angular planes to her face and eyes as hard as the turquoise stones he had seen Reginald Ash setting into a silver torc.

'Or they seek to ruin our good name,' Mistress Corviser offered, 'but it is the quality of his work as makes my husband sought after, and we will ride the storm.' The last words were an assertion.

Bradecote noted the 'we' and had the feeling that what she said applied as much to herself. Even if he strayed, she would keep up the appearance of the ignorant wife in public because he had wealth and position in Worcester, and without him, she was nothing.

'Where were you the night before last, Master Corviser?'

'He was in his own bed,' declared his wife even as he opened his mouth.

'Of course he was.' Bradecote looked at her, and that look showed his cynicism. He wondered about letting them know that he was also considering that Ricolde was killed upon the instruction of a moneyed man, or woman, and by one who would kill for silver. No, he would keep that quiet for a while yet. 'Thank you for your help. I am sorry to have kept you from your work, Master Corviser, for my feet are eager to be well shod once more.' With that he turned, but then halted. 'One more question to you both. Do either of you have kin a little up the river, in Northwick, Claines or Hallow?'

'My wife's brother lives in Hallow, my lord.'

'But I have not seen him since the Feast of the Ascension,' added Mistress Corviser and folded her arms, daring them to ask more. They did not do so, but left, Walkelin in Bradecote's wake.

'If you carved her likeness from a stick there would not be much to take off,' murmured Walkelin, the whittler.

'So, you did not like Mistress Corviser. Nor did I, and not just her looks. I want you to stay here, Walkelin, and keep an eye on them for an hour or two, see if you hear raised voices, or either leaves. Report to me at the castle when you hear the bell for None.'

'Yes, my lord. Er, if it sounds like it comes to blows . . . ?'

'Then you intervene.'

'And if they both leave?'

'I would think it unlikely. In fact, I very much hope that Corviser would not think of leaving, and is right now working hard upon my boots, since I gave him a hint.'

'Ah, that was a hint, my lord. Yes, of course.' Walkelin's lips twitched. Just occasionally he felt bold enough to jest with the lord Bradecote. His superior looked at him, and his eyes held humour though the face was impassive.

'It was. I shall now go and see Roger the Healer, to see what he "brews" as his excuse for his visits to Ricolde. He sounds an unlikely man with an axe, yet we must speak with him. He is but along the street, yes?'

'Yes, my lord.'

* * *

Roger the Healer's home was redolent of so many different smells it was hard to discern one from the other, and it blended the sweet with the rank. He was not the only one of his calling in Worcester, and rivalry was fierce. This he admitted to the lord undersheriff.

'It is all down to reputation, my lord, and one rich patient who cannot be saved by any remedy can cast a good man's name into the midden for months. Mistress Ricolde, now she was a patient worth keeping, for she never looks – looked – unwell, and indeed showed a fine bloom of health.'

'Yet you attended her, at her home.' Bradecote gave no stress to his words.

'I did visit, to replenish a pot of salve, my lord. I . . . I do not talk of those I treat, but the lady is dead and . . . Mistress Ricolde bore scars, old scars that I doubt any man who . . . well, he would not be looking at her feet, from preference now, would he?'

'Her feet?' For a moment, Bradecote acted as if perplexed.

'There were burn marks to the soles of her feet, very old, but the skin had tightened and twisted, and gave her some discomfort from the contraction. I believe she had soft fur inserted into her shoes, to give a little softness as she walked, but she lived with it all the time. I made up a salve, of comfrey, onion and dogwood, to my own mixing, and it gave her ease when she massaged it into the skin, as she said. She certainly bought it from me often.'

'But refilling a pot of salve would not take all night, would it.'

'No, my lord.' The Healer coloured. 'She was a remarkable woman. We would talk, or rather she would let me talk, until the candle guttered. She was always interested, always understanding.' The man chewed his thin lip, then murmured, 'I am not a man of lust, my lord. I do not know why. Perhaps it is that I minister to the flesh so much that it is different to me. Yet that does not mean I do not crave a little company. I am a lonely man. I shared her bed, Ricolde's, but as a place to sleep, not to . . .' His voice faltered, cracked. 'She was an angel.' His hands covered his face, and he wept. Bradecote, taken by surprise both by the revelation and depth of his feeling, just stood there and waited. Gradually the man took control of his emotions. He wiped his cheeks with a shaking hand.

'I would not, could not, have killed her, but I could kill the man that did. Find him, my lord, and hope that I do not.' The vehemence in his voice gave it a strength at odds with his weak frame, and Bradecote did not doubt his intent.

'We will try, try our best.' He paused. 'Do you have kin? Upriver, Hallow way, perhaps? Or this side of the river?'

'None, my lord. There is nobody, nobody at all.'

'Thank you. You should speak with Father Anselm of All Saints. I think you both held her in respect in different ways, but he would understand.' Here was a lonely man, facing more loneliness, and with nobody to tell of his grief. Who better than the priest to give him solace in his sadness.

Serjeant Catchpoll did not believe in letting the general populace know that the sheriff's men were less than omniscient, or, as he phrased it to Walkelin, 'Let 'em think we see everything, hear everything, know everything.' He spoke briefly with the bellmaker and then went hunting the gatekeeper, who turned out to be upon his watch and not at home. He declared that new information had come to light, and that any man of Worcester entering the gate on the early morning of the murder was to be named to him, so that questions might be asked. In the face of this very official-sounding demand, the gatekeeper dredged his memory very carefully.

'I can name but three, Serjeant. There was Edwin the Turner, who had left the day prior to visit his sick oldmother in Northwick and returned long of face because she is like to die. Then there was Osric Boldman's eldest lad, and from the look on his face he had been out to meet a wench and either found her bed the softer or was too late from his wooing to get back in. Sheepish, he looked. The third, well he does not really count, because he lives outside the wall anyway.'

'But his name?'

'Godfrid, journeyman to Will Fellman, as has his business just out yonder beyond the gate. Not like the tanners, of course, but the smell of pelts and salt and oils—'

'Yes. Does he come in often of mornings?'

'No. I would have to say he keeps to himself and the work. Rarely see him, at least I have not, and our watches change, so I have been about most times of day, and the night too, in case there is something important that has to get to the castle. We would open the wicket for that, but nought else, mind.'

Catchpoll frowned and held up his hand to silence the watchman as he gabbled further insistence that none but those with authority ever gained entry after dark. He was still frowning when he went to revisit the homes upon Brodestrete where they had asked their questions the day before, but there was a grim smile gashing his grizzled beard when he met with Bradecote at the castle. He said nothing was to be gained from Gerald Bellmaker except that he regretted Ricolde's passing, and then gave the more interesting news.

'This Godfrid rarely comes within the walls, so it was an odd thing. But, if he lived outside, why come in at all, that early? I have not discovered if he came in the evening before, before the gate was shut, but we must ask the other gatemen that.'

'So, how does a man who lives without the wall have an evening at an inn, Catchpoll?'

'Easy, my lord. The wicket gate is very rarely opened to let anyone in, but since whoever is leaving is known, the gate can be opened safely to let them out.'

'I see, so . . .'

'The thing is, my lord, that one of Ricolde's neighbours does recall a man at her door on the morning of her death, when she must have already been upriver. We asked about the past, not a man on the day of the death, and a man knocking to enter in daylight was unlikely to be one who paid her.'

'Why should he knock upon her door if he knew she was dead, though?' Bradecote's brows knit.

'Habit, I would say, my lord, in case anyone might be within unexpectedly.'

'And why would he have returned to . . . ? You think he dropped something, left it behind, and feared it would lead to him?'

'Aye, my lord, it makes sense. We found nothing.'

'If he did find something it was swiftly found, because he had not looked beneath the cot and discovered the box of silver. If a man has committed murder, what is theft to add to his sins?' Bradecote could be as cynical of his fellow man as Catchpoll. 'He could at the least take the scrip of coin that was to have gone to Father Anselm and none would have been the wiser. Who would say, "She was robbed of some of her money"? We would have seen the loose silver and thought her "treasury" intact. He buries it, hides it and over the next few months he has a little more money than usual, but not so much as to raise suspicion among the suspicious.'

'You mean me, my lord.'

'I mean you, Catchpoll. I think we need to go and—' He stopped. 'It is not like the tanner's, is it, Catchpoll? I swear if it is, then you go alone.' The undersheriff could still smell the stench of the Sutheberi Hill tannery in his nightmares, many months after having had to visit it.

'Well, it is not sweet-smelling like a flower, my lord, but not as bad. They tread the skins to soften them and work butter and salt into them to keep the fur from moulting from the hide. There are bits to scrape off, of course, a bit ripe, but they do not cure in piss and—'

'I need no more. I told Walkelin to meet us at the castle by the bell for None. He is watching Corviser's place. That wife is not one I would care to cross. I wondered, since there was some cause to think her involved, if she would do something unusual, even meet someone. It was worth an hour or so of Walkelin's time.'

72

'He will not be kicking his heels for long, my lord, even if he is returned before us. We can have our words with the journeyman and decide if he is worth bringing along or not, and no, my lord, I do not think this one would be better handled by me alone, just in case you was thinking it.'

'Only fleetingly, Catchpoll. Only fleetingly.'

Chapter Five

Will Fellman's premises backed upon the wall, not more than sixty or so paces from the river, and Bradecote and Catchpoll exchanged glances, thinking the same thing. They knocked upon the door, and a woman opened it. She was comely, in a tired way, and clearly advanced with child. Her face was very pale, but her eyes were red, eyeball and rim both.

'Yes?' The voice was a lifeless whisper.

'Mistress Fellman? We would speak with your husband.'

'So would I, but he would attend you the more.' She looked at Catchpoll. 'You are the thief-taker, yes?'

'Yes. And this is the lord Bradecote, undersheriff.'

'He is not here. Gone upriver to buy pelts and will be back when he has done so.'

'Well, we would also speak with his journeyman.'

'With Godfrid? He is out the back, treading a skin. You

had best come through . . . my lord.' She gave an awkward bob and led them into the comparative gloom of the chamber. It was sparsely furnished and showed no great wealth, but for the addition of an assortment of pelts that made up a covering for the bed and one upon which a child of about three sat, sucking its thumb. All the furs were patchy, skins that had lost too much hair to be sold on but might still keep in warmth. There was also a small boy of about five and a girl of seven or eight, who had the same desolate look of the mother, and shrank back at the entrance of the two unknown men. Thrust into a corner was a cradle, and in it, linens for an infant, folded neatly, though Bradecote sensed it was not in anticipation. There was a silence to the chamber, heavy with melancholy.

'I am sorry, mistress, that we come at such a time,' offered Bradecote, who was not slow to understand the situation. She just looked at him, then nodded. She led them through to a yard at the rear, where a well-set-up young man, with a mop of thick, brown hair, was treading skins in a wide, coopered half-barrel. He looked at the woman questioningly, and also, thought Bradecote, with a kind sympathy.

'This is the lord Bradecote, Godfrid, and the lord Sheriff's serjeant.'

'My lord?' The man stopped treading and stood still. The picture he presented looked vaguely ridiculous.

Bradecote cleared his throat. The smell was not as bad as a tanner's, but there was an odour of rotting flesh and salt and butter tending to the rancid.

'You were seen entering through the Foregate yesterday,

when it opened. It was noted because you are not used to do such a thing. Where were you going?'

'I . . .' Godfrid glanced at the woman, his eyes questioning, and then colour suffused his cheek. 'I was upon an errand, my lord.'

'From your master? He sent you to the house of Ricolde upon an errand?' The undersheriff's disbelief was audible.

'I sent him, my lord,' Mistress Fellman said, listlessly. 'My husband left the day before yesterday, as I said, to buy skins up the river, but . . . I am not a fool. I sent Godfrid to that house to see if he was there, so that he might be told his child was dead.' She caught her breath on a sob. 'He would not have cared much, for it was "but a girl", and she was in a raging fever for the two days before. He said there was no point in him delaying his journey, but if he was in Worcester, well, he might have found the time to attend her burial.'

'I see. I am sorry, Mistress Fellman. These questions have to be asked. The woman Ricolde was foully murdered, yesterday morning, so . . . What you say makes good sense. We will not trouble you further.' Bradecote looked at Catchpoll, whose face was grave and also thoughtful. He nodded. They left the way they had come, and heard a child begin to cry as the door shut behind them.

'Well, we could never have guessed that for a reason, but it is a good one,' said Catchpoll.

'Poor woman.'

'Aye.' Catchpoll hawked and spat into the dust.

'I should have asked why she thought her husband was

there. I mean not for what purpose but . . . He knew her, at least he sold things to her. There was that fox-fur-lined hood and the mole-lined shoes. I should have told you what I gleaned from the Healer.'

'And what was that, my lord?'

'That he adored her, but did not use her, not as other men might. I think he might be the third man Father Anselm mentioned. He said he lacks desire, desire of the flesh, but he is another man you would term "a poor lonely bastard" who went for companionship and a little human comfort. He also made her salve, salve for the old burn scarring upon the soles of her feet. You do not think those came from an accident.'

'No.'

'No more do I. Well, he said he made this salve for the discomfort and that she had fur linings in her shoes to give them something softer to press upon, as we found. So on two counts she would have come to Fellman, unless there is another of his trade hereabouts.'

'He is the only one here.'

'And he was "going up the river", which implies a boat, Catchpoll.'

'It does. The only thing to spoil this idea I see growing in your mind, is that he comes from Gloucester, so has no connection with Bevere Island.'

'Ah but wait. If he uses the river when he goes to buy pelts that are trapped by men along its length, he must have got to know the part near here very well indeed, whether he was born in Gloucester or not.'

'But you still have to ask why he would want to kill the best whore in Worcester, and on the island. There is no "why", my lord, and that worries me. Until we have the "why", I do not see my way clear to the "who".' Catchpoll paused. 'My lord, I doubt Fellman is a good man or a good husband, but being a faithless bastard who finds a whore because his wife is too full-bellied to please him is not a hanging offence.' He glanced sideways at the undersheriff.

'You think I want him to be guilty because of that, Serjeant Catchpoll?' Bradecote snapped. His mouth was full of the taste of a bad stench, he had just added further upset to a woman lost in grief for a dead child, and it was true, part of him did want it to be this unseen man who might well betray his wife and had left his family with a child sick to death, without showing any care. It was true, and it got in the way.

Catchpoll, wisely, did not answer.

Undersheriff and serjeant walked in grim silence from the Foregate and along Bocherewe, the main thoroughfare that ran north to south towards cathedral and castle, and the silence was isolating rather than companionable. Bradecote was angry with himself, and Catchpoll was trying to tease threads of possibility from the tangled mass of question and knowledge. It sometimes helped him to think of it as the wool of a fleece that had to be teased and carded so that it could be spun on the twirling distaff. It started off as a bundle and ended as a long thread. So far, they still had but a bundle of thoughts and ideas, and isolated truths.

As they walked, Catchpoll felt eyes follow them, wondering. All Worcester must know by now that they were hunting a murderer. Fellman's wife had been in ignorance more from her cocoon of deep grief than living outside the walls. Nothing would have touched her in the immediate aftermath, nothing would have had meaning. For everyone else it was still a gem of news to discuss at street corners, or when buying and selling, but it would not last long. The ripples upon the surface of Worcester would smooth out and Ricolde would become a 'Do you remember . . . ?'

They entered the castle bailey and saw Walkelin leaning against the wall of the stables and talking with 'his' young woman from the kitchens, who moved away, blushing, as they drew near.

'I hope that your head has not cast your duty out when wenching thoughts entered, young Walkelin.'

'No, Serjeant. And I was just talking and—'

'Looking, eh? Well, looking is all you could do in the bailey in full daylight, without attracting a crowd.' Catchpoll grinned at Walkelin's discomfiture. 'So, has Mistress Corviser hit her husband over the head with her skillet?'

'Not as I heard, Serjeant, though there was some loud talking and all in a female voice. I do not think she was complimenting him on the neatness of his stitching.'

'Sounds unlikely. Neither left?'

'Not really.'

'And what does "Not really" mean, Walkelin?' Bradecote, who had been scowling, did not sound in the mood for vague answers.

'Well, my lord, Mistress Corviser did come out, but only to cross to the place across the street, where she spoke with Oldmother Stane, and then went back indoors.'

'I see. Then you are—'

'Oldmother Stane, whose daughter keeps house and cooks for Robert Mercet, Walkelin, is not some kind old woman who dispenses wisdom and a good way with barley broth.' Catchpoll shook his head at his apprentice serjeant. 'You have to rid yourself of the idea that every woman with white hair and a doddering step is kindly and innocent. Her husband went off when the children was small, and she swears he followed in the train of some lord to Outremer, but I knows as he was hanged in Ludlow for stealing sheep.'

'Many a decent woman has been married to a man who ends that way, Catchpoll.' Bradecote folded his arms and looked at the serjeant.

'Indeed, my lord. I would be the first to say it, but Widow Stane, as she was known before age gave her respectability, bred bad 'uns. One son was a bully of Mercet's until he was killed in a fight, another disappeared when he was declared without the law, and the daughter married another of Mercet's men, who drowned in the river six or seven years back, while trying to take forcible possession of a man's boat, a man who owed Mercet money. Her son is near a man now and works in Mercet's warehouses, lifting and carrying, being big but not bright. You have to wonder what Mistress Corviser was discussing, faced with that.'

Reluctantly, Bradecote agreed.

'So, you want us to pay a visit to Robert Mercet, Catchpoll?'

'I would feel the happier knowing one way or another if there was any connection, my lord. Then we can go back to Bevere and Claines and dig deep into what went on years back that might link to what happened to Ricolde. Once we has everything from here, and from there, well, there is just a chance there will be a link that gives us our answer.'

'Then we go and knock upon Robert Mercet's door.'

Robert Mercet was one of the wealthiest men in Worcester and liked everyone to know it. When he gave alms, it was in front of as many people as possible and to the prior of the cathedral priory, not his parish church, and when someone got in his way, he made sure that everyone knew it had been an unwise decision, whilst keeping himself out of the castle cells. The antipathy between him and Serjeant Catchpoll was mutual and of very long standing, but he was a generous man and extended his loathing to the undersheriff and 'the underling', Walkelin.

His very substantial oaken front door was opened by Serlo, his household man. Serlo stepped back, not so much to allow them to enter as out of dread. If he feared Catchpoll, he was terrified of the undersheriff, in which terror Catchpoll was happy to encourage him. Hugh Bradecote was a very reasonable man, but it served Catchpoll's purpose the better if Serlo believed that, however unpleasant Serjeant Catchpoll might be, he was as nothing to his superior. Serlo, used to men with power being always ready to kick the lowly, believed the lord Bradecote would consider an afternoon spent watching torture was an entertainment. He shrank against the wall.

'The lord Bradecote, to see your master,' announced Catchpoll, with aplomb.

Serlo made small mewing noises as he bowed so low the back of his greasy neck was visible. The sheriff's men strode past him as if he were invisible. They entered the hall chamber, where Mercet conducted his business, most frequently using duress. The man looked up from a vellum scroll, his pale aquamarine eyes narrowing. He set one pudgy hand upon the table.

'Ah, the lord Undersheriff, and his . . . minions.' He stressed the 'under' and made 'minions' sound like dogs. He half rose, with the ghost of an obeisance. 'How may I assist the law today?' His voice was smooth, like the skin of his face, above which angelically pale, wavy hair attempted to disguise his pink scalp. It was fighting a losing battle.

'You make it sound as if "assisting the law" was something you do frequently, Master Mercet. I am not sure the law sees it quite the same way, but we will leave that.' Bradecote could sound just as smooth and insincere. Meetings with Mercet were always conducted upon the thin ice of politeness over depths of loathing. 'We are here concerning the death of Ricolde, of Brodestrete. You will know where she lived, since you were her landlord, and I am sure you visited to see that your property was in good order, personally.'

'A sad loss. She was a good . . . tenant.' He sighed.

'A good tenant from whom you were trying to extort an increase in rent before you had the right.' Bradecote was still matter-of-fact.

'Alas, you have been misinformed, my lord, as so often. The "increase" of which you speak was required because I had

82

to have a new door made for the property, the previous one having been kicked in. It must be one of the risks of those engaging in her . . . trade.'

'The damage was not reported to the castle,' growled Catchpoll.

'Do not tell me you would have searched all Worcester for the man that did it? For me? I am touched at the thought, Serjeant.' Mercet laid his hand over his heart and smiled, but his eyes glittered.

'Since I have little doubt it would have been one of your own men, yes, I would.' Catchpoll kept his temper in check, but it was there.

'You know, my lord, it is one of the risks of dealing always with the law. A man becomes so very suspicious, suspicious to the point of madness. Do be careful it does not affect you too.' Mercet looked straight at Bradecote, whose gaze did not falter. The merest hint of a frown appeared on Mercet's brow, for there were few who could outstare him.

'And one of the dangers of dealing always with the edge of the law is that one can so easily overstep it,' replied Bradecote. 'Do you have kin outside Worcester, on the north side?'

The question clearly took Mercet aback.

'No. I am a Worcester man, and my father and his before him. We have no hint of pig-herding and haymaking in my family.' He clearly regarded rural life as unworthy of him and even the suggestion of having connections to the soil an insult. There was no attempt at dissimulation.

'And where were you the night before last, Master Mercet, just so that we know?'

'In my own bed, my lord, having said my prayers.'
Mercet trying to sound pious made Catchpoll give a crack
of laughter.

'Can anyone swear that for you?'

'Serlo and Agnes, the woman who keeps me fed.'

'We would speak with her. Have her fetched.' Bradecote
could be autocratic in a way Mercet never managed, as if it was
natural. Mercet had to work at it.

'Serlo,' said Mercet, still looking at Bradecote, 'fetch Agnes.'
He said it the same way that he would have had him fetch a
dog. Serlo, who had been standing by the chamber entrance,
disappeared and returned with a woman, who was probably
younger than she looked, and who wiped wet hands on her
skirts and dipped in a wary obeisance.

'Master?'

'The Undersheriff, sorry, the *lord* Undersheriff, wants you
to tell him I was here the night before last.'

'No, I want you to tell me whether Master Mercet was here',
corrected Bradecote.

'He was, my lord, all night.'

'All night? You were with him all night?' Bradecote's mobile
eyebrow rose.

'No! I am not his . . . I am not!' Her outrage was swift
enough, and her cheeks went scarlet.

'Forgive me, but then you cannot vouch for him all night,
can you.' Bradecote did not pose it as a question.

Catchpoll controlled himself with difficulty.

'I set the latch upon the door, and I sleep in the passage.
Master could not have left.' This was Serlo, nervous, fearful

of angering his master if he did not say something and the undersheriff if he did. Mercet relaxed, visibly.

'That is much more reasonable. Now, Agnes, your mother lives opposite Robert Corviser, in the Corviserstrete, appropriately.'

'Yes, my lord.'

'Have you, or your son, been to visit her this last week?'

'I . . . She is my mother and old.'

'Have you visited her?'

'Yes, my lord.'

'And have you spoken with Mistress Corviser?' Bradecote was persistent but slightly casual, as though this were some polite social interchange.

Agnes took a slightly deeper breath before making her denial. 'No, my lord.'

'Think again, Agnes, and give me the answer.' There was a hint, just a hint, of steel in the voice now.

'I may have . . . just to talk about my mother and her bad leg.'

'I am glad Mistress Corviser hides a kindly heart beneath that . . . firm exterior. Did she mention Mistress Ricolde?'

'Mistress? Her? Not fit for the title she was and no mistaking. We agreed, as any goodly women would, that such as her, flaunting themselves, well, they deserve flogging.' Suddenly, Agnes was not concerned about what she said or to whom she was saying it.

'And did Mistress Corviser arrange, shall we say, for such a thing to happen? Your son is a big, strong fellow, isn't he?' Bradecote was guessing, wildly, but it seemed worth trying.

'He never touched her. He never. She wasn't there when he went. He never touched her, and he is a good son.' Agnes's voice grew more and more shrill as she repeated herself. Mercet shut his eyes. Some people did not so much fall into traps as leap into them.

'When was she not there?' Catchpoll had kept silent until now, seeing as she was sufficiently overawed by his superior, and he was doing a good job.

'Day before yesterday, hour after sunrise. Didn't want any man there, one who had . . . He never saw her.'

'Thank you, Agnes. As his mother, you should teach your son that justice is dealt with by the law, not whoever is prepared to pay to have it done.' Bradecote stole a swift glance at Mercet as he said this.

'Oh, he is a good boy, my lord, as would not do nothing to shame his name.'

Bradecote looked unimpressed but did not mention that the lad's grandsire was hanged and his sire drowned in the act of playing the bully.

'I think, Master Mercet, that that is all.' He nodded at Mercet, turned on his heel and walked out without another word, with Catchpoll grinning behind him and Walkelin looking out of his depth.

Some yards along the street, Catchpoll spoke.

'Seems as it is not just me you is learning off, my lord. The lord Sheriff himself could not have been more commanding or cold. I was watching Mercet all through, as well as the woman. You rose in his estimation there, and he will be the more cautious of you in the future. Pity the bastard has nothing to do with the murder, but I cannot see how he could. Having one of his men kick her door in and then increase the rent because of repairs, well, that is typical of Mercet. I would wager he had the door made by a man as owes him or is afraid and charged but a half its worth, and the increase in rent would be far more than needful. Yes, typical Mercet, and hacking Ricolde to death is not. Oh well.' He sighed. 'And we know why Mistress Corviser was so quick to go and see her neighbour. She must be quaking in her well-made shoes lest we take her up for murder when she was planning a step less.'

'But the folk in Brodestrete spoke of seeing one man, a young man, at her door in the morning.' Walkelin was letting things process through his orderly brain.

'I think, if we was to ask what they looked like, we might get two answers,' replied Catchpoll. 'These people do not spend their every waking moment peering through cracks in their shutters. It is just odd coincidence that at a time when you would least expect a man to be knocking to get in, there were two, one after the other.'

'The only real problem with all of this is that we no sooner think we have a reason and a person than they prove to have no reason and not to be the murderer.' Bradecote grimaced.

'They only laid her in the earth this morning, my lord. We needs not think all lost for a while yet, and we have not gone back upriver to discover what lay in her long-distant past.'

'I cannot see a man from a generation ago killing her now, that is my problem with looking outside of Worcester, Catchpoll.'

'There ain't much more of Worcester where we might look though, my lord.'

'No. Since we are not leaving until the morning, let us stand down for the day. I am sure Walkelin's mother, and Mistress Catchpoll, will both be delighted to see more of you both.' Bradecote toyed with the idea of riding back to Bradecote for the night but thought Christina would not enjoy him leaving before cock crow. Of late she had not been contented in the morning.

Chapter Six

As it turned out, any plans he might have entertained would have come to nothing. Shortly after he had settled himself in his chamber with a beaker of wine and removed his now very-dilapidated boots that were fast giving up the ghost upon the cobbles and packed earth of town streets, a servant came to tell him that there was a man below, with an urgent message. Hauling on his boots with a groan, and leaving his wine with some regret, Bradecote went to the hall, where the Foregate keeper was not so much stood as half crouched, his hands braced on his knees.

'My lord!' The man was gasping for breath. 'My lord, he is returned.'

'Who is?'

'The swordsman who gave me no "good morrow", the day you found Ricolde dead.' The man crossed himself even as his chest heaved.

'And is he kept at the gate?' Bradecote asked.

'Well, not what you would call kept, my lord.'

'Where is he?' The undersheriff sounded as though he expected to hear 'I do not know'.

'I followed him to The Goose tavern, my lord, and then ran here.'

It could be a lot worse.

'Then you will have to run again, because we need to reach him before he quaffs his ale and moves on.' Bradecote ignored the man's groan and strode quickly from the chamber, exhorting him to hurry up.

The undersheriff did not actually run through the streets, having decided that the gatekeeper would never keep up and his boots might fall apart, but even at his swiftest walking stride the short-legged man was panting as he followed at the double. He knew his way to the sign of The Goose, now repaired after the lightning strike fire of the year before. They reached the tavern, and saw a man leaning against the outside, a beaker in his hand, clearly unconcerned with more than ensuring no thief tried to steal from his belongings upon the pack pony.

'That is the man, my lord Bradecote,' managed the gatekeeper, pointing at the man, and collapsed to sit in an exhausted heap upon the ground.

Bradecote looked at the man, looked intently. There was something he recognised in him.

'I know you, I would swear it.'

'I reckon as you do.' The man did not look either delighted or disappointed, and his voice was without emotion. 'You have changed the more, but the snivelling lordling become the lord fits face to title. I would not have known you else.'

Bradecote was trawling through memory, and the man's comment sent him to hunt among the memories of his squiredom. There it was that he found him.

'Jehan of Ullenhall. Yes, older, heavier of jowl perhaps, but Jehan. So, what brings you through Worcester, and once in each direction, north and south, when your kin should surely live to the east?' Bradecote paused. 'You were described as a man who lived by his sword and with all his worldly possessions with him. A visit "home" to kindred would not need that, unless you trust your lord's other men so little you think they would steal your goods in your absence.'

'Ha, well, there are a couple I wouldn't put past trying something, but they would think twice with me, for I am still swifter than they are.'

Yes, he had always been swift, in action and in taking opportunity. Hugh Bradecote, at the age of eight, had been sent to his father's old mentor, Henry de Beaumont, Earl of Warwick, for his training, although the earl was far from young and had died the following year. That left his son Roger, a youth only eight years older than Hugh himself, as the new earl, and a widow in her mid thirties. The Countess Margaret was, even with five children of her bearing, both a competent and comely woman, and a support to her son, only just man enough at seventeen to take his father's powers and wield them with any success. She had 'mothered' Hugh when he had arrived, homesick and rather lost, and junior to all the other squires of the earl, and it was upon her bosom he had wept at fourteen, when his own mother had died. He had idolised her as a surrogate in those early years, and Earl Roger, who used his wits more than physique, and was a thoughtful, even gentle young man, showed him that there was more to being a lord than just being a warrior.

Jehan, somewhere in age between his new lord and the widowed lady, had proved himself as more than a merely capable man-at-arms under the old earl and had been given advancement. He wore power as badly as Earl Roger wore it well, and one evening, after too much wine, had decided that the lady must be in need of a man, after a year of widowhood. He had staggered to her chamber, where young Hugh was being physicked after the drawing of an ageing milk tooth that had given trouble, and entered, swaying. He had not been pleased to find the child there, nor that the Lady Margaret was both unwilling to accept his advances and quite able to defend herself against an inebriate. The ten-year-old Hugh had also tried to defend his lady and been clouted round the head in the attempt. The lady could have had Jehan flogged, or worse, but took the pragmatic view that he had probably had as little control over his brain as he had his legs and contented herself with making sure he got the worst jobs and little respite in which to make merry for the next six months. He could do nothing but accept his punishment, except that when he got the chance, he took out his discontent upon the smallest squire. When none might see, there were blows and kicks for errors that did not exist, and Hugh Bradecote learnt that there were penalties for doing the honourable thing. Thankfully, at the end of the year, Earl Roger had sent Jehan and his sword arm to assist in the increasingly unsuccessful holding of the family's lands in the Gower Peninsula, and he had not returned, at least while Hugh Bradecote remained in the earl's service.

'In whose service are you, if any?'

'The Lord Henry, Henry of Gower, Earl Roger's brother, not that it is any business of yours.'

'Ah, but there you are wrong, and as I well recall, you got a lot of things wrong, however good your sword arm. Forget the squire. I am Hugh Bradecote, Undersheriff of Worcestershire, and my business is discovering the man who murdered a woman of Worcester. Which again means I ask why you have travelled through Worcester twice these last few days? Your kin are not local.'

'I carried a message for Henry of Gower, to kin of his.'

'One that meant you took all your baggage with you?' Bradecote sounded unconvinced. 'Messengers tend to travel light and fast.'

'It was a . . . heavy message.' Jehan's manner challenged. In truth, knowing his identity and from whence he had come, there was no possible reason to associate him with Ricolde or Bevere. Whatever it was he was doing, and whether or not it was upon Henry of Gower's instruction, had no relevance to the task in hand. Nevertheless, Bradecote was not going to make things easy.

'You left at the opening of the town gate two days past, so you stayed overnight in Worcester. Where, and with whom?'

'I can give you no name, other than "Brother". I stayed in the guest hall of the priory. You can check, and I do not suppose you would think they lie. I left early, wanting to reach my destination early enough to rest my horses, and set off back today. There is never peace in Wales, and I prefer it where I am most useful.'

'Yes, I am sure Henry of Gower finds you useful. Best you get yourself back to the priory, if you rest there tonight, before the holy brothers take to their beds.'

Bradecote turned to the gatekeeper, thanked him for his diligence and walked away, in the certain knowledge that Jehan's eyes followed him all the way.

Walkelin, who had kept the lord sheriff's business from his mother the previous evening, was confronted by her over the cooking pot, demanding to know if he was involved in what was now the talk of Worcester. Had he stepped into 'the whore's lair', and was it true that she had manacles of silver and a tapestry with lewdness depicted upon it? What did it show?

Her son's jaw dropped. He told her that there was nothing that a decent woman would have been ashamed of, and in fact it was very respectable within.

His mother, disappointed, berated him for entering a house of such sin, despite it being his duty, and told him off for mentioning 'decent women' in the same breath as 'that Ricolde'. She then sat silent for much of their meal, wondering whether it was better to reveal the truth to her friends or pretend that their assumptions had been all true and thereby have more happy hours to discuss the iniquity of Ricolde the Whore.

By contrast, Mistress Catchpoll did not talk about Ricolde at all, not directly. Besides, if there was a killing, then Catchpoll would be involved in the hunting of whoever did it.

Catchpoll himself, after a few minutes' discourse with his old friend Drogo the cook, and a beaker of ale, had returned to his own hearth, but not to the women's gossip that was trickling through Worcester. Mistress Catchpoll was not one inclined to be charitable to the late Ricolde, having a strong view on 'women of her sort'. She had that spark of jealousy, prevalent in most of the women whose looks, if they ever had them, were faded with the marks life had put upon them over decades, for the few whose beauty was so evident it would be stupid to deny it. She had no fears of Catchpoll being under some spell to the murdered woman, in any physical sense, but he had been quiet the previous evening and had said not one word against her. He looked pensive again this night. It irked his virtuous wife that he could admire, in any way, a woman to whom virtue was unknown, but she was not stupid enough to carp about her. His expression did make her lay a hand on his arm as he stared at the hearth.

'It is not like you to worrit yourself over a killing the way you do over this one, Catchpoll.'

'It's wrong, that's what it is,' mused Catchpoll, half to himself.

'I do not deny it, but at least it was not some goodly soul and—'

'You ought to have been at All Saints and heard Father Anselm. He valued her.'

'He is a priest. His charity is . . . great.'

'So was hers, as has come to light, but I am not talking the "wrong" of killing. It is the way it does not fit together. Those outside the wall have the connections to Bevere and the place

95

of killing, and those inside have the connections to the woman, and not only do neither overlap, but neither gives us a reason why a man would commit a murder with some forethought and then . . . She was not just killed, Wife, she was slaughtered. None of it fits, and yet it has to.'

He stared into the cooking pot, as if the pottage might give him inspiration. He also had 'that' expression, which long years of marriage meant she knew when best to leave him to his thoughts. She offered him another ladleful.

The morning found all three of the sheriff's men trotting northward out of Worcester, but they got little further than the Foregate when they were hailed by a female voice. They halted and turned to the sound.

'My lord, my lord, I must speak with you.' Mistress Fellman, white of face but with a bruise that was fast becoming a black eye, broke into a shambling run and stumbled towards them. Bradecote dismounted, and she nearly fell into his arms. She was shaking.

'He is returned. He is returned, and look, upon his cotte . . .' In her hand she clutched a bundle of cloth, which now dropped to the ground. Her voice was trembling as much as her limbs. 'He returned last eventide, quite late, and I saw not this, for he cast it aside and . . .' She caught her breath and looked at the ground.

'Mistress Fellman, are you all right?' Bradecote, looking down at the top of her coif, felt the trembling in her arms as he held her from him. His first thought was of the fragility of a woman in her state of carrying. She nodded.

Catchpoll picked up the dropped cloth and held it wide

in both hands. It was a man's cotte, and the front was heavily stained with darkish marks, marks that had not come out with washing. He peered closely at it to be sure.

'Blood,' he said, laconically.

'They say she was slaughtered, my lord,' whimpered Mistress Fellman. 'Whore though she was, to do that . . . My children are not safe! I am not safe!' Her eyes pleaded.

'Be calm, mistress. Are you sure . . . ? Perhaps there is another—'

'It is him. I know it. But why? He knew her, provided moleskin for her shoes, fox pelts for her cloak. She was a rich . . . woman. She was good business, beside ought else. Has he stolen from her? Why would he kill her otherwise and why . . . ? He goes up and down the river several times in the summer months. If there is an island, he will know that too, but I cannot see . . .' She was breathing very fast and becoming incoherent.

'Where is your husband now?' Bradecote kept his voice very flat and measured.

'He . . . he went to see Alnoth, Alnoth the Tailor, but he too may be in danger, for he knows as Will had dealings with her, with the dead woman. They worked together upon the cloak, a cloak fit for a queen. I was coming to the castle, my lord, thinking I had time. He must not know it was me who . . . He will kill us, assuredly he will kill us.' Her voice rose to become a shrill wail.

'Walkelin, you help Mistress Fellman to her home, and you guard the door until I send relief or news that Fellman is taken.'

'Yes, my lord.' Walkelin held out his arm to the shaking woman. 'You will be safe. You will, mistress.'

She looked to Bradecote, who nodded, and set her hand upon the proffered arm. Then he looked at Catchpoll.

'We leave Walkelin's horse with the gatekeeper. Alnoth the Tailor. Do we ride or run?'

'We run. Follow me, my lord.'

Serjeant Catchpoll disliked running, not least because he hated opening a conversation whilst gasping for breath, and it made him look old. Alnoth the Tailor could be found in a little courtyard off Crokkere Strete, and it was both close enough to reach on foot and the thoroughfare not wide enough to take a horse at speed. He led the way, with Bradecote's long stride easily keeping up with him, but at Alnoth's open frontage, with the shutter up to let most light into his workplace, Catchpoll suggested, in a wheezing undertone, that the undersheriff do the talking.

The good thing was that they did not find Alnoth in a pool of blood. The bad thing was that they did not find Will Fellman.

'Has Will Fellman been with you?' enquired Bradecote, with urgency but without panic.

Alnoth the Tailor blinked owlishly at the undersheriff, for when he had been focused upon his needle, he needed a moment to readjust.

'Why, 'tis you, my lord. Yes, he was here but a very short time past, discussing some fur trimmings I want for the lord Sheriff himself. You have just missed him.' He sounded perfectly calm and clearly had not been threatened in any way.

'Yet he has not passed us as we came from the Foregate.' Catchpoll had his breath enough for speech.

'You would not, Serjeant, for he is gone on to William Cooper, right next to you, Serjeant. He was saying as one of his half-barrels has a leak.'

Catchpoll groaned. Now they would be haring off almost as far as they could from one end of Worcester to the other. Bradecote grinned as they departed, striding swiftly but not quite running.

'It keeps you young, Catchpoll, all this chasing about.'

'I don't know about that, my lord. What keeps a man young has little to do with the streets and more to do with his bed, and it don't cripple his knees neither.'

Bradecote gave a bark of laughter and lengthened his stride, which meant Catchpoll's creaking knees had to move the faster. Looking purposeful was good and showed the law was active, but by the time they reached Catchpoll's own front door the man was wheezing and swearing by turns. His good wife was upon the step, talking to another woman, and stopped mid sentence.

'It is a long time since you came running just to see me, Catchpoll.' She nudged her neighbour, who giggled.

'Will . . . Next door,' he managed.

'Got that sullen man Fellman with him,' she said and was surprised to see the relief upon her husband's face.

Bradecote wasted no time and knocked upon the cooper's sturdy oak. Mistress Cooper opened it and dipped into a curtsey, recognising the undersheriff.

'My lord?'

'Will Fellman is with your husband, mistress?'

'He is, out the back, my lord. Shall I fe—'

'No, thank you. We will see him there.' He brushed past her, followed by Catchpoll. The cooper was about his business, and a broad-shouldered man, with a mane of dark brown hair and a long mouth, lounged against a wall, talking to him. His expression was surly, that of a man always ready to be disappointed with what life gave him, always ready to find fault, just as Will Cooper's was open and inclined to find something about which he could smile. It was that smile he gave to his neighbour, as he gave a respectful nod to the lord undersheriff.

'Morning, Catchpoll, or, since you have my lord with you, is it "Serjeant Catchpoll"?' He spoke as one with nothing to fear from the law.

'Morning, Will. You have the right of it. This is sheriff's business. Could you leave off your work a while and let us speak with Master Fellman here?' It was a question, but only just.

'What need can you have to speak with me?' Fellman folded his arms and looked belligerent.

'Well now, that is what we knows and you is about to find out.' Catchpoll's voice lost the friendliness, and Will Cooper made himself scarce.

'I come by my pelts honest.'

'None says otherwise, Master Fellman,' remarked Bradecote, equably. 'It is not about your furs we want words with you.'

'Then . . .'

'You went upriver, three days past.' It was not a question.

'I did, and no secret was it. There's men as far as Wribbenhall who sell me skins and know as I comes upriver time of St Mary Magdalene. They trap for me that week and bring me what they catch, as they do about St Luke's and Lady Day. The animals is still fresh enough so as the hairs keeps in the skin for me to cure. I got me some good fox, a marten, plenty of squirrel and mole. Keep me going that will.' He omitted a couple of coney that a warrener up by Holt might miss.

'Where did you stop, the first night?'

'It was warm, so no need of cover as such. I slept 'neath the stars, on the bank of the river.'

'So none can swear an oath to where you were?'

'None, but none need do so.'

'Ricolde, of the house on Brodestrete, was hacked to death on Bevere Island the dawn you say you awoke on the riverbank.'

'Well, I saw nothing, being upriver of Bevere by then . . . my lord. First I knew of her death was when I returned, yesterday eventide.'

'You knew her?' Catchpoll's words could have both meanings.

'She bought furs off me. A good customer, she was, and is missed as such, no more. Ask Robert Corviser or Alnoth the Tailor. They will tell you all she had from me.'

'And you never shared her bed?'

'No.' The man shuddered. 'I am married.' He did not sound joyous about that either.

'So was most who paid her coin,' said Catchpoll, calmly.

'And this morning your wife was seen washing a bloodstained cotte in the river.' Bradecote was as cool.

'My work—'

'She was shocked, it seems, at what she saw,' continued the undersheriff.

'She had no cause to be.' He sounded sulky.

101

'And there is little doubt Ricolde was taken to her death up the river by boat.'

'I left the day before, from what you have said.'

'No, you left home then, that is all that can be sworn. Your journeyman was seen thumping upon Ricolde's door, the morning she was found, and it seems because he was seeking you to tell you of the death of your child. Why do that if he thought you already upriver?'

'Because my wife is a suspicious bitch,' he spat at them, 'and Godfrid is a weak-willed dog who will lick her hand and do her bidding without using what little brain he possesses.'

'This is the same "suspicious bitch" who has borne you four children and a fifth coming?' Bradecote sounded unconvinced.

'She is mine. I do not have to like her to use her.' Fellman shrugged. 'The church does not account the getting of children a sin within marriage. I am spared a penance for doing what any man does, and she cooks well enough.'

'Why would even a suspicious wife think of Ricolde, the most expensive whore in Worcester, not some other?' enquired Catchpoll.

'Because she bought furs, of course.'

'But if she had done only that, why, most men in Worcester would have seen her as often over time.'

'Then cast your suspicion at Alnoth, or Corviser, or any other man.' Fellman was losing his temper. He looked one who did so easily and frequently.

'Alnoth has no boat, nor Corviser. You do. You were not seen at the time Ricolde was butchered and you cannot prove where you were. It is enough to hold you until the lord Sheriff returns, at the least.' Bradecote sounded calm but he wanted this man in a cell. Whoever killed Ricolde had lost his temper, at the end at least. This man felt 'right', and everything pointed towards him. At least if he were safely in a cell, they could continue their hunt for anything that might make his guilt sure and get his confession in the face of it. That was the only problem at present. Unless he did so in a fit of anger, he did not look likely to admit to anything at all. 'Take him to the castle, Catchpoll,' he said, as if bored with listening to excuses.

'You cannot.' Fellman braced himself to resist, but had not noticed the way that Catchpoll had gradually manoeuvred to his side, and was taken unawares as the sheriff's serjeant took his legs from under him from behind with a stave taken from the pile that Will Cooper had ready to hand for his barrel.

'Amazing how wrong a man can be,' murmured Catchpoll and grinned at his superior, whilst tying Fellman's wrists behind him.

Chapter Seven

Fellman protested loudly, all the way to the cells, not in a fearful way, but in pure anger. It gave Hugh Bradecote pause for thought.

'His anger was genuine; I would swear an oath upon it. Would a guilty man be that angry, Catchpoll?'

'He is an angry sort of man. You find them sometimes. They rage against life from start to finish.' Catchpoll shrugged.

'And are they killers?'

'Not all, but I would say they had the greater inclination to violence so . . . Look, my lord, we have things which link him to the river upstream: he has a boat,' Catchpoll began to tick things off on his fingers, 'he had contact with Ricolde, and his wife thought him likely to be tupping her, whatever he says, there are bloodstains on the cotte he wore when he went up the Severn, and he is a man who snaps.

104

What was done to Ricolde was the act of such a man.'

'Yes, and that makes me think he is her killer, and yet . . . For that same reason does it not exclude him? Would he have been cool enough to take her from her home and all the way up to Bevere Island to execute her and then, only then, go wild? Surely he would have cut her throat, or throttled her, there on the bed?'

'It does not sound most like at the first, and yet whoever did it was capable of both things, so it has to be possible.'

'And even if it was him,' persisted Bradecote, 'and he could plan and also loose his rage, there is no sense in taking her upriver to kill. Better to have killed her and taken her upstream a little and dumped the corpse in the river if he wanted no sign of him upon her. It is still a mess, Catchpoll, say what you will.'

'Not everything in life is tidy, my lord, nor in death neither. We goes upon what is most likely, and the lord Sheriff and the Justices in Eyre will decide if that is good enough.'

'So, I await my boots and sit here looking lordly, do I?'

'You might not do the sitting, my lord, since the castellan is due back from his manors today.'

Bradecote groaned. The last few days had at least been free from his fussing.

'That might make me return home even without the boots.' He grew serious again. 'Is there anything we have neglected, Catchpoll?'

'What about the axe?' Walkelin, just relieved from his guard upon the fellman's home, entered as the question was asked. Undersheriff and serjeant frowned at him, but he had learnt not to be put off. 'The thing is, my lord, when I was there, I asked his wife if he took his axe with him, when he went upriver. She looked at me as if I was brain-sick, well and truly she did. What cause would he have? she asked, and then went and fetched the axe from the rear yard, where it is always kept.'

Catchpoll swore.

'If he stole another man's axe, he would need to know where it was kept, and besides, nobody has reported one missing.' Bradecote rubbed his chin, thoughtfully. 'Could it possibly have been a cleaver? It is smaller to carry and—'

'Whatever he used, he would be bloodstained, but if it was a cleaver, then he would have to be kneeling by the body. You saw the ground. Even at the time his braies would have been soaked with blood and spattered if he used an axe.' Catchpoll shook his head. 'Kneeling and hacking at a corpse? To dispose of in bits perhaps, but she was just left there. No, my lord, I do not see a cleaver.'

'And if his cotte was stained, what about his braies anyway? Unless he was very prepared, he would not take a spare pair with him, and do the ones he has on look any worse than a man's whose labour is outdoors?' Walkelin raised the awkward question. 'And,' another occurred to him, 'what would the people he met upriver think of a man soaked with blood? They might not run to us crying murder, but they would surely remember it if asked. If we go upriver and they look blank, then it cannot be him.'

'Agreed. At least that way we know if he is innocent there is no doubt.' Bradecote did not conceal his relief.

'And if they saw blood then that is our final proof he is guilty,

106

my lord. Do we go now or on the morrow?' Walkelin was keen.

'The advantage of tomorrow is that I ought to have boots that are not about to fall off my feet, and we can still ask at Claines and Bevere, in case of some early connection we have not discovered.' Bradecote sighed. 'He is not even local. That adds to the problem in my head. I grant he knew of Bevere Island if he uses the river, but that killing had significance, being there. I would still like to find the answer what and why, for it niggles. We visit there first and then go up that side of the Severn, cross at Wribbenhall and come down the western side to Hallow and then back to Worcester. We can be back if not in one day then two at the latest. I would feel the better for knowing we have this right, however much it is not our final decision.'

'When we asks there it may be some link arises. I think as you are poking around too deep, my lord, and you'll end with a pain in your head to match that in your badly shod feet. Rest both and be fresh for the morning.' Catchpoll's advice was pragmatic, and his superior, running his hand through his hair, could not but agree it was the best course.

Hugh Bradecote went up to the battlements, where the man-at-arms on duty was feeling the sun even though it was past its zenith and inclined to the somnolent. He made every effort to look fully awake when he saw the lord undersheriff and ostentatiously began to walk to and fro. The merest hint of breeze seemed to taunt rather than give relief. The undersheriff looked past priory and cathedral at the secular dwellings. He realised, with some surprise, that he was beginning to feel like

Catchpoll. Worcester was 'his'. He was becoming more familiar with the streets, and from this height could have pointed out not only thoroughfares, but where some of the most important, or most interesting, townsfolk lived.

'I really am getting to be like Catchpoll,' he murmured, under his breath.

He saw Walkelin striding purposefully from the castle gate and watched him until he disappeared from view between the houses, and then he sighed. Simon Furnaux, the castellan, was approaching from the Sutheberi gate, his showy chestnut followed by mounted men-at-arms who were not so much security as ostentation. Bradecote wondered whether Furnaux would be more shocked by a very violent death or the identity of the victim. Either way he would be sure to bleat, and all through the evening meal too. It was almost worth fasting, but he had to be faced at some point. It was as he was about to turn to go back down to the bailey that he saw Robert Corviser, with something wrapped and clutched to his chest. Well, he might have to listen to Furnaux, but at least he would be wearing his new boots.

Corviser was being escorted across the bailey to the hall as Bradecote emerged from the gatehouse tower.

'You seek me, Master Corviser.' It was not a question. Both men turned.

'My lord, I have your boots, as promised.' Robert Corviser looked very keen to please the undersheriff.

'A good job too, or I would have soon been barefoot. Come with me.' Bradecote led the shoemaker into the hall, as yet blessedly free of the castellan's presence, and went to the dais where he could sit upon a chair and drag the sorry remnants of his boots from his feet. One worn sole was cracking across from the hole that had previously given access to stones, and the other was little better. 'These have given good service but are beyond all hope.'

'You will find this pair will last as well, my lord, I promise. Of course, being new, they will take a little time to become as comfortable as "old friends", but as with any friendship, both sides must give a little, getting to know each other.'

Bradecote pulled on the new boots. They lacked the softness of the old leather that had moulded over time to his feet, and although they certainly fitted, he wondered how much his flesh would have to 'give' over the next few days. Thankfully, he hoped to ride more than walk.

'I am sure that they will, Master Corviser. Now, here is your payment, as agreed.' He dropped coin into the man's hand and expected him to bow himself out. However, Corviser lingered, uncertain or unhappy, perhaps both. He gazed at the boots, given 'life' by becoming things that moved.

'My lord, concerning my wife . . . She is a good wife in many respects . . . keeps house well, has a good memory for who owes me, but . . . sometimes her memory is too good and her imagination too vivid, and she is unforgiving. When you asked me about Ricolde, I did not tell you all the truth, her being there, but I doubt anything I know will aid you in finding who killed her, and that is something I pray for.'

'Then tell me now, since I would have truth before concealment, and you may yet have some small thing which proves a help.'

'My lord, I did go to her home, though I stayed the evenings only. I told my wife I went to play at dice with two friends, but she did not truly believe. You see, Ricolde was everything my wife is not, and I do not just speak of her beauty. My wife lacks softness, she has neither ear to listen, gentle tongue to soothe, nor hand to caress. Ricolde, God rest her soul,' Corviser crossed himself, 'provided that. I never actually lay with her, but . . . she was worth the coin for her other skills. I had an affection for her, truly I did, and she . . . Her poor feet. They were like the rest of her, beautifully proportioned, but the soles . . . I asked her what accident befell her, and she said none. It was done with intent, and by her own flesh and blood.' Corviser stared at Bradecote, and the revulsion on his face was very genuine. 'She said her father did it to get her mother to tell him something. She was a small girl and all she recalled was him yelling "Tell me" over her screams as he pressed her feet to the hot ashes of the hearthstone.' He shook his head. 'We have not been blessed with children, but what father does that to his child, my lord? How could he? What amazed me then, and does even now, is how Ricolde could be what she was, when a man had done that.'

Bradecote did not say that it was not the only evil inflicted upon her by a man, nor that when men such as Corviser or the Healer came to her, it was they who were suppliants and she who had control of the situation. Had it all been an act? Perhaps, though since Roger the Healer never made any demands upon her for sexual gratification, she might have felt genuine compassion for him. For the rest, she who was 'used' actually used the men to give her a comfortable life in terms of goods and chattels, and as her secret rebellion against being the victim.

'I cannot give you answers to that, Master Corviser.'

'It is all the truth, my lord, I would swear an oath upon it.'

'I believe you.'

'Good.' The man sounded relieved, as if he had made confession and eased his conscience. 'I will be away then, my lord. May the boots do good service.' Corviser made obeisance and left.

Hugh Bradecote sat for a while in thought. It took a strong spirit to survive the evils Ricolde had endured, the same spirit he found in his Christina. She was at last cherished, and it occurred to him that Ricolde was cherished also in a small way, by men who would pray for her. It was a thoughtful undersheriff who was drawn from his cogitation by the strident and complaining voice of Simon Furnaux, who wanted all the goriest detail, and at the same time was denouncing the victim and bemoaning that if it was true that Fellman was the culprit then who was to supply the furs for his next winter robe?

Bradecote resigned himself to a poor evening.

Walkelin, not wishing to return to his mother's questions, or further moralising upon the late Ricolde, chose the far more pleasurable option and headed for the castle kitchens, where he hoped to be able to draw the maid Eluned into a storeroom to enjoy a few minutes of whispered nothings and wandering hands. His wooing of Eluned was hampered by the fact that, despite his youthful instincts, he was naturally rather shy once it got beyond honeyed words and fluttering eyelashes, and his previous encounters with the opposite sex had been mere fumbling dalliance. His feelings for Eluned were not merely lustful, though she certainly had an effect upon him. She had a fine figure and a face that he found beautiful, and if her normal tone was soft and liltingly Welsh, she had enough spirit to stand her ground when annoyed. This was both attractive and a little frightening, since she reverted to her native tongue and Walkelin had no idea what she was saying, or for what he ought to apologise. Had he asked his serjeant's advice, Catchpoll would have grinned and told him that most of the time man's 'crime' was being a man, so apologise for that for a start.

He found Eluned shelling peas, so he offered to help, since he was less likely to be sent about his business by Drogo, the castle cook, if he was doing something useful. In fact, the kitchen despot just shook his head and murmured something about the wench not letting her hands stray to Walkelin's 'pod', which made them both blush.

'So, is it true?' Eluned cast Walkelin a sidelong glance.

'Is what true?' Walkelin was dreading her asking about some 'detail' of the inside of Ricolde's home, just like his mother.

'That the man who killed the . . . you know . . . is taken.'

'Oh, well . . .' His relief was pushed aside by the lord undersheriff's lack of confidence that all was yet proven likely. 'A man is in the cells, but there are things we still want to know.'

'Such as?'

Walkelin was not sure what 'things' would help, other than knowing whence Fellman got the axe and where he disposed of the bed covering. He might easily have burnt that and left no trace but ash upon the bank of Severn somewhere upriver.

'The actual weapon he killed her with. Mind you, his cotte had bloodstains upon it, dried and faded, but definitely there, so perhaps we do not need the axe.'

Eluned shuddered at the thought of the axe, and then sighed.

'Hard work are bloodstains, to get out. You need to get to them fresh, see, and best if you rub salt into them first. You can almost get rid of them with salt and good, cold water, but once they are set dry, you can scrub till your knuckles are raw and get nothing but a change in colour. Still there, they are.'

'Salt?'

'Yes, salt, the stuff we put in the cooking. That salt. What other is there?'

'And it gets rid of bloodstains?'

'Are you not listening or have you onions stuck in your ears, Walkelin?' Eluned looked at him with exasperation. 'You have never washed anything other than your feet, have you.' She shook her head at men.

'So if there was lots of fresh blood on something and you, say, put it in the river for an hour or so, the marks would be faint, anyone seeing you would not exclaim at the sight of blood? Especially if you rubbed in salt as well?'

'They might see marks, but you could not say they were blood, unless you knew or had seen lots of bloodstains before, and if the cloth was dark, perhaps not at all.'

'Eluned, *cariad*, you are a gem among women.' He leant to give her a peck on the cheek.

'There's pretty.'

'Meet me in the brewhouse, after the bell for Vespers, and I will say nicer things,' he whispered in her ear. She giggled, and he abandoned culinary tasks.

'Much help he is in the kitchen,' grumbled Drogo, as he left.

Walkelin crossed the bailey and left with a purposeful stride. He was not heading home, but to see Mistress Fellman, and he had a question.

Serjeant Catchpoll did not dwell upon the lord undersheriff's worries, though he did not dismiss them out of hand. The lord Bradecote was a man whose ability to blame himself for things was far too acute, and doubtless he was countering that by trying to make sure that he was certain in his own mind of guilt. The 'problem' of the killer having to be cold and calculating, and yet a man who snapped, was insoluble by reason, but then men did not always behave according to reason. Besides, Catchpoll's gut instinct was that Fellman had committed the act. If any niggle remained in his own mind, it was why he had done so, but that question would arise with any man they took. There had been no theft, bar the bed covering; a man could not be jealous of her lying with other men, since that was her trade, nor was she going to reveal his infidelity to his wife. Walkelin had originally suggested that a man might love her, and kill her so that she remained 'his' in death and he would no longer have to share her, but that would be either very cold-blooded and planned or of the moment. Catchpoll also thought if that were so her killer, when caught, would admit the crime without any pressure. No, this was one of those untidy killings, where one piece of the broken pot of truth had slipped from view and would not be found.

By the time he reached his own doorstep, Catchpoll had set it all aside, and his wife looked up from peeling onions, her eyes watering. It was not often that he was home before a meal was ready.

'Greeting me with tears, wife?' He grinned at her.

'You've scarce been away so long I would weep with relief to see you back.' The words could have been cutting, but she too smiled. 'So, this early return is because you have upset our neighbours by finding a brutal killer in their home and not because you were overcome by the urge to watch me chop "tear makers".'

He came and stood behind her and slipped an arm about her waist.

'Could be you were right earlier, and I just had to come running to see you.'

'Hah! No sign of you running now, Catchpoll. Stop that, I am cooking.'

'Won't be long before it is set to boil though. A wife,' he declared, magisterially, 'is for four things: keeping a man's house tidy, keeping him fed, providing him with children and warming his bed.' She could feel the rumble of mirth in his chest behind her.

'Is that all?'

'It covers most things. Now, you have this place always clean enough I could eat off the floor were it not for getting rush stalks in my mouth, you are a fine cook and have this pottage going on, and our children have children of their own. That just leaves . . .'

* * *

Walkelin went back to the castle, not sure whether he had solved a problem or tied further knots to untangle, and Eluned found him a slightly distracted swain. When he returned to his home, a faint crease was between his brows, and his mother berated him for not attending to her.

Mistress Fellman had not been delighted to see him, regarding him with some suspicion, as he thought. She clearly thought he doubted her word, and her answers were at first cautious.

'Does your husband take anything with him, when he goes to buy pelts from those up the river, mistress?'

'Bread and cheese, for the first evening, if he is fending for himself, and he does so in the summer if it is fine.'

'Does he need anything for the animal skins though?' Walkelin did not want to actually ask about salt in case she gave the answer she thought he wanted rather than truth. He had learnt that much from Serjeant Catchpoll.

'Most are quite fresh, and he takes salt for those and to recompense in kind where his best providers have skinned the animal a week or so back, and he has shown them to lace it well with salt to preserve it till he collects. He does not take the butter or oil, for it is too messy, and he likes to work the pelts here where everything is to hand.'

'And are the braies he wears today the same ones he was wearing when he went upon his journey?'

'Aye. He has his other workaday cotte upon his back, and he keeps a cotte and another pair of braies apart, for holy days and such, since his working garb tells all his trade by the smell. There's some as cannot bear it, but after a while you do not notice it. I grew up with it, so I do not smell it at all, really.'

At that moment someone came into the chamber behind him, and Walkelin saw the woman's expression soften, and the girl-child was there, with Godfrid behind her. The child looked tearful.

'She has grazed her knee, mistress,' said the journeyman, calmly.

'Thank you, I will look to her.' Mistress Fellman reverted her gaze to Walkelin. 'Do you need more of me, sheriff's man?'

'No, thank you, mistress.' In truth, Walkelin wanted space to think. He wandered back to the castle in abstraction, and even cuddling Eluned did not take his mind entirely from the problem.

Will Fellman had the means to have cleaned the worst of the blood from his clothing, and if his braies had been stiffening with gore, then he had but to swill them in the river before he slept upon the bank, and on a warm summer night they would have dried enough to put on, even if damp, next day. Would he have known about salt water and blood? Since he used it in his work, and sometimes blood got upon his garments, he might well know, from seeing his wife take salt to make a paste not unlike his own for the furs. This pointed to Fellman's guilt, and yet . . . the bloodstains on the cotte that the wife had waved under their noses had quite dark staining, as though it had been allowed to dry and had simply then been ducked into water. That would mean Fellman had done nothing about the blood on him, nothing at all. Surely he would not have wanted to be seen like that? At the very least he would have rinsed the worst of it off.

Walkelin went home, frowning, and the frown deepened after his evening meal, when his widowed aunt turned up to join her sister in pressing him for interesting details about the death and about the victim.

Chapter Eight

'It is being said she had chests of silver coin and the bedcovers of silk, and I had it from a tongue I trust. Living like a queen she was and upon the gain from her sinning. Mind you, she will pay for it in the Hereafter, for God sees all, and she will be judged for her actions. Much good will silk and silver do her now where she is gone.' The Widow Hedger, Walkelin's aunt, was in full flow, and he wished she was not. There was a relish to the woman's words, as though glorying in being shocked and in being pious where another fell short.

Walkelin thought of what he had been told of Ricolde's charity, generous but secretly given, but he said nothing. Somehow he thought she would have wished it kept a secret still, rather than passed to be gossip among the sharp-tongued women of Worcester.

'She always went about in finery, her head held high, as

though better than decent women,' Walkelin's mother added, corroboratively.

'Shameful. Mind you, a flogging would have been right, but chopping her up—'

'Leave it.' Walkelin was not one to shout at his elders, but he had recently eaten, and he had been there, seen the corpse.

'No need to—' his aunt began, and then halted at the look on his face. She recognised male implacability when she saw it.

'Well, it will be less the talk of Worcester now that a man is taken for it. Bellowed all the way to the castle, did Will Fellman. His poor wife, what must she be thinking, having a man who could do that for a husband.' Walkelin's mother sighed.

'She'll be thinking her prayers have been answered, and that's a fact,' her sister responded, instantly, and was gratified that she had the full attention of both her listeners.

'Why?' It was Walkelin who gave in and asked the question.

'Because he makes her life a misery, finding fault with her for no reason, treating that poor little thing, their eldest, as if she was vermin, beating the both of them at will. The times I have seen her bruised something terrible . . . I think she has only kept the child she is carrying because he has held off her, in the belief it will be another son, but there is the sweetest jest of all.'

'She cannot know whether she will bear a boy or a girl, surely?' Walkelin was in happy ignorance of what went on with producing children once male involvement was over.

Both women laughed at him.

'Of course not, but she does know it won't be of his siring.'

'What?' Walkelin's exclamation was as loud as his previous admonition, and the women jumped.

'Oh, come now, boy, you cannot be so foolish as to think every babe is born to the husband who earns the bread. Husbands stray often enough and with poor reason. Sibbe Fellman's reason might not please a priest, but has sound sense to it, though if he ever found out . . .' Widow Hedger shook her head.

'You are guessing. You cannot know.'

'Can I not? Well, that is where you are wrong, sister-son. I have known her since long before I was left widow, and many's the sound piece of advice she has taken from me, having neither mother nor female kindred. When her elder lad had that fever last wi—'

'If Fellman is not the father, who is?' Walkelin was not interested in childhood ailments.

'Does it matter, as long as Fellman never catches him or her?' snorted his aunt.

'It may matter an awful lot. Did she say?'

'No, she did not, but I know where I would look, and it is not in another household.'

Walkelin groaned.

'What is the matter, my son? It has nothing to do with the death.' Walkelin's mother was dismissive.

What he could see, and they could not, was that it might have everything to do with the blame falling upon Will Fellman.

'But he is a violent man, a nasty, cruel man, and the poor soul would be well rid of him,' declared Widow Hedger, when Walkelin explained.

'He might well be so, but that does not mean he is the killer of Ricolde, and it does mean that his wife has a very good reason to make it seem he is steeped in guilt. She even has some security for both the business and her children if he, as the breadwinner, were to die upon the order of the law.'

'Leave well alone, I says,' grumbled his aunt. 'This is a woman's problem, and women's business. If he did not kill . . . her . . . then I doubt not he would kill someone else, some innocent person, in time.'

'Listen to yourself.' Walkelin was horrified. 'You are saying both that the law should be used to remove those who you think "might" commit a crime and that Ricolde the Whore was "guilty" because of her whoring, and that what . . . she deserved to die? What justice would there be if we followed that rule? No. This is all wrong. Come the morning, we take this to the lord Bradecote and to Serjeant Catchpoll.'

'You cannot make me speak' – Widow Hedger looked belligerent, through worried – 'and who do you think you are to demand it of me?' This was the nephew she had known since he was a swaddled babe.

'I am Serjeant's Apprentice to the Lord Sheriff of Worcestershire.' Walkelin had never named himself thus, formally, ever before, but he did so now and stood tall as he did so. Both mother and aunt were surprised, but also rather overawed. 'We go, early, to the castle, and if you refuse, why then, I shall go to Serjeant Catchpoll myself, and he will come and take you before the lord Undersheriff in shackles, and all Worcester will see you. What gossip would that start?'

Widow Hedger dabbed at her eyes, and Walkelin's mother, her arm about her sister's shoulder, accused him of disrespect, cruelty, and being self-important.

Come the morning, however, both he and his aunt went to the castle.

Undersheriff and serjeant were talking quietly by the door to the castle hall when Walkelin came upon them next morning, and he was not alone. The serjeanting apprentice looked rather embarrassed but determined. With him was a woman in her middle years, rather cowed by being before the Undersheriff of Worcestershire and with her hands gripped together, but also with a firm look to her mouth and the tension of one about to perform a disagreeable duty.

'This, my lord, is Widow Hedger, my mother's sister. She has information that . . . changes things.' Young Walkelin sounded very serious.

Bradecote, judging whatever would be said was not for a wide audience, invited them into the cool gloom of the hall and looked at the woman.

'Then tell us this information, mistress.' He was authoritative, but not bullying.

'It is about Will Fellman and his wife, my lord.'

'And is it information or is it gossip? The difference is important.'

'Information, my lord. I live but a step along from their place, and I have known her, the wife, for some ten years. She confides in me, and . . .' Widow Hedger bit her lip and then took a deep breath. 'The child she carries is not his, not Will Fellman's.'

There was silence for a moment. Walkelin, having already heard this news, was not shocked, but his superiors were, and it showed upon their faces.

'She has said this, to you?' Bradecote wondered why a woman would reveal such a dangerous secret to anyone.

'Yes, my lord. She has been beyond sorrow with the death of the babe and angry that her husband cared so little. I went to comfort her, for she has neither mother nor sisters, and the grief broke from her like a flood. She told me as how he cared nothing for the girls, the eldest child nor the youngest, and beat the girl as he did her, but was determined that the next child would be a son. She gave an odd laugh and said even if it was, it would not be his.'

'Did she name the father?' asked Catchpoll.

'What need? That Godfrid is a good-looking fellow, but more important, he has a kind nature. He would not beat a wife for the pleasure of it, over nothings. Sinful it is, what they have done, but you can see how . . .'

'And so you think the wife is getting revenge upon the husband and also finding a way that means she can be with her lover?' Bradecote frowned, and the woman paused, not knowing if her answer would bring wrath.

'I . . . I do not know, but I saw her with her basket of washing this morning, and it was as if all care had gone from her and even the memory of her new-buried babe, my lord.'

Bradecote's frown deepened, and his dark brows met.

'And why have you brought this to me? You clearly think little of Will Fellman, who is, you believe, a cruel husband to a long-suffering wife. So why speak when your words may free him?'

'Because' – the woman looked daggers at her nephew – 'I value the law.' If she had told truth thus far, this was an

124

obvious lie, and Walkelin seemed to be inspecting the beams of the hall roof.

'It is good to hear,' said Bradecote, taking the statement at face value, though Catchpoll heard the equal falseness in his response. 'Thank you for your information, mistress. It may yet have importance in our taking of the murderer of the woman Ricolde.'

At this the woman's face hardened. She did not like to think of herself as helping bring such a man to justice, even if what was rumoured, that he had cut the woman into small pieces, was grim beyond imagining.

'You may go.' She was dismissed, made a bobbing obeisance and left, glad to distance herself from her own words and their consequences.

'So, keen to see the law upheld, your aunt?' Catchpoll grinned at Walkelin.

'What really happened, Walkelin?' Bradecote leant back against the wall and folded his arms before him. 'Have you been asserting yourself as man of the house?'

Walkelin looked uncomfortable. His mother was much inclined to treat him as she had when he was a lad and mothered him with a combination of maternal bullying and fussing. He generally gave in and was a dutiful and respectful son. He did not like upsetting her.

'You see, my lord, what she said, she said before me and Mother, chatting about it all. When I said it was important, she tried to deny it as "women's business". But I could not let it lie. I told her if she did not come with me and tell you, I would

125

tell you, and Serjeant Catchpoll would be banging on her front door and dragging her through the streets in chains.'

'What for, exactly, Walkelin?' Bradecote sounded mildly interested.

'Er, I did not give a reason of law, just said he would, and I meant it, too. Then she burst into tears, and my mother said I was a bully and . . .' Walkelin shook his head. 'I will get nothing but hot words from her this evening.'

'But you did not give in. That is what matters. Your mother will no doubt be secretly pleased you have shown yourself iron-willed.' Catchpoll nodded approvingly.

'The thing is, what does it do to our happy belief that we have Ricolde's murderer in our cells?' The undersheriff pulled a face, and Catchpoll sniffed.

'It brings in doubt, sure enough.'

'There is more, Serjeant. Do you know how to get bloodstains out of cloth, either of you?' Walkelin looked at his superiors.

'Er, water, rubbing?' Bradecote made a simple guess.

'What are you a-getting at, Young Walkelin?' Catchpoll's eyes narrowed to slits.

'Well, I did not know, but it seems all womenfolk do. You rub a paste of salt into it and then wash it, and if the stain is fresh, it almost disappears. If the stain is not dried and set in, but drying, well then it fades the stain more than just washing and pushes the darkest part to the edges. On well-dried stains it fades them sort of brown to even a greenish colour.'

'Thinking of changing your trade and becoming a washerwoman, Walkelin?' enquired Catchpoll, but he was clearly impressed.

'No, Serjeant. You see, when I found out about the salt, I went back to Mistress Fellman. I did as you have taught me, Serjeant, and did not ask her if her husband took the thing I wanted to know about, but just asked her if he had taken anything with him when he went to buy skins upriver, and she said he took a crock of salt. He took it so that he could pay in kind to those who had used salt on the pelts to keep the hairs in, and also to do the same on any fresh caught until he could cure them proper back here. He had salt with him, and although you would say a man would not know about salt and bloodstains, he might well, since his is such a trade, using it for curing the skins and with him sometimes getting blood upon his clothes.'

'So you are saying that having given grounds to let him go, we also have better grounds to keep him under guard.' Bradecote pulled face.

'Not exactly, my lord, because just when I was excited about that news, I had another thought. The cotte we have has large bloodstains on it, clearly blood, blood that had dried and then been no more than perhaps wet in the river. There had been no attempt to get them out properly.'

'But if she took it to the river to wash and then found the marks . . .' Bradecote's brain was catching up.

'What I do not understand,' continued Walkelin, in full flow, 'is that the wife did not know of Ricolde's death, you said, Serjeant, and unless you said to her she was hacked—'

'She only had to ask anyone by that stage,' Catchpoll interjected. 'She might have been new to it, but all Worcester knew Ricolde had been killed, aye, and bloodily too. That knowledge, making it not just a simple killing, loosened tongues, and we likes them loose.'

'Why would a man with water all about him and even salt, if he knew its use, not make some attempt to clean the signs of violence from him when it was fresh? Why make people wonder?' Bradecote was following his own thoughts. 'The man deals in dead animals. If they are fresh caught . . .' He shook his head. 'Would they have seen it as part of what he does?'

'But wait, my lord. Have you ever skinned an animal?' Catchpoll looked at him and questioned.

'I . . . Not as I can recall, no.' It was not something the nobility did. They hunted and they ate. They did not prepare food, nor watch its preparation.

'Well, there ain't much blood, if done proper, and he would have experience. You might get some smears of blood, taking off feet and claws, but them was good-sized bloodstains.'

Bradecote put his hands to his brow and groaned.

'What proof have we even that it was Will Fellman's cotte, other than his wife thrusting it at us?'

'You mean the journeyman killed Ricolde?' Walkelin looked disbelieving. 'Why would a woman defend a man who—'

'That may be one step too far, Young Walkelin,' Catchpoll interrupted him. 'It need not be that the blood came from a body, at least not a human one. Think on it. We come nosing about, asking questions about the murder of Ricolde, and the mourning mother has no knowledge of it. She is angry, she is miserable, and her husband beats her. Added to that she is going to produce a babe that may yet show who fathered it in its looks as it grows. She only has to find something with blood in it . . .'

'Such as what? I cannot see them with meat beyond feast days, Catchpoll.' Bradecote did not want to be persuaded, not deep down.

'There were fowl in the back yard, my lord. Kill a bird past its best for eggs, take what blood you can and then the giblets, and mash 'em and it would make for a bloody enough look. She then takes the cotte, one of her husband's or one of the journeyman's, and gets as much into it as she can, lets it dry in the yard and then washes it, so that the stains remain, but faded. Her husband has returned in a poor humour, treated her roughly, and next morning, lo, she is before us with "proof" of his crime.'

'That is all very good, Catchpoll, but my worry is this: you have been looking at how people are killed for years. If anyone could plan a killing it is you. This is a woman with three children, a fourth just buried and a fifth in her belly. Is she likely to have thought this through, made such a clever plan? She has put up with this man for years, why revolt now?'

'Because here is her chance? Because she fears he has suspicions about that child to be and fears for it, and her own life? I grant a beaten wife would be more likely to kill in hot blood, taking things one step further than defending herself, but . . . My lord, are you not seeing her only as victim in this? Victims can turn.'

It was true, he thought. He did see her as the victim, sympathised with her plight, and much of her fear of the man, the fear that she had shown so obviously, need not have been feigned. It could still be real even if the cause were different, and she feared her husband discovering that

129

she was unfaithful. What Walkelin's aunt had revealed even increased his loathing of Fellman, who beat both wife and small daughter, but it did not mean he was a killer, nor that the beaten wife might not send her husband to his death. He heaved a heavy sigh.

'Fellman denies he did more than provide fur for Ricolde's shoes and garments. He is not a local man, which was always the problem, and now we have an even bigger one, which casts great doubt upon the "evidence" brought to us that connects him to the killing. We did not think too much of the doubts because they got in the way of our convenient idea. I say we let him go.'

'And what of the wife?' Walkelin wondered.

'We did not tell him it was she who brought us proofs, only that she was seen washing bloodstains from a cotte.' Bradecote grimaced. 'He has no cause to know of her involvement, and if we accuse her of lying to see him hang, then he will, and we have suspicion, doubt but no proof beyond her looking the happier when he was in a cell, and her admitting her adultery to a woman friend. If we act, what would you give for her life?'

'Not much,' grumbled Catchpoll.

'So she gets away with plotting his death?' Walkelin persisted.

'Perhaps, but if we do anything, another death, plus that of a babe unborn, are probable. We let it, and Fellman, go.' Bradecote rose from his seat, looking grim-faced. 'Let us get this over with.'

Will Fellman was not all gratitude when he heard that he was to be freed.

'You had no right to take me, take me from my family and my trade, no right at all. You make this cry of "justice", but there is none for me, and why? Because you can link me to a dead woman through selling her furs? You might as well have taken half the tradesmen in Worcester, aye, and with them having other dealings with her, the filthy whore.'

'But—' Walkelin was about to ask a question, but a tug on the back of his cotte from Catchpoll silenced him.

'I work hard, I pay my taxes, and you would see me before the king's justices because you have nobody else. That is the truth of it.' The man gave vent to his pent-up feelings.

'I have said you may go, and there is an end to it. Get back to your business and to your family, and do not come to our notice again.' Bradecote was not going to justify himself to this man.

'You can be sure that I will not . . . my lord.' The title was thrown more as an insult. Walkelin held the cell door open, and Fellman stalked out, mumbling his grievances still.

'Why did he say he had no dealings with Ricolde, other than trade, when his wife sent the journeyman to find him there?' asked Walkelin. 'That could not have been part of some plan.'

'She might just have believed it if he had let slip some admiring word about her,' suggested Bradecote.

'Then why call her a "filthy whore" now?'

'Because, Walkelin,' explained Catchpoll, 'that sets him even further from her and among the "virtuous" tradesmen who only sold her their wares, not sampled hers. He was not seen at Ricolde's door, his name was not mentioned. We have only the wife sending the journeyman to look, and he would not have

131

found him there. What we need to worry about now is not Will Fellman, but what we do next in our hunt for Ricolde's killer.'

'What we do is easy enough, Catchpoll. We go as we intended yesterday. We go to Claines and the manors near to Bevere Island. You may yet avoid your mother's hot words, Walkelin, for we may not be back tonight.' Bradecote rubbed the back of his neck. 'Come on. Let your womenfolk know of your absence and we will be away. The problem is that the trail is another day colder, and we want this man who butchered a woman, want him badly.'

Chapter Nine

Hugh Bradecote was already mounted, his steel-grey horse fidgeting and mouthing the bit, and Catchpoll was adjusting his horse's girth, when Walkelin returned, rather out of breath and pink-cheeked. The undersheriff looked sombre. He was trying to set aside all the information that had led them astray, sift from it the facts and consider how that would influence what they would ask when they made their way up the banks of the Severn.

Their first halt had to be at Claines and Bevere manors, and he felt deep down that something in Ricolde's childhood past held the key to everything. Whether anyone would remember with such a passage of time was not certain.

The trio trotted through Worcester, and a surprising number of eyes followed them, wondering at their stony expressions. Had they not just caught a killer? Once out beyond the Foregate, Bradecote set his horse to a steady canter. It actually felt good to be on horseback and out in the countryside after a few days in the stultifying heat of the Worcester streets and the smell of massed humanity. Bradecote preferred the warm summer smells of field and copse, and thought briefly of his manor and whether little Gilbert might be about to take his first steps.

'Do we begin in Claines, my lord, or go to the reeve at Bevere, since it is a smaller community and closer to the river?' Catchpoll asked, dragging him back to the present.

'Well, we need not explain to him what set us hunting, and he is old enough to know any ancient "gossip" hereabouts. That is our biggest problem. At least half the folk are going to be too young to know what went on.'

'Not our only problem either, though, my lord. If what Ricolde told the priest is true, and I doubt she would lie to him, then what went on here was much of it concealed and what was known shied away from. Even at years' distance, none would be keen to bring that to light.'

'What if the uncle is still living?' Walkelin posed a valid question. 'We can have no "proofs" other than the words of a woman now dead, and he has but to deny all and we get nowhere.'

'I for one will have trouble keeping my hands from his scrawny throat,' growled Catchpoll. 'Kin are there to protect, not mistreat. Ricolde had a father who beat her, a small girl, and then an uncle who did worse. May they both rot in hellfire.' He spat into the trackway dust.

'And if the aunt lives, then she would say it was not his fault,' sighed Bradecote, 'since she threw the girl out. If she did not quite believe it back then, she will have learnt to believe it over the years for her own peace. You are right, Catchpoll. We stir up what all will want to lie still and fade to nothing.'

'We don't do this to be popular,' muttered Catchpoll, with a grim smile that lengthened the thin gash of his mouth in the grizzled beard.

'No, we do not.' The undersheriff did not smile at all.

They slowed to trot through Claines, not wishing to show any undue urgency, and were very shortly afterwards at the wooden palisade of Bevere manor. A woman looked up from drawing water from the well, and chickens scattered with agitated clucking.

'Where will we find the reeve?' called Bradecote.

'He'll be in the far field, my lord,' replied the woman, recognising rank from garb and the voice of authority. 'Towards the river and to the south. The pease is being weeded.'

The same activity would be going on upon his own strips, thought Bradecote, and they would be praying for rain to plump up the growing grain before a couple of good dry weeks to see it ripe for harvest. He thanked the woman, and they left their horses and headed in the direction she had pointed. They found Heribert overseeing the weeding of the priory's selions, before the villagers looked to their own strips, young and old with weeding sticks to cut down thistle and dock. When he saw the sheriff's men he broke away from his task and came to them, making obeisance to the undersheriff. He did not look overjoyed to see them, since they were associated with something he would far rather forget.

'My lord? You have need of me?' He clearly wished the answer would be negative.

'We have need of your memory, Master Reeve.' Bradecote smiled, but it was a very contained smile.

The man relaxed a little.

'Then I hope it is up to the task, my lord, but I told you at the time nothing was seen on the island until—'

'No, no, you mistake. This is not recent memory of but a few days ago. We are come to ask about things that happened in Bevere and Claines many years past. I would speak to all on the manor if you can gather them.'

'As you wish, my lord.' Heribert turned, called to a lad of about thirteen and sent him about the field, gathering workers as a dog might be sent to gather sheep. They actually huddled like sheep before the undersheriff, people who viewed rank as dangerous and shied from contact. Bevere was not a large manor, and there were comparatively few of any age that might recall the gossip, if nothing more, of a quarter-century past.

'I am the Undersheriff of Worcestershire, seeking the man who killed a woman by name of Ricolde, of Worcester, upon the island in the river, some days ago. We have found she was born here, that her mother drowned, and her father and brother then left her with kin. She parted from them and went into Worcester the better part of twenty years since. Somehow this has bearing upon why she was killed on Bevere Island, and who killed her also. I need any information, any memory, that helps us with what went on all that time ago.'

There was silence, as the import of what had been said sunk in.

'Now, we are talking twenty or five and twenty years back, so those of you with under a score years to your name may return to your labours. I know that the pease harvest is important, and you need a good yield.' Bradecote spoke as a good manorial lord. The youthful filtered away, and they were left with about twenty souls, watching them warily.

'To all of you that remain, I say this. We need to know about what happened then to find the answers now. It is not "dead and buried" because it has brought about a fresh death.' Bradecote spoke solemnly.

'It is many years, lord.' The voice was a woman's.

'Indeed, but some things linger. A drowning, a family parted, these must have been remembered.'

'They were of Claines, not Bevere.' The speaker was a man in late middle age, with thinning hair and a missing front tooth.

'And the names?'

'You must speak of Wilferth and his wife, Ranild. Thing is though, the girl was not called Ricolde, I am sure. Sad business. Some say as Ranild took her own life, but Father Benedict in Claines said there was no proof and gave her ground in the churchyard like any good Christian soul.'

'He wanted to think it an accident,' added a woman, with a sniff, 'because he was a kindly man who thought the best of folk.'

'And others did not?' Bradecote looked at her, and she dropped her gaze, aware not only of his eyes but those of her neighbours, interested and judging.

'It was common enough knowledge that Wilferth was a harsh husband,' she said, quietly.

''Tis a man's right,' grumbled a male voice from the back of the group.

'Aye, it is, but not to strike a wife for pleasure, because the humour is upon him, nor a mite of a child neither, and he beat wife and daughter both.' The woman had roused at this. 'Broke the girl's arm when she scarce walked. The river might well have seemed a better end to that sort of life.'

'But in that case, would not the woman have taken the child also, to spare it that future she dreaded?' This was Catchpoll, his tone measured. 'Would she leave a little girl to face wrath that she could not?' This obviously caused some thought among the community, with some nodding and others sceptical. 'Tell us what actually happened, and when, by season and year if you can.'

'It was spring,' came a voice.

'And in the year that we had late snow that killed many of the lambs, coming unexpected.'

'My Osmund was born that year, in the summer, and he has just come to six and twenty years.'

By this process a date was discovered.

'And what happened?' The undersheriff spoke before there was too much reminiscing about who was born when.

'Nobody knew, lord. She went to the river, but not with any good reason as was known, and her body was found a mile downstream next day.'

'Do the women of Claines go there with washing?'

'Some do, in preference for the stronger flow and cleaner water, but neither washing nor basket was upon the bank or found.'

'Did any of you see the body?' It was a slim chance, but Catchpoll wondered if there was something to be discovered.

'I did.' An old woman stepped forward. 'She was drowned right enough. I saw a drowned man when I was young, floating in the river. The skin was the same, bar the marks on her arms where she must have knocked into branches as she went down. In spring there is often more floating in the current.'

'Both arms?' Catchpoll was interested, very interested. 'Scratches or bruises?'

'Both arms as I recall, and dark marks, black bruises. Logs and tree limbs, you know . . .'

Catchpoll glanced at the undersheriff, meaningfully. Bradecote gave a barely perceptible nod.

'And the husband and son left afterwards.' The undersheriff was almost talking to himself.

'Yes, lord. You would not think him a man to be overset by the loss of a wife he cared but little for, yet who is to say?'

'And the girl-child, she was left with kin. Do they live?'

'No, oh no.' This was said with, thought Bradecote, a touch of relief.

'And they were Claines, not Bevere.' There was clearly something from which these people sought to distance themselves. 'Best ask in Claines, my lord.'

'Aye, ask in Claines.' This was followed by much nodding.

'Then thank you for your help and may your pease flourish with the weeding.' Bradecote gave a nod of dismissal, spoke a few words of thanks to Heribert the Reeve, and then the three sheriff's men began to retrace their steps.

'Well, long past proving, but my guess is the husband drowned the wife and then left.' Catchpoll was quite matter-of-fact.

'But does a man who beats his wife do something like that?' asked Walkelin. 'Would he not kill her in temper rather?'

'He would risk hanging if he did, and this way . . . Well, he proved he could get away with it.' Bradecote shrugged.

'But what Walkelin says has merit, my lord.' Catchpoll sucked his teeth. 'He might beat her, but she would still be useful, cooking and such, and I think some men like having someone to lord it over, and I do not mean "lording" such as you do, neither.'

'Which begs the question: "What made him kill her?"' Bradecote was thoughtful.

'She was going to run away?' offered Walkelin.

'To what? Starve in a ditch?' Bradecote was unimpressed with the idea.

'Another man,' said Catchpoll, confidently. 'The angry husband would snap at that. My only surprise is that whoever it was did not meet with a "nasty accident" too. What do you say to the husband drowning her by, or on, the island?'

'It gives us a link, but only if whoever killed Ricolde was her father, and why now, not years back if it was him?' Bradecote had serious doubts.

'What if he took up work upon the river, went down to Bristow, travelled the sea and came back only now?' Walkelin was more positive.

'But why come back at all if that were so? I am not convinced.'

'Because sometimes, more times than you would wish, people act not according to sense but just plain thought of the moment. Makes our task the harder, and sometimes easier, since they leave traces when not thinking.' Catchpoll liked Walkelin's

140

idea. 'And you see, my lord, there is a possible link. We never caught up with Thurstan Shippmann.'

'You are not saying he and Wilferth are one and the same, surely, Catchpoll?'

'No, my lord, but what if something Ricolde let slip to him he then passed to someone on his craft? What if, perhaps, when he talked of his love of the river, she had said she disliked it, because her mother drowned in it, upriver? The father-turned-sailor is curious, goes and watches, sees the mother in the daughter's looks, sees her trade . . . There, you see, is motive stark and true.'

Bradecote had to admit this was so.

'And yet it relies so much upon the slimmest of chances. The father would have to have returned, been on a particular boat, at a particular time, and overheard one piece of information.'

'It could be the son, my lord.' Walkelin was frowning, concentrating in his methodical way.

'It could, and part of me feels it more likely, but what father tells his son he murdered the lad's mother?'

'A twisted one, and none but a twisted man would have done as he did to Ricolde's feet.' Catchpoll grimaced.

'But he took the son with him. That shows the boy was important to him.'

'If the father has died since, might it have been some deathbed confession?' suggested Walkelin.

'If it was, surely it would have meant the last place the son would wish to see would be Bevere Island, and even if the father "vindicated" his actions . . . Son more likely than father, yes, but even so, the odds are very long.' Bradecote shook his head.

'Only odds we have though, my lord. We agree what happened here to the mother has bearing on how Ricolde died, so it has to be someone who knows about that.'

'And we needs to find out why the folk of Bevere are so glad that Ricolde's kin are no longer alive and were not from their manor. You would think they carried a plague,' remarked Walkelin.

'Yes, I noticed. The aunt blamed niece not husband. I also noticed that they talked about the priest in the past tense, so whoever ministers to them now is newer. Pity.' Bradecote frowned.

'Let us hope not too new, my lord.'

They bypassed the manor buildings and carried on to the church in Claines, in search of the priest. They were fortunate, since he had returned from the fields to say the office in the cool of his little church.

'Father, may we speak with you?' Bradecote had waited until the Latin phrases ended, and there was silence.

The priest turned and saw the three men.

'Of course.'

'I am Hugh Bradecote, Undersheriff of Worcestershire, and these are Serjeant Catchpoll and his apprentice. We are hunting the killer of a woman who lived in Worcester, but was born here, and died upon Bevere Island.'

'You mean the horrible killing before the Sabbath?' The priest, who looked about the same age as Bradecote, crossed himself, and his brows drew together. 'The evil that men do . . . I did not know the poor soul came from here. Nothing was said.'

'We only discovered it in Worcester, Father. She left many years ago, before your time, but in circumstances that have meaning. We have asked in Bevere, and her family is named, though none remain here. It concerns a woman who drowned, six and twenty years since. She was buried in the churchyard, though some wondered if she had taken her own life. Your predecessor did not share that thought.'

'Father Benedict was a man of compassion.'

'Did you meet him, or were you sent after he died?'

'Oh, I came when he was too infirm to continue his ministry. He was afflicted with a shaking of the limbs, but I think what killed him was not being able to do God's work. He lived but three months after I came.'

'And when was that?'

'Eight years ago, come All Hallows.'

It did not bode well for positive answers, but Bradecote asked anyway, if the priest knew anything of a couple, now dead, who were kin to one Wilferth.

'I am sorry, my lord. I have buried many in eight years. Without names I cannot answer you. We must ask the reeve. He is—'

'Out in the pease field.'

'You know?'

'It was not hard to guess. Will you introduce us?'

'I will. Come with me.'

The priest, whose name was Father Laurence, took them to a scene that was almost exactly the one they had witnessed in Bevere, though there were more people. The reeve, a stocky man with ruddy cheeks and large, capable hands, was respectful but guarded. He called together those labouring in the field, and the sheriff's men saw the same look upon all the faces when it was declared who they were and why they had come to Claines. It was a closed look. These people had something to hide.

'You can give me the names of the kin who took in the girl, and her name, since it was not the one she used in Worcester.' The undersheriff looked at the reeve.

He nodded but paused before opening his mouth.

'The girl's name was Eadild. Gytha was Wilferth's sister, a few years older, and with no child of her own outside the churchyard. Wilferth said he had no way of caring for a small girl.'

'Said he had no use for her, you mean,' came a mutter from within the group. 'She was too young to do a woman's work.'

'And Gytha's husband?'

The silence hung in the air. After a long time the reeve growled the name 'Cuthwin', and several men spat into the dusty earth at their feet.

'He does not seem to have been popular, my lord,' commented Catchpoll, loudly, but it drew no response. The silence was sullen.

'So, Cuthwin and Gytha took in the child Eadild, until she was thrown out at about twelve for . . . wickedness.' Bradecote was looking at the villagers. There was some shuffling of feet. They knew just what 'wickedness' had been the reason for her being thrown out of her adopted home, and nobody wanted to say a single word about it. Eventually, he abandoned the line of questioning, and returned to Wilferth and his put-upon wife.

'Let us talk about Wilferth then and the drowning of his wife. There was suggestion in Bevere that some thought it might not have been an accident.' Bradecote did not say she might have gone into the Severn of her own free will, and Catchpoll hid a smile. He was being 'serjeant wise'.

'She would not have abandoned her little one,' said a woman, firmly. 'I said it then and say it now. Wilferth was a hard man, a hard, hard man.'

'So, if she did not take her own life, what was she doing by the river? Bathing her feet?'

'She went there often enough, but not to wash.' Another female voice scoffed. 'Why should we worry all these years after to say it and her long buried? Wilferth was a brute, a callous, hard-fisted, hard-hearted brute, so what wonder she sinned.'

'She had a lover, then?' Bradecote could feel Catchpoll's smugness without seeing it.

'I am sure of it, my lord.'

'And had he a name?'

'None I knew. He was not local. My thought was he came from the other side of the river and Hallow. She had kin over there.' It sounded as though the other side of the Severn was a foreign country.

'So Wilferth found out, did he?' Catchpoll stepped to stand beside the undersheriff. 'It's what you think, I can see it on your faces.'

'He had the right, if she betrayed him,' said a man.

'And you wonder why no woman ever took you on after your wife died,' a female voice mocked.

'It is true.' The reeve did not want discord in his village

over things long buried. 'At first it seemed a mishap, but when Wilferth and his lad—'

'Called?' Bradecote interjected.

'After his father. Well, they left the day she was put in the earth, and he gave Eadild to his sister. There was rumour Ranild had been seen up close with a man shorter than Wilferth and thin-built. There was no proof, and Wilferth was gone who knows where, so it was let lie, and so it ought to remain. It was not a man of Claines, and them that sinned, if they sinned, was beyond us.'

'But not beyond God.' They had all forgotten the priest, who looked troubled.

'No, Father, not beyond God, to be sure.' The reeve coloured.

'And nobody has any further idea as to who the other man might have been?' Bradecote looked about him at the shaking heads. 'How tall was Wilferth if he was shorter?'

''Bout the height of your serjeant, my lord, but very broad of chest he was.'

'And when he went, he said no direction?' Walkelin was thinking along his own path.

'None, though our first thought was Worcester, but nobody ever saw him thereafter and there are times we go in, to market, or to the cathedral upon a holy day.'

'What would he have done in Worcester, though, a man of the land?' A younger man asked the question, being one who could not imagine working within the confines of walls of any sort.

'Aye, there is that.' Several thought this sensible.

'Did none of you ever see Eadild, the girl, when she went to Worcester?' Bradecote asked.

The faces went blank, the heads shook.

'I see. Well, Father, I would ask that you have Eadild, or Ricolde, as she was known when grown, in your prayers tonight, for she got neither kindness nor charity here in life.'

'But the name, Ricolde, is known here, my lord. It is a rare one hereabouts, and the only one any of us ever heard of in Worcester was a whore.' The voice, which was male, sounded dubious.

'She was not "a whore". She was the finest whore in Worcester,' growled Catchpoll, 'because whoring was all she had that she could do, thanks to her childhood. She was also a benefactress of the church, and' – he paused to get the right words – 'a comfort to the elderly.' He did not specify the type of comfort offered. 'You pray for her, Father, and have every man, woman and child in this manor pray also. She deserves that.'

'Yes, yes, I will, for we all sin.' Father Laurence was shocked, but then this day had given him several shocks about his flock.

Bradecote thanked the reeve, nodded a dismissal to the gathering and strode away with Catchpoll and Walkelin in his wake.

There were several things to ponder.

Chapter Ten

They retraced their steps to the manor at Bevere without speaking, each man cogitating upon those aspects of what they had learnt that stuck out the most to him. When they reached it they were offered beer, for the day was hot, and went to the hall, where they sat upon a bench with their beakers. Catchpoll gazed into his as if it might give him inspiration.

'Well, we have confirmed what we hardly doubted and already suspected,' sighed Bradecote. 'Ricolde spoke truth to Father Anselm, and her mother was drowned by her father. The father was violent and found out she was playing him false. They are all deeds so long ago committed that only God can judge, as the priest said.'

'Yes, my lord, but there is the chance we may find something in Hallow. If Ranild, the drowned woman, had kin there, then someone would remember her, and her lover . . . Hallow is close enough to be his likely origin, and we have a description.' Walkelin looked eager.

'My height and thin. Not many men like that about, to be sure,' said Catchpoll, sarcastically. 'Even if we could find the man, and who would choose to hold up his hand and cry that he was an adulterer, we do not learn anything that helps with finding the killer we seek in the here and now.'

'All we have is that it is more likely that Wilferth or his son killed Ricolde, assuming as we do that Ranild was drowned at Bevere Island, or her husband assumed she had sinned with her lover there.' Bradecote ran his hand through his hair. 'There is no other reason why a man would have brought Ricolde to the island to kill her.'

'No reason we know of, my lord, but there might yet be a man who had a reason that does not link to anything we have discovered.' Walkelin gave voice to caution.

'If that was meant to be encouraging, Walkelin, think again. It would mean you are saying we have not even narrowed down the number of men who might be the guilty bastard.'

'We have to work with what we possess, my lord, and I am with you.' Catchpoll scratched his ear, thinking. 'Sense says Ricolde's place of death had meaning to the man who killed her, and he had a reason in his head to kill her. Which means we are looking for an old man who still has strength in his body, or a man in his late thirties. That means the son has to be more likely, and with either one, where did they disappear to after they did the deed?'

'And that brings us to the idea you and Walkelin share about Thurstan Shippmann, or rather some member of the crew of his boat, and they could be anywhere up or down the river, or even down the sea coast from Bristow.' Bradecote was gloomy.

'So, do we go back to Worcester, now, my lord?' Walkelin enquired.

There was a pause.

'No, not yet. We can ask along the river about Thurstan Shippmann, who went upstream in the last few days. And we can finally dismiss Will Fellman from our thoughts by speaking to those with whom he traded, and who would have noticed if he was blood-soaked and behaving like a man who had just hacked a woman to death.'

'And how would that be?' Walkelin looked interested.

'Don't ask fool questions, lad.' Catchpoll glared at him.

'But I am serious, Serjeant. Would he be furtive or . . . excited or . . . calm?'

'Take your pick. All I would say is he would not be straightaway just as before, as though nothing had happened, but you might need to know the man well enough to make the comparison. I doubt any who met him just to trade would see that, but there is a chance.'

'And at least we will be doing something, rather than kicking our heels in Worcester waiting for a boat that may or may not tie up sometime in the next month. Not that I am remaining there to wait, just so that you know.' Bradecote emptied his beaker and set it down with a thump on the bench beside him. 'Let us be on our way.'

It was as they emerged into the sunlight that a young woman came before them. She looked nervous, almost furtive, and her voice was hardly more than a whisper, as though she wished nobody might hear her. She made a deep obeisance.

'I am come from Claines, my lord. I . . . The woman who was killed, Eadild, I would have justice for her if I can help.' She plucked at her skirts, and her breathing was unnaturally fast. Whatever she was going to reveal, it was costing her dear.

'Then tell us, but sit. You need not be afraid of us.' Bradecote spoke gently and indicated the shadow of the hall, where they would not be staring into sun glare. It was a little cooler.

'They none of them wanted to say, my lord. Can I have your promise no harm will come to them?'

'You speak in riddles. What is your name?'

'I am Tilde, to all, my lord.'

'Then who is "them", Tilde?'

'The others, the men of the village.'

'I do not think the lord Undersheriff is interested in old justice,' said Catchpoll, his eyes narrowing. Bradecote glanced at his serjeant and thought he understood where this might lead.

'No, I am not. Will that ease you?'

'Yes, my lord. You see, Cuthwin was . . . He died a dozen years ago, and I give thanks every day of my life that it is so. He . . . I was seven years old . . . He tried to throttle me to keep me quiet, but my brother heard, and he tried to fight him and made such a noise that others came, the men, and . . . they saw his foulness, and they put a rope about his neck, and strung him up in the big barn, and my father cut off . . . It was just and it was right. What he did . . .' She covered her face with her hands.

151

'I am sorry. It was indeed right and just, for he was taken in the act of . . . a capital crime, though it would have been better had the lord Sheriff been told of it thereafter.

'Nobody spoke today to save my shame, and for fear of the law, my lord. My shame cannot be set aside, but at least the other part can be so. What he did to me, if he treated his wife's blood kin that way, and for years . . . No wonder his wife said she blamed herself. She sort of faded away and died the following winter from a chill.'

'The shame is his, not yours, Tilde.' Bradecote spoke firmly, as if giving judgement.

'Tell that to the village. They pity me, but I am tainted. I am nineteen and unwed. No other family would see their son husband me.'

'Would you wish to be married?'

'No, but I am a burden else.'

'What of taking the veil?'

'My father has but few strips of poor soil in this manor. My dowry would be too small.'

'Does he know you have come here?'

'No.'

'If you would be content with holy sisters, there is a way that you could be dowered without your father's coin. May I speak with him?'

'No, oh no. He would be angry, he would—'

'What you have said is not going to become the gossip of Worcester, Tilde. It carries no further, and there is no action the law would take against those who dealt with Cuthwin. Let me speak with him, and you have a future assured, and

152

through the kindness of Eadild, who shared your suffering.'

Tilde looked him in the eye for the first time.

'You mean this, my lord?'

'I would not say it otherwise. Take me to him.'

She took a deep breath and nodded, and he followed her from the courtyard. Walkelin and Catchpoll said nothing, even after they had left, for some time. Eventually, Walkelin spoke, and in scarcely more than a whisper.

'Truly, one can be ashamed to be a man.'

'Aye, but you had best get used to the feeling, lad, because in this job you finds out just how bad men can be.' Catchpoll shook his head and went to ready the horses.

The sheriff's men let their horses walk on a loose rein, since the sun was now beating down upon them, and when they encountered people in the fields it was far less intimidating if the riders did not seem intense and urgent. Bradecote gazed between his horse's ears as it twitched them with the flies buzzing about its head. He was aware of an irrational sense of disappointment. There was no good reason to think that speaking to the folk of Claines and Bevere would make the answer to their problem blindingly obvious. What he had held to was a foolish hope. Everything that made sense made no sense. The facts just buzzed about like the damned flies.

Even the marshy river margins were dry enough to barely take the imprint of the horses' hooves after a dry summer spell, and they forded the Salwarpe, the river level being low enough for the horses to splash across without having to swim. Then, where it was shallow, they let the animals drink, but not too deeply.

There were few villages close to the eastern bank of the river and the ride was quiet. They spoke to a boy herding swine in the shade of a thicket, a few men fishing from coracles, and one gutting his catch upon the bank, but got nothing but frowns and then shaking heads, except for one man who said he had seen a man rowing upstream a few days past, but whether it was the day Ricolde was murdered or the one before he could not be sure.

'So it could be Fellman, innocent man about his business, or not.' The undersheriff was getting a headache. Hot weather and a tangle of information conspired together to leave him tetchy and with a dull thudding within his skull.

'We'll find more upon t'other side, my lord, at Holt and Grimley and Hallow. If Fellman did sleep upon the bank I would reckon it would be this side, and he would go into Wribbenhall first thing in the morning, before everyone was out to the fields, so as to catch at least some of those with pelts for him in their homes. Trouble is, he would not need a fire these nights, so unless he caught himself a fish and cooked it, there might be little trace of him or where he dragged his little boat from the water. The only thing we have is that the bank must be shallow enough for that.'

In the end it was Walkelin's sharp eyes that saw the mark of the shallow keel leading up to what Bradecote had mistaken for the trail of a wild animal going to the river to drink.

'No, my lord, it is not just the grasses crushed, but a mark into the ground, just here and here.' Walkelin pointed where a small craft was dragged. 'No footprints, but . . . yes, ash. It wasn't a big fire, just enough for a fish to cook over it, and there is that coppice a short way back. If Fellman had a good knife he could cut a few thin branches if none was upon the ground already. Nice place to spend a summer's night, I reckon.'

'We're not interested in whether he enjoyed himself,' muttered Bradecote, morosely, and Catchpoll gave Walkelin a look and the hint of a shrug which indicated that short of finding a man running towards them confessing all, the undersheriff was not going to be pleased by anything at present.

They reached Wribbenhall as the shadows lengthened, but before the workers returned from the fields. It was a royal manor, not that any king had trod upon its soil in the last two centuries, and there was no hall as such, but the king's reeve would have the largest dwelling, so they made for that and found a girl of about ten nursemaiding three siblings, one a babe on her narrow hip. She nearly dropped the baby in horror at the sight of Catchpoll and a scowling man dressed all lordly, and was struck dumb, answering their first questions with nothing more than a nod or shake of the head. She was clearly unwilling to let them step over the threshold, however, and stood her ground in the doorway. She then had the bright idea of sending the child nearest her in age to find a parent, and a boy of five or six slipped past them and went running as fast as his legs could carry him to wherever they were to be found.

A short while later a slightly breathless reeve arrived, dragged his cap from his head and apologised that he could offer no more than shelter for the night and a share of their own meal, which was a pease pottage With three extra mouths to feed, and grown men at that, there was more bread than pottage, since the lord undersheriff refused to have the children eat but bread alone. The reeve's wife, seeing him wince at the sound of the baby crying, offered him a wet cloth for his brow and her mother's remedy for a headache, madder root tied to the head with a thread of red wool.

He took only the cloth.

Catchpoll, meanwhile, was asking about Fellman and frowned. The reeve knew of him but had not seen him for some months.

'It does not mean he has not been here, but I . . . No, I have not seen him.' He gave no further information and turned the conversation to being hospitable.

Walkelin brought up Thurstan Shippmann, but the reeve could only say that quite a few craft put in at the little quay to overnight when it was too dark to see the way clear, and some goods were transferred that were going to or from Kidderminster, but he had not real dealings with the traders. He knew of the name but would not be able to tell you the name of his boat, nor recognise the man.

They rose with the dawn, since those who headed to the fields needed to use every fine hour of daylight. The morning was cool, Bradecote's headache was gone and with it his short temper. He thanked the reeve for his hospitality, surreptitiously pressed silver pennies upon the wife and had the reeve find them someone to ferry them across the river. They would have the sun in their eyes later, but for the first miles it was pleasant and even their mounts were eased, with fewer flies to annoy them, and where willow and hazel did not bar their way there were places where they could travel a little faster.

When they reached Holt they had better luck than the previous day, for Fellman was known to several of those who lived with the river as a neighbour. Three men told of selling him skins from animals they had trapped, and a lad who was proud to say he had killed a fox with his slingshot as it tried to wreak havoc among his mother's hens. He revealed that he had no knowledge of how to skin it, but a neighbour had helped him and got a good price for the skin for him. Having heard what other men were paid for a fox it was clear the 'kind neighbour' had pocketed most for himself. When he was pointed out by the boy, the man spent an uncomfortable few minutes with Serjeant Catchpoll, who not only drew all he could remember of Fellman from him, but indicated that cheating a boy of his pennies was not 'good business' and that, whilst not illegal, would put him at odds with the rest of his community if they got to hear of it. Perhaps, Catchpoll suggested, he might find three silver pennies had been temporarily mislaid and would now be handed over to the lad. This was accompanied by Catchpoll's broadest death's head smile, which assured compliance.

What was clear was that nobody in Holt had been concerned at Fellman's appearance, even when pressed to say if there was anything unusual in his manner or look. He was, said those who knew him, not a friendly man, fair in business, but not one they would wish to cross.

'Bit like having a bull,' said one man. 'You know, does the job, generally stares right through you, but you are always a bit cautious when up close with him. Will Fellman is like that. You surely would not invite him to feast with you. He seemed no different to normal is all I can say.'

'Has Thurstan Shippmann been seen in the last week, going up the river?' Bradecote asked, though he knew the man's direction, and was both surprised and interested in the answer.

'Ha! In a foul humour he was and no mistake. He was heading up to Shrewsbury, some few days past, that was, and was a good steersman short. Something about a death in the family, and the man he had hired to take his place on the trip being useless. He was announcing it to half the shire as he passed through, and a good pair of lungs he has in him. As I reckon, his crew must have ringing in their ears come nightfall.'

'Was this change made in Worcester?'

'I could not say, my lord, for it was but his bellowing.'

The sheriff's men looked at each other. It was tantalising information, that might mean nothing or everything.

'So we know that Fellman is just as we have found him ourselves, not a man you would call "friend" and one you would be careful not to annoy, but there is no sign of him bearing marks upon his clothes or his soul that say he committed a brutal murder.' Bradecote swung himself up onto the saddle and looked at Catchpoll. 'Looks like his wife's pointing finger was nothing more than that. And the theory about a crewman of Thurstan Shippmann's is looking ever more reasonable.'

'Aye, my lord, and if he was heading upriver, at least he will be back in reasonable time. '

'And we can ask in Worcester if any local man took the place,' offered Walkelin.

This pleased his superiors.

'Very true, Young Walkelin. And if it proves to be that the man came off there, then someone will know who and why. We make some progress.' Catchpoll urged his horse to a trot.

It was a trio in better mood who rode into Grimley, where a man had sold Fellman half a dozen weasels and three squirrel skins. When asked when that was, he frowned and said it was five or six days ago but was vague.

'It was a hot day, I can tell you that. Sweating hot it was, and Fellman, well he had the better of it on the water, a mote cooler there, and he had his back bare. I warned him as he would catch the sun, but he said he had it all planned, and his cotte was in his craft, and he would dip it in the river and put it on wet once he set off again.'

Since every day had been hot for a week this was not a huge help, though Walkelin's eyes brightened.

It was as they were leaving that they saw a woman laying a good-sized blanket over the bushes in the sun. It was a good time of year to wash bed coverings, since the nights were warm, but this one took their attention. It was a good wool, dyed yellow, and had a border of red stitched about it, which was rather grand for a village peasant. It was also noticeable that there were discolourations on one part of it.

'Fine weather for washing, mistress,' acknowledged Catchpoll.

''Tis that.'

'Pity them stains won't come out. Must have cost a fair sum, a fancy cloth like that.'

She looked a little uncomfortable.

'Tell me, have you had this long?' Bradecote leant forward, his arm across his pommel. His voice held interest, but no threat.

'I . . .' She looked from one to the other of the three strangers. The man who had just asked the question looked important.

'Come, mistress, we do not think you stole it.' Bradecote spoke softly.

'We thinks you . . . found it. By the river.' Catchpoll smiled, which was the last straw. The woman burst into tears, interspersing sobs with vehement protestations that she had nothing to do with anything wicked. How they knew so much scared her.

'Just tell the lord Undersheriff when and where you found it, mistress,' advised Walkelin, thinking he was the one man of the three who might not scare her witless. 'That is all we need to know. The blanket is yours, and we do not seek to take it from you.' There was something about Walkelin that was reassuringly ordinary, even if his red hair was not a common colour.

Her sobs abated. She had found it caught among the reeds at the river's edge, a few days ago, when she went to wash clothes. It was sodden and the stains in it were faint.

'Come off one of the boats that ply the river, I thought.' She did not say why it had been 'lost overboard'. However, the only thing of which she was guilty was deceiving herself that those stains were not blood. 'I may keep it . . . my lord?' She looked to Bradecote.

'You may keep it, and the person who owned it before would not begrudge it to you, I am sure.'

She looked relieved.

They wished her good day and trotted the short way to Hallow.

'If we asks them as went to Ricolde, I am sure they would remember a covering like that,' Catchpoll said, confidently, and then grinned, realising what he had said. 'That is, I mean the missing blanket she was wrapped in to get her to the boat, not what they did with her.'

Walkelin choked.

'And the bloodstains? Washed out they were, but . . .' Bradecote grimaced.

'Thinking on it, the killer might have wrapped it about his body like a flesher's apron. It would keep the worst of the blood from splashing on his braies and his cotte. It was discarded afterwards, and, mark you, above the island, since a woman of Grimley would not be walking to Hallow to do her washing.'

'Which means the man headed upriver, at least a mile or so. He might have then walked back to Worcester, all innocent-looking. If it was Walter's boat, as was found downstream, would that work, Catchpoll?'

'It adds a little time, my lord, but not much. Yes, I think it works, though I do not see why he came upstream to lose the blanket. It was hers, not his, so does not link any particular man to her.'

'And there is still the axe,' noted Walkelin.

'But a blanket floats, at least long enough to get caught in reeds, and an axe sinks. I doubt any will see that axe again, unless they are a fish.' Bradecote felt remarkably pleased. Even if there was still no name, here was another missing piece. Catchpoll often said catching wrongdoers was like putting together the shards of a broken pitcher, and this had been a big, missing shard. 'Once we are back in Worcester, we find out what we can from the river men about changes to Thurstan Shippmann's crew. Things are starting to make some sense at last.'

Chapter Eleven

The people of Hallow knew all about the murder on Bevere Island, for all that those on the other side of the river treated them as 'strangers'. It had provided much food for chatter as they worked the fields, and, unlike upon the eastern bank, they were eager enough to talk about it in front of the sheriff's men, which was telling. It had that aspect of being shocking but not quite connected to them. It was clearly a revelation to them that the murdered woman had originally come from Claines, and it was this which drew old connections to the surface. A weather-beaten woman sighed, crossed herself and remarked as how history repeated itself.

'Why do you say that?' asked Bradecote, hoping he knew the answer she would give.

'Because it is not the first death there, and I doubt the last. The priest should say words over it. I say as the island invites death.' She shook her head.

'And what other death was there?'

'Oh, many years back it was, before your time, my lord, and the Severn has flowed past and taken all memory with it, as most hope.'

'This woman who has been killed, her name, when a child, was Eadild, the daughter of Wilferth.'

'Wilferth? Him? Sweet Jesu!' The woman paled.

'What of him?' Catchpoll thought that the undersheriff was treading too softly, though the approach was sound.

'It was him who . . . and this the daughter?'

'Her mother drowned, but it was put down to accident,' stressed Bradecote.

'No accident, my lord.' It was a man's voice, but a dead voice also. There was nothing in it, neither anger nor shock, nor a desire to shock.

'Why say you that?'

'Because Wilferth drowned his wife.'

'That is but gossip.'

'No, it is truth before God.' Several people muttered and shook their heads at the man, who looked the sort of wiry fellow in whom toughness and strength abounded, though in him strength had dwindled. His hair was greyed, his shoulders sagged a little as though he bore a heavy weight upon them and his voice held no life.

'You cannot know.'

'I can, for I saw him do it, near as I could.'

'Leave what is past alone, Oswin. It does no good.' A woman said, not unkindly, and laid her hand upon his arm, but he put it from him.

'I saw Wilferth of Claines drown his wife, and I had not the courage then to tell it before any but the priest, and my penance has been living with knowing I let him get away with it. You are the law, my lord, so I tell you now. I was there. I did nothing, nothing except save my own worthless neck.'

'Who are you?'

'I am Oswin, son of Alfric the Smith, and I was her lover.'

There was a moment of total silence, before Bradecote broke it.

'Then we would speak with you, Oswin, and alone, not because you can get justice for the mother, but because you may yet help us get justice for her daughter.' He indicated with his hand that he should step away from his neighbours and speak with the sheriff's men privately. They moved aside and sought some shade beneath an ash tree's boughs at the field's edge.

'I cannot see how that can be, my lord, for I have not set foot upon Bevere Island in six and twenty years. I can tell you nothing about what happened upon it more than what is common knowledge, that a man killed a woman and tried to cut her into pieces.'

'We would hear more of Wilferth and his family and what happened those years ago, for we believe there is some link between them, not mere chance.'

'You won't hear a good word about the man, from me or anyone here in Hallow. Ranild was a good woman, and a good wife if he had but let her be. She was my mother's cousin's daughter, and I knew her from childhood. She was happy and laughing then, all coppery chestnut hair and sparkling eyes. I would have wed her, but her father thought

Wilferth a better match. I was a second son to the smith here, and he thought Wilferth a bold man who would do something with his life. What he was in reality was a bully who liked hurting people. He beat her from the beginning, and she made excuses at first, till she lost a second child because of him. When the little girl came along he used to use her to hurt her mother, because doing anything to a child is worse for a woman than doing it to her. He held the poor thing on the hot hearth stones once so that her feet were burned. All of Claines must have heard her scream, but nobody interfered with Wilferth, not if they valued their skin. It was after that we met, one time she came over here to see kindred when he was in Worcester. First time it was just talk, because she had nobody to listen to her. Over three years we saw each other, secretly, perhaps a dozen times, and by the end we were lovers. I was no strapping, handsome man, but I cared for her, and she had not been cared for at all in years.' He shook his head.

'I have wondered since if Wilferth had his own suspicions, or whether a "good neighbour" saw something and told him. Either way, the day after Ascension we had hoped to meet upon the island. He was meant to be taking a pig to market, but he did not go. He came over to the island, roaring like a bull, thinking we could not escape him.' Oswin hung his head. 'I played the coward. I can swim, see, and I told myself if he did not find her with a man, he would do nothing. It was a lie to my conscience. He did not need to find her with anyone. He went there to kill her, and had she been picking flowers and singing psalms he would have killed her just the same. I heard her beg and I heard a splash, and the next day her body was found downstream. He killed her. I heard rather than saw, but she never drowned by accident, and he and the lad left the village next day.'

The sheriff's men looked at this shell of a man, hollowed out by his own guilt. From what had been said of Wilferth he would have had no chance against him in a fight, but each of the three agreed with him; he had taken the coward's way and paid thereafter.

'Have you any idea where they went?' asked Catchpoll.

'None, other than it was not Worcester. Nobody ever saw sign of them again.'

'And the lad, was he beaten? Would he have gone his own way as soon as he could?' Bradecote wanted something, anything, that would help them take one killer if the other was beyond all but the judgement of Heaven.

'That was the odd thing. Wilferth idolised the boy, and I never heard from Ranild that he ever raised a hand to him, but he did worse in some ways, to my mind. He showed him how to be a man, and can you imagine what one in his image would be like?'

'Having seen what happened to Ricolde, yes, we can, since sense says he or the father would be the only ones to link her to what happened there,' growled Catchpoll.

'Ricolde?'

'It was the name the daughter took in Worcester.'

'Ah. Only Ricolde I heard of there was a grand sort of whore, not that anyone here could afford her sort.'

Catchpoll opened his mouth, but then shut it. Why tell him?

They thanked Oswin, for what little he had given them, and he returned to his labours.

'We have lots of proofs for the past and little help for the present,' grumbled Catchpoll.

'Everything he said, though, makes it even more likely that the son, if not the father, is our man, surely.' Bradecote took comfort from that. 'We know Thurstan Shippmann is lacking his steersman and that may yet be significant. Once we are back in Worcester, we may get a name, or a description and be on his trail like hounds.'

'But the bedcover appearing upstream, my lord? He could be out of the shire by now,' Walkelin reminded him.

'He might be but think on this. If he works upon the Severn he will stick to the Severn, and even if he goes as far as Shrewsbury, he will come back. If we have to check every craft that comes through Worcester for two or three weeks, we will find him, taken back by Thurstan Shippmann if his replacement was less able or as a new man upon another boat. I doubt he will think us that close to discovering him or that dogged in hunting him.'

The undersheriff's good mood plummeted, however, as a rider came towards them; a large man in a hurry. Hammon was not a man-at-arms one easily forgot. His face was red, where it was not blotched with dust, and that dust was turning to muddy streaks as it met with the sweat from his brow. His horse's flanks were heaving and its nostrils distended, showing scarlet within.

'My lord. I come with news. There is another woman dead

in blood.' Hammon wiped the dust from his face, though in fact he merely moved the streaks. 'The lord Castellan sends to you to return straight away to Worcester.'

Bradecote felt his stomach turn over and offered up a prayer that it was not Mistress Fellman. If they had got it wrong . . .

'Has she been named, Hammon?' Catchpoll voiced the question.

'No, Serjeant, leastwise I have not been told it. A man came running to the castle, shouting that a woman had been killed, and the serjeant of the guard went and saw it was true. He reported to the lord Castellan, and he sent me to find you. He said as you would likely be heading south on the west side of the river.'

'I told Furnaux, in case the lord Sheriff returned,' explained Bradecote. 'This may cast all our ideas into the dust, Catchpoll, and the alternative is that we are hunting two killers and Heaven forfend that is so. But it may also mean our man still lies in Worcester.'

He set his heels to the grey's flanks, keen to find out what had happened in their absence and at the same time dreading the truth.

They returned to Worcester at speed and with the summer dust of the trackway in their throats. Bradecote wanted to get straightaway to see the body, but even as they clattered into the bailey Simon Furnaux emerged, as though he had been lying in wait for them, and was berating the undersheriff, which was not his role, before he had even dismounted.

'You leave Worcester, abandon it with a madman on

the loose killing women, even if they are women of no importance, and—'

'Not here and not now, my lord Castellan.' Bradecote handed his reins to a groom. 'I have more important things to do than listen to your complaint. But we did not "abandon" Worcester, there is no proof the killer is "mad" and to the law, as to the Almighty, every life is of importance.'

'That is blasphemy.'

'No, it is not, but by all means go and argue the fact with Father Prior if you wish. Serjeant Catchpoll.' Bradecote did not turn to look at the serjeant.

'Yes, my lord. She's in an alley off Brodestrete.' Catchpoll had already got the word from the serjeant of the guard and did not need to be asked the question. He cast the castellan a look which indicated how glad he was not to be 'his' man.

'Then let us be gone.' Bradecote turned on his heel and strode from the bailey with Catchpoll and Walkelin in his wake.

'If ever you wants someone to hold the lord Castellan down while you cut out his tongue, my lord, just remember I am always glad to be of service,' Catchpoll growled as he drew abreast of the undersheriff. He was not jesting.

'I will bear that in mind, Catchpoll.'

The body had been found in an alley at the other end of Brodestrete to Ricolde's house, and a man-at-arms stood at the entrance, placed there by the serjeant of the guard, who thus earned Catchpoll's thanks. He knew that Catchpoll always complained if 'half the shire has prodded the body and trampled all about' the site of a death.

It was not Mistress Fellman, and a wave of guilty relief flooded Hugh Bradecote. She was young, grubby, her clothes, those not saturated in her blood, were probably all she possessed, and she was crumpled like a discarded rag. It spoke of her being a thing of no importance whatsoever, and yet a few hours past she had been a living woman. She was not so much lying as curled up, having collapsed forward, her head touching her knees. He crossed himself. It was patently obvious that her throat had been cut.

Catchpoll crouched down, muttering about his aching bones as ever, and closed the staring eyes.

'He cut her throat from behind, because that took her unawares and would mean less blood on him, and I reckon he held her as she went down, which is why she ended like this. It is a hot day, but even so, she has not been dead many hours for there is a touch of warmth to her still and no sunlight shines here.'

'Who is she?' asked Bradecote.

'That I can tell you, my lord. Her name is Berta, a whore who plies her trade about the quayside mostly. She is, or was, not the choosy sort and was picked up by men who weren't too choosy either.'

'And where was she from, I wonder?' Bradecote spoke his thought aloud.

'Town born and bred, was Berta. She was one as enjoyed her work, or so it was said. Mind you, that was mostly by the dames who said the shame of it killed her mother, and a whore who looks miserable all the time will not get much business.' Catchpoll sounded very matter-of-fact. 'She wasn't one who came to it by necessity, you might say.'

'Er, no.' It was not a subject the undersheriff had considered, but it made sense. He was still a little taken aback at Catchpoll appearing to regard whoring as just another trade like baking or brewing, 'Was she . . . expensive like Ricolde?'

'Middling sort, to my mind. Used the alleyways until her mother died, then the room she lived in, at least by night, so not the cheapest who survive meal to meal on the streets, but not at all like Ricolde. I doubt there was a whore like her, Ricolde, for three shires. Ricolde was not open to being bought by day, not these last ten years, and woe betide the man who thought otherwise. Berta earned her bread on numbers, day or night. Her dwelling is nearer the quay so perhaps the man who killed her acted as one who did not need long or care where.'

'She ended the same way as Ricolde,' remarked Walkelin, trying to sound more casual about the body than he felt.

'Not the same, Walkelin, other than her trade and that he made sure there was a lot of blood. If the killer wants us to know he is removing sinful whores, you would think he would make it more the same.' Catchpoll's brow was furrowed. 'Someone who kills to "say" something wants to be understood, wants it clear. Keeping the method the same does that, and I am not yet sure this is close enough.'

'Or he wants us to think it is just someone else, doing as he did, so we divide our efforts.' Bradecote was thinking ahead.

'Fair point, my lord, fair point. I don't like killers who think they are cleverer than we are.' The serjeant sounded as though this was a matter of honour.

'Well, we seem to prove them wrong, Catchpoll, and the more they try to be "clever", as you call it, the more they are likely to make a mistake.'

'Ah yes, that is very right.' Catchpoll was obviously much cheered by this thought.

'It feels wrong, but I feel relief that there is none to mourn this poor girl, other than possibly the men who used her.' Bradecote shook his head. 'Her life was of the same worth, when all is said.'

'Careful, my lord, or you will be sounding like Father Anselm. Now, she was slashed with a knife, clear enough, not with an axe or heavy blade, and it need not have been a big knife either.'

'But a man with an axe, a bloodied axe, would be very obvious walking the streets in daylight, Catchpoll, so that difference need not be proof it was a different killer.' The undersheriff rubbed his hand across his chin. 'Though he cut her throat, which would be the nearer to an execution than just stabbing her, and Ricolde's death had overtones of that.'

'Aye, my lord, but only a fool would slit a girl's throat in the middle of the day here, in the streets. The blood would spurt, sure to, and keeping it off himself would be nigh on impossible. You would have expected it to be a planned killing and under cover of night. He likely clamped a hand over her mouth to prevent her screaming and then slashed her throat. Being behind her would help him, but his sleeve would surely have got blood on—' Catchpoll stopped suddenly.

'What is it?'

'I was wrong.' He had moved the body onto its side, and there was a tear across the gown from hip to hip. 'He drew the knife across her belly first, not deep. There was no attempt to get her insides outside, but he cut her there, not enough to kill, and then cut her throat. Bastard.'

'So it was intended as a sign, rather than an act of frenzy or rage.' Walkelin flapped his hand about, wishing there were fewer flies buzzing about in the narrow alley. 'And the wound, low like that, looks meaningful.'

'Thus it was designed to disguise, or it was another man, who, not knowing the details of Ricolde's injuries, simply guessed and made poor copy.' Bradecote grimaced. 'That helps us not at all in deciding if we are after one man or two.'

'If it is the same man, why did he kill Ricolde on Bevere Island and Berta here on the street, and but a few days apart? That is what I wants to know.' Catchpoll was still staring at the two wounds. 'And this was probably just with an eating knife such as everyone carries. It was kept well honed. The edge of the wound is very clean and sharp, and we are definitely talking a knife not a dagger, mark you, because this was a blade, not a sharp tip that made the cut, with a fine edge. If a man had a dagger he would use that and stab with it. Less blood about and tidier.'

'So we discount any dagger-wearers. That's a great help, Catchpoll. It discounts me, the castellan and about a dozen men of the town.' Bradecote was not delighted.

'One of those being Mercet, my lord. He wears a dagger in the belt about that fat belly of his.' Walkelin sounded suitably disappointed. 'I know he would not do the deed himself, but . . . You has to hope, as Serjeant Catchpoll says.'

'Good to see you are training Walkelin in Mercet-loathing,' remarked Bradecote, drily.

'Comes with the job, my lord,' replied Walkelin, instantly.

'So, same man, a man using the first death to "cover" his own act, or just a mischance of time, Catchpoll?' Bradecote was serious once more.

'I am not a great believer in "mischances", my lord, not when it comes to killings. I discount that. It is so different to Ricolde's killing that it ought not to be linked, but two whores within a week . . . And also, if it was a man trying to do the same, all that has been spread through Worcester is that Ricolde was cut up. To hear the whispers, you would think we brought the body back in many parts. He might as well have slashed her across the stomach or her arms. The lower wound has meaning.' He sucked his teeth. 'For all that I have said, I am inclined more to the same man, but the idea that what one man has started another might continue cannot be utterly discounted.'

'Which means if it is Thurstan Shippmann's missing steersman he actually returned to Worcester, which is not quite as expected, with the bedcover being dragged out of the river at Grimley.' Bradecote looked puzzled. 'And why kill here again? My dread now is that I think we need to find out if this missing man even left the boat at Worcester. Very foolish we will look waiting to take a man for the killing if it turns out he parted from the craft at Gloucester. Walkelin, you go to the quays and see what you can find out. Catchpoll, you and I will take Berta's body to Father Anselm, who is losing parishioners to violence far too often, I fear.'

Walkelin departed upon his task, and Catchpoll went to the man at the alley entrance and told him to fetch a handcart and something to cover the body.

'We are faced with the same problem as last time, Catchpoll, in that those who saw her last today are not likely to be queueing up to tell us exactly where and when,' sighed Bradecote as he returned.

'But since she was outdoors more, and this was a daylight killing, we might still hear of sightings that limit when she died and with whom she was seen, my lord. If nothing else, every whore in Worcester will be fearing for her life and keen to have this man taken. When we have seen Father Anselm, we can head down Gropelone and speak with any of the "sisterhood" plying their trade there, just for a start. The news will spread like summer fire on a heath.'

'But will it only be hard upon the heels of panic?'

'I cannot say, but they may go together, my lord.'

'We have been seeking Ricolde's killer based upon the motive being her person, not what she did. Do we have to look at everything all over again from a different angle if it was not "her" but just that she was the most well-known whore in Worcester?' Bradecote was a worried man.

'Put that way, my lord, perhaps, but if that were so, Ricolde would have been found in her bed, as dead as this girl, but not miles away. I cannot make that fit, but then I do not see it as two men, so . . .'

'Start with the most known and make that death "spectacular", then work down?' offered Bradecote.

'That still does not sit with the ferocity of the blows to

Ricolde. If what you say was true, it would have been simply cold-blooded, and that man was raging by the end of it. We find things that work, that fit together, and they in turn break other links. Somehow in this, my lord, there is one path that takes us through the muddle, joins everything. It is just that at present we are stumbling about with dead ends.' Catchpoll grimaced at the remains of Berta. 'We need that path.'

Chapter Twelve

The man-at-arms returned with a handcart, and he and Serjeant Catchpoll lifted the corpse to place upon it, where it was covered with an old, oiled cloth. With Catchpoll to the front and Bradecote behind like some bizarre mockery of a funerary procession, they made their way to All Saints, and took the body within to lie in the cool of the north transept. Catchpoll then went in search of Father Anselm, whom he found praying with a woman over her sick child, and when the pair entered the church, the priest was already aware of what awaited him. He crossed himself.

'Poor Berta. She was, I admit, rather a lost soul. Her mother, a very pious woman, died despairing and ashamed, and Berta did not even come to her interring. I did wonder if it was some rebellion against her mother's strong belief that first set the daughter upon the path of sinning, but there was no reconciling the pair.'

'Father Anselm, we are asking ourselves if this woman died because of those sins and Ricolde before her. Has any man of your parish shown sudden signs of ranting against such women? If he was poxed he might "blame" them, or if he became mad and believed they were all tempting him, just him, to sin to damn his soul.' Bradecote thought it worth asking, and Catchpoll nodded in agreement, though both wondered if the priest might refuse to consider such a thing. Father Anselm frowned, but in thought not anger.

'I have a parishioner who keeps wanting me to cast spirits out of the swans on the river, because the other rivermen have told him some tale, and he is frightened of the women who ply their trade upon the streets because his mother told him they "bewitch" men, and he now thinks that means they are witches.' He shook his head. 'He is not aggressive though, in any shape or form, and in fact keeps very much out of their way. He would not dare get close enough to one to harm her.'

'Ah, we have encountered Walter of the Possessed Swans.' Bradecote managed a smile but glanced at Catchpoll.

'There is no malice in him, my lord.' Father Anselm was very sure of this. 'He is merely rather simple of wits and very credulous.'

'Could any man lead him to do misdeeds, by persuasion, Father?' Bradecote looked apologetic. 'We need to consider everything. If he is slow of wits, he might be biddable and unable to see that he was being used.' He could not see Walter doing what had been done to either woman.

'No, my lord. I realise you must think me too inclined to see

179

the good in souls, but Walter is an innocent and his only vice is ale, because he always thinks he is not drinking much, and alas, he cannot hold his drink at all. I think others encourage him because it is funny to watch him fall over after but three beakers.' The priest paused. 'Mine is not the only parish within the walls, my lord. I preach against sin, but charity towards those who commit the sin. It may not be the message preached to every congregation.'

With bitter memories of a previous priest in a neighbouring parish, Bradecote nodded his understanding.

'Then we had better be about trying to find who saw Berta today and if she was seen with a man, though that might be several. We will leave her to you and your prayers, Father.'

'Do we trust the good Father's judgement?' Bradecote looked at Catchpoll as they left the cool of the church into the mid-afternoon heat.

'It was Walter's boat that took Ricolde, but if we were to ask, and we will, there will be someone from his favoured tavern who will swear he was snoring unconscious in the small hours when some man was with Ricolde, and from what was said, the last place he would have gone is in her dwelling. That bed covering is the final proof she was taken from that bed, and Walter would not have been the man to do it.'

'No, I agree. So, we have to knock on doors and try and talk to the other women who sell themselves, and—' He halted as Walkelin arrived, a bit breathless.

'Well?' Catchpoll looked at the red cheeks that clashed with the flaming bright hair.

'The man left at Worcester, but the thing is, he was unknown to the men at the quayside, which is odd if he came from here. He was replaced by Siward, who told Thurstan he had experience on large vessels.'

'But Siward couldn't give a word straight and true if his life depended upon it,' grumbled Catchpoll. 'I only wonder Thurstan did not know better.'

'Perhaps he had to sail and had little choice,' offered Bradecote. 'What may be interesting is if the man was not living in Worcester, how did he know of the death of a relative, one close enough for him to leave his employment and with no guarantee of returning to his work, since it angered Thurstan? Was he really meaning there would be a death, a thing in the future, because he had heard of Ricolde from his captain and intended to do away with her if she proved his sister?'

'Her long-lost brother killing Ricolde makes sense, my lord, but why then kill again today?' Walkelin was frowning.

'Simple distraction. He has not got another craft to sail upon and may indeed hope to rejoin Thurstan after all. In the meantime, he has to avoid us. What better to do than keep us chasing a trail of dead whores?'

Catchpoll grunted. There was sense to it, a lot of sense to it.

'Did any say what this unknown man looked like, Walkelin?' Bradecote looked at him.

'Nothing out of ordinary in height or in build, brown hair, sort of chestnut, and,' Walkelin kept the best till last, 'a tidy beard.' He was clearly pleased.

'Hmmm. Very useful, except for one small thing.' Catchpoll

looked at Walkelin's keen, open face. 'Sorry to break this to you, lad, but a man may lose a beard very easily using a thing called a razor. If we only go about staring at men with beards, we might yet miss him.'

'The trouble now, then, is to find out who this man is and before he adds another victim to that trail. He might try that.' Walkelin sagged a little.

'Let us pray to the Holy Virgin he does not get the chance.' Bradecote crossed himself. 'But think on this. Ricolde had deep chestnut hair. Might his colouring not be a sign of their shared blood? And might not a razor have been used on Berta?'

'I had not considered a shaving blade, but it would work well enough. So, we keep our eyes open for men of the right colouring, but best we also start asking about Berta's last sightings. If you and Walkelin take one side of the lane, my lord, since you alone might make a whore nervous, and I can take the other, then we meet and work up Brodestrete. They will be getting used to us thumping our fists on their oak there, though we will get no warmer a welcome.'

The serjeant had no fear that Bradecote would object to his making the decision. It was simple sense. At times being the undersheriff of the shire was an advantage, since some things could not be refused and some people overawed, but when it was possible for people to close like oysters, the fear of saying the wrong thing was an impediment. Walkelin was approachable, 'one of us' to the ordinary folk, but he had no power. Combine the two and they offset each other's disadvantages. As for Catchpoll himself, well, he had just enough power, a lot of experience and the people of Worcester knew just where they stood with him, which was one step back and acceding to his 'requests'.

The street women of Worcester knew that Serjeant Catchpoll was not the sort who could be 'persuaded' to look the other way if what went on was more than an exchange of money for favours, but at the same time he was not one to hound them when they plied their trade quietly. He had taken a couple of men for killing one of their number over the last dozen years or so, and they knew that they were safer in Worcester than Bristow or Gloucester. They would not normally choose to speak with him, but the news had, as he had expected, travelled fast, and he found quite a few women standing around in pairs, feeling safer that way. There was also less lurking in the shadows, so it perversely seemed that Worcester possessed more whores than usual. At least they were not afraid of him, not wondering if 'it might be him'. These things combined to loosen tongues in the loosest of women.

One had seen Berta with a man just after the cathedral bell rang for Prime, but only saw them from behind. He was a head taller than Berta, with dark brown hair and broad shoulders, but she could give no name to him, nor a better description. Her companion remarked that Berta, God rest her poor soul, did not generally have 'regulars'. There was a touch of pity in the tone, but it also set the dead woman in her place. A whore to whom men did not return could not, in the opinion of her peers, be very good.

'I warned her to be more cautious, I did, 'specially after

Mistress Ricolde,' the woman crossed herself, and even Catchpoll was surprised that Ricolde was referred to with deference by the other whores, 'but she would take any as paid the penny, be they roaring drunk or the creeping, hole-in-a-corner sort afraid of being seen by someone as knows them. But is it true, Serjeant, that the man who did for Berta cut her throat?' The whore shuddered when he nodded. 'Then it was no violent drunk, was it, but a man who wanted a death. Heaven protect us all.'

'All the more reason to aid us in catching the man and not just hoping to Heaven's aid. Has there been any man lurking, watching you all, these last few days?'

'None. We gets watched, of course we does, but just for a few minutes while a man makes up his mind.'

'Or gets up his courage,' added the other woman, with a wry look.

'If you sees the man you saw with Berta, or sees his back, you send to me, right away, understood?'

'Yes, Serjeant Catchpoll.'

'And be careful.'

'We will. Before God, we will.' They meant it.

It could not be said that Walkelin and the lord undersheriff were finding it as easy to elicit any information, since the people they wanted to speak with shrank into the shadows, and Walkelin had to follow and 'flush them out' like a hunting dog. They then looked very edgy and were initially monosyllabic. Hearing 'no' repeated in a reluctant manner was not heartening. Walkelin did his best, and although some were of no help, they managed to find one person, a fisherman, who had seen Berta talking to 'a man yesterday about sunset' which they would have thereafter discounted had he not said their conversation was not amicable. The man was not, he said, a man he could name, so he would assume him a trader visiting Worcester and taking advantage of what it had to offer for entertainment when far from home.

'Mind you, if Berta was the best entertainment he could find, he was either poor, blind or has a miserable life at home. Not saying a word against the wench, mind, but . . . Ah well, poor thing never deserved an end like that, God be merciful to her.'

'The stranger was not the man who left Thurstan Shippmann, was he?' asked Bradecote.

'Could not say, my lord, for all that your man here, Walkelin – the son of Hubert, ain't you? – was asking about such a man and others saw him. I was on the river then.'

It was a pity, but what the fisherman did not know he could not tell.

'Thank y—' Walkelin began, but the man said one thing more.

'Why don't you ask the Healer? He was hanging about her a lot these last weeks. He might have seen something.'

'Roger the Healer?' Bradecote's response was swift.

'Aye, Roger, the thin, pale one who looks in need of one of his own potions.'

Bradecote's mind reeled. The man connected two dead women, yet surely it made no sense. It was left to Walkelin to repeat their thanks.

* * *

Meeting Serjeant Catchpoll at the bottom of Brodestrete, the undersheriff revealed the surprise revelation before all else.

'I cannot see Berta paying for his cures, Catchpoll, and he is a man who would not want the sort of comforts she provided.'

'We only has his word on that, though, my lord, and though I agree he looks the last man for bloody violence, he has links to both the victims.'

'I believed him, totally.'

'Well, that might be sound enough. All we has is doubts, so best we find out more. Then, and only then, my lord, can you beat your own back for taking a man at his word. Let us see what the good people of Brodestrete can tell us, meantime, and then we will have the whole of it and can plan our moves from there. I wonder how many will invite us in for a beaker of ale and the chance to take the weight off our feet?' He grinned, since last time three women had nearly beaten him with their brooms, and one had gone so far as to threaten that her husband would complain to the lord sheriff about him. Imagining what William de Beauchamp would say to such a complaint had made Catchpoll anger the woman even more by laughing and telling her to try first with the lord undersheriff, since he was before her door.

As expected, the doors opened upon people who spent a lot of time ignoring the seedier side of life going on almost outside their own doorsteps, or at least pretending to do so. Catchpoll knew they would be a lot more forthcoming if Berta had been a solid member of the community, but although it was tempting to suggest that failing to find the killer swiftly put all women at risk, he was also aware it would mean complaints to William de Beauchamp that his men had been remiss, having had nigh on a whole week in which to discover the man.

Bradecote, having trodden this weary path before, tried a new tack, realising the women would like something to gossip over and the men to be set apart from any hint of interest in 'that sort of female'. He therefore focused not on Berta but on the man with whom she had been seen.

'We are asking if anyone saw the woman Berta with a man today, because we know that one left a boat plying the river trade, a man unknown to those at the quayside, before the death of the woman Ricolde, and he may still be in Worcester. He is a man with chestnut brown hair and has, or had, a beard. If any saw a man like him with the woman Berta, killed this morning, then we must know, or if you saw a man with blood upon his sleeve and no wound to give reason for it. A man who kills women will eventually not only kill cheap women. We need to catch him, and the more we know of how he looks, and where he has been seen, the quicker will we take him.'

It opened doors the wider and mouths also. Catchpoll, always cautious about giving out what they knew or did not know, passed from an initial feeling of horror to realising it was quite clever. There was threat, but not too immediate, there was the positive tone that the killer would be found, and they were not being asked about a woman who had sold her body for silver pennies and about whom they cared nothing, but about a man who was 'dangerous'. He looked at the undersheriff with a new respect. Not only had he learnt a lot about the methods of 'serjeanting', but he was using his own wits to achieve the ends.

The only difficulty with what they learnt was in timing. A man said that he had seen a man with 'a cheap woman who might have been the one who is dead', but the look in his eye said he knew it was her and his words were to keep his wife from asking awkward questions.

'He had a beard, not a wild one, and his hair was brown or black. It was the day before yesterday that I saw him, not this morning. I could not name him.'

'Which is even further proof he knew it was Berta, because he described the man's face not his back,' murmured Catchpoll, as they moved on, 'so he saw hers too, and she has worked these streets several years.'

'And if it is the man from the boat, then he has not shaved his beard, unless today itself,' added Walkelin. 'He seemed unsure about the hair.'

'It is still an "if" though,' cautioned Bradecote.

At the next house the man and his wife both shook their heads, but as the three sheriff's men moved along, the door opened again. A girl of about fifteen, and clearly the servant, slid out, made a low obeisance to the lord undersheriff, to whom she had obviously been told to be very respectful, and said that she thought she had seen Berta that morning, or rather had heard her, since the man's back kept her from view.

'I knows her voice, my lord, for her mother and my oldmother lived but a few doors apart, my lord.' The girl had her head slightly bowed and her knees slightly bent as though ready to drop another curtsey at any moment, and was thus gazing at Bradecote somewhere below the level of his belt. It was oddly disconcerting. 'The man was strong, my lord, broad, not skinny and weak. His hands were upon his hips like this,' she placed her hands upon her own hips and stuck out her elbows, 'but he was not angry and shouting at her, my lord.' She paused, then added, 'There was something about him made him seem frightening though, even from behind.' This had made such an impression that she forgot to add 'my lord' to the sentence.

'Can you tell us what he wore, what colour of hair he had and when you saw them?' Bradecote kept as much command from his voice as he could, but the girl still trembled at being addressed directly by one so important.

'Sort of darkish brown, that was his hair, and he had plenty, and his cotte was the colour when you use onion skins for the dyeing, my lord.'

Bradecote had no clue as to what that might look like, so asked her to point out something similar. She pointed along the street to a woman's gown in a brownish-yellow, a slightly dull gold. It was a common enough colour.

'But it was a little brighter and darker than her gown, my lord. I saw her some time past, halfway between now and when I got up, my lord.'

'Thank you. That is of use to us.'

She remained in the 'ready-to-curtsey' position, until Bradecote actually dismissed her, when she dipped twice and then crossed herself for good measure. Bradecote had to bite his lip as she flitted away.

'If either of you say "my lord" when you open your mouths

I shall hang you by your thumbs from the battlements. What did her mistress tell her about me? Do I look that terrifying?'

'Not to us, be assured, my—' Catchpoll grinned, the gash of his mouth lengthening in the grey stubble of beard as he stopped, intentionally leaving the last word implied. 'Trouble is, if that is our man, what chance he is still wearing the cotte if it is bloodied? That, combined with plenty of hair and build, would be a good pointer to him.'

'It was most certainly not the thin Healer.' Bradecote felt relieved.

'It gives less time for it to have been him that saw her last,' Catchpoll conceded.

'So, what do we do?' Walkelin looked at his superiors, from one to the other. 'Do we search Worcester for the man in the onion-dyed cotte or keep asking at doors?'

'You, Walkelin, are to scour the streets for any man that is as the girl described. It is but a chance, yet worth taking. We will continue to the top of Brodestrete, to be thorough. Serjeant Catchpoll and I will then seek out Roger the Healer so that we may glean anything that lies in his knowledge and cast him also from suspicion. If you do not find him before the bell for Vespers rings, return to the castle and we will think upon our next move.' It sounded decisive enough, but Bradecote was painfully aware that the chances of it proving successful were slim.

Walkelin nodded respectful compliance and headed back down towards the quayside, so that he might work away from the river more systematically. Undersheriff and serjeant continued their way up the street, but although there were some who 'confessed' they had seen Berta recently, every sighting seemed to be earlier than the man in the yellow-brown cotte.

'The more we hears, the more it is like to be him as did for her, unless of course, he was her last "customer" and the killer, having watched where they went, slipped into the alley after he left. The women always seem to let the men depart first, not walk away themselves. I am not saying as that was the way of it, but it is possible, and if so, we have little hope.'

'On which depressing thought, let us seek out Roger the Healer, upon the chance that he might have the cure for our low spirits, namely details of some man with whom Berta was at odds.'

What had not occurred to Walkelin was just how common a colour a cotte dyed brownish-yellow might be and how many variations might yet still be accounted within the bounds of what a servant girl might have seen. Having dismissed a man with a bent and crippled leg and straggling grey hair, known throughout Worcester as 'Twisted Tovi', a gangly stripling and a short, thickset man with a sweat-beaded pate showing less hair than a tonsured monk, he was getting to think that every man in Worcester possessed a cotte that colour, and most were wearing it today to spite him. It was then that Heaven was merciful, and Walkelin duly offered up thanks as he lengthened his stride and came up behind a broad-shouldered man with thick brown hair and a cotte as the girl had described. He had just come out of the tavern by St Andrew's Church and was not steady upon his legs.

'Here, let me give you a hand to keep you from the gutter,' offered Walkelin, coming abreast of him and taking his arm. He looked at the man's face and knew him in an instant. It was Godfrid, Will Fellman's journeyman, and there was blood upon his sleeve.

Chapter Thirteen

Roger the Healer was hunched over a pestle set upon a bench, grinding the fresh leaves of some plant into a pale green mush. The air was redolent of herbs and wild garlic and odd smells that came from nothing one would eat. A healer's shop was something vaguely mysterious to most people. He looked up as the sheriff's men darkened his door and bade them welcome in a voice in which the cheeriness was a standard 'mask'. He spoke the same way to those for whom he thought his remedies might be efficacious and to those for whom no cure was possible. Bradecote saw through it now, to the sad man within, a man who lived in the gloom without a warming sunshine upon him.

'Have you been at your pounding all afternoon?' Bradecote gave him a slight smile.

'Indeed, my lord. There are some remedies that work best if made when it is hot and sultry and others I would only make when it is cool or rains. How and when we make a preparation is important to the way that it works upon the body.'

'Then you may not have heard the news that is upon the tongues of Worcester. The whore called Berta has been found with her throat cut.'

'Sweet Jesu!' Roger dropped the pestle and crossed himself. 'But I was only speaking with her yesterday.'

'And it is for that reason we would speak with you today. You have been seen with her several times recently. Was there anything she said which made you think her afraid of anyone?' Bradecote did not lay any stress upon the fact that he had been seen with her.

'None. She was upset, with clear reason, after the killing of Mistress Ricolde and afraid a little, but not of any one man, my lord, I would swear to that.'

'She was not afraid of you, then.' Catchpoll made it sound a reassuring confirmation, not a question, but Roger the Healer heard the question nonetheless. He was quiet, but he was no fool.

'Me? No. No, Serjeant Catchpoll, she was not afraid of me. I might almost have wished she was, just a little, for she owes – owed – me coin for an unguent I provided for her some weeks past. She was afflicted with a rash girdling about one half of the body, such as I have seen often enough before. She had pains and then blisters, and men were afraid when they saw it. She feared she was poxed, but I told her true enough it was not the ailment common in her profession. She was very ignorant, as are so many.' He shook his head. 'I provided the unguent, whereupon she' – the man blushed – 'offered me payment other

194

than in silver. I told her that I was only to be paid in coin, and she said she would bring it to me shortly thereafter, but for the last three weeks I have been pestering her for the money and she has always given an excuse. I shall never get it now, of course, but . . . I will not go hungry because of the debt.'

'When you "pestered" Berta, were there ever any other men you saw hanging about her?' Bradecote realised, as he spoke, the question sounded foolish. Of all women to have men hanging about them, whores were the most likely, or else they were whores that went hungry.

'None more than you might think. None persistent, if you follow me, my lord.'

'I do. Thank you. We will leave you to pestle and mortar, and your potions. Good day to you.'

'And to you, my lord Bradecote, Serjeant Catchpoll.' The healer took up his pestle, and as they departed, the rhythmic pounding resumed.

'You know, my lord, I think he made no association whatsoever between the death of Ricolde and that of Berta,' murmured Catchpoll when they were outside in the sunlight.

'No. To him they were entirely different. I mean, he knew what Ricolde did, with other men, but when he was with her, she did not play that role and was not that woman. I imagine she rather liked an evening where she just acted homely and wifely.' He paused, suddenly missing his own home comforts. 'Do you think any of the women plying the trade in Worcester will seek to step into Ricolde's place, Catchpoll?'

'Not soon, for sure. I think perhaps some youngster might be told the tale of her and aim high, but most on the streets now could not change, nor make themselves into what she was, and her skill was that she was so many different things to differing sorts of men, from the lusty to those without any lust, like Roger, and she knew just how to be for each. That marked her above the rest, God rest her. I do not think—'

Catchpoll got no further, for a man-at-arms was coming towards them, and for the second time that day, in haste. At least on this occasion it was with good news.

Walkelin had taken the unresisting Godfrid to the castle and sat with him in the guard chamber until the man-at-arms he sent to the house of Roger the Healer returned with undersheriff and serjeant. Since he was no longer a man-at-arms but a serjeanting apprentice, he felt he had the rank, but he had selected one of the more biddable men who would be unlikely to argue the case with him. What he did not realise was that the better part of a year under Catchpoll's tutelage had given him a greater confidence in dealing with others, after all he could now speak with the lord sheriff himself and not quake, and he wore his assumed authority with remarkable ease. While he waited, he watched Godfrid. The man fitted the description given except that Walkelin was hard-pushed to imagine him as seeming threatening. Even drunk he exuded a sort of indefinable trustworthiness. However, he had been seen from behind and by a slip of a girl. She might assume all big men were aggressive, and of course the man was now sleepy with ale. Walkelin wondered why he had been in a tavern and drinking when he ought to be at his labours, but thought letting his superiors think up the questions would be better than asking them himself and having to recall and relay the answers. Perhaps he had got to the more demonstrative stage of being ale-sodden and gone looking for a woman, and had been seen then, louder, more agitated. It would be an odd man, though, who murdered a woman in cold blood and then went back to his beaker.

Both serjeant and undersheriff had looks of relief upon their faces when they entered the guard chamber and looked decidedly 'warm', having returned at speed. Their expressions froze, however, as they looked at Godfrid. Walkelin could almost hear their doubts.

'I know, my lord, but he fits the way the girl said, and I have seen more men in cottes the right colour this last hour or two than you could imagine, and none but he fitted in hair and form.' It did not alter the look of vague disappointment on the faces of his superiors. 'And, my lord, there is blood upon his sleeve, as Serjeant Catchpoll said there would be if he had his hand across her mouth to silence her.' That improved matters.

'What have you to say for yourself, Godfrid?' Bradecote looked at the man, who was gazing into space and frowning, probably wondering where he was.

'He cast me out, he did. And me near finished my years as journeyman too. Not that it matters. Not when you think what he's done.'

'Fellman, your master? What has he done?' Catchpoll's voice was calm, and he concealed his urgency.

'How could he? A poor woman with a child near to coming into this world!'

'What has he done?' This time it was Bradecote, and he did sound urgent, very urgent. He had fears of another death.

'He hurt her. He was shouting at her and shaking her and . . . and I told him he must stop. I told him he was wrong. He hit me, dragged me out the back and hit me till my wits near failed, and then he threw me out, for ever. I cannot protect her, not any more.' Disconsolate, Godfrid gulped and then sniffed.

'And the child she carries is yours.' Bradecote spoke more softly now.

Godfrid nodded. 'She thinks it is so for he takes her at his own pleasure, and that might be often or not at all for some weeks. He has no thought to her, no care at all. There is sin upon my head, but I think his the greater for the way he mistreats wife and child alike. He is a bad man, a bad man.'

'So, what happened after he threw you out?' Catchpoll brought the questioning to more pertinent matters.

'I went to the tavern by the quay. I had no work, and it was hot. I drank. Then I went for a walk.'

'A walk? Where? Why?' Bradecote frowned.

'I don't know. I wanted to think, but I could not think, not things together, only that Sibbe is on her own, and I cannot help her.'

'Did you meet a woman in Brodestrete? A whore?'

'I bumped into a woman. She shouted at me.' He sounded surprised, even offended. 'I shouted back, perhaps. She made my head spin, being all loud and shrill. I do not know where it was. Then I went to the tavern up towards the Foregate, and I had more ale to make my head feel better, but it does not.' He slumped the more. 'It feels worse.'

The sheriff's men looked at each other. He was not feigning his inebriated state, of that they were sure. Whilst it might affect

198

his answers, it would also make him less able to intentionally disguise the truth. What he said sounded true enough and perfectly feasible.

'How did you get blood on your cotte, Godfrid?' asked Walkelin.

'Wiped my nose on my sleeve, see?' Godfrid held up the sleeve. The bloodstain certainly had a linear shape. 'The master punched me on the nose, and it bled a bit. I did not notice at first because other bits of me hurt more. Fair doubled up I was, so I did not see the blood drip on the ground.'

Catchpoll leant and lifted the man's chin, looked at his face. He had swelling to the left cheek and the left side of the nose also. Then he looked at the cotte. It was not a good light in the guard chamber, so he took Godfrid by the arm. The man stood with reluctance, gave a great groan and vomited. Bradecote sighed and then coughed as the smell hit him.

'Take him outside and, Walkelin, fetch some water and swill this, before I have the castellan telling me his men cannot use the chamber for the stink.'

Outside, the less-than-fragrant Godfrid presented a sorry figure, wincing in the sunlight, head bowed, knees bending. Having assured himself that the man was unlikely to retch over him, Catchpoll crouched a little himself and studied the cotte more closely. The obvious stain was along the sleeve and matched what Godfrid had said. It was also smeared rather than sprayed or splashed, and there were small flecks of blood on his chest.

'Not enough blood, my lord, not really and truly. You cut a throat and the blood is scarlet and spurts out. This, this is as he

199

says, where a man has wiped a bloody nose upon it in a streak.'
He mimicked the action.

'Which means not only is Godfrid not our man, but that the one good pointer we had is meaningless. We have got nowhere, unless we return to thinking it was the bearded steersman.' Bradecote sighed and rubbed the back of his neck. 'I think my head is spinning, Catchpoll, like Godfrid's here, but without the excuse of ale. Everything we have been told is muddling into a sort of whirlpool and sorting any line to follow is near impossible.'

'We need to go back before Berta's death, my lord. We had our path then, even if it had no clear end to it.'

'But does that not mean leaving her death out of our reckoning?'

'No, my lord, we just weaves it in without the things that led us here to Godfrid.' He looked at the man and sniffed. 'Kindest thing to do would be put him in a cell, without chains, and let him sleep it off in the cool before we lets him out, and if we make that tomorrow morning he has a night's lodging, of sorts.'

'That seems very generous, Catchpoll.' Bradecote's lips twitched.

'Put it down to me thinking he is right about Will Fellman. He may stop short of law-breaking, but it does not mean I like the man, one little bit.'

'So he goes on your list with Mercet, does he?'

'Ah, but they are very different, my lord. Mercet sets out to be a bastard as if it were a trade. If there was a guild of bastards in Worcester he would be at its head. He probably spends his evenings working out how to be a bigger one. Fellman is just the same nasty bastard all the time and puts no effort into it.

There's decent men with a temper, and they keep it within themselves as much as they can. Those like Fellman do not bother.' Catchpoll's philosophy was fairly straightforward. 'I will go and speak with Master Fellman, just so he knows we knows what happened and as a tidying of strands.'

'Walkelin could go.' Bradecote nodded towards the serjeanting apprentice.

'Yes, my lord, he could, but seeing him will not annoy the man as much as seeing me.' He smiled with anticipated satisfaction. 'I doubt as I will be very long.'

Will Fellman was leaning against the frame of his own door, stripped to the waist and enjoying the warmth of the sun as it dried him. The worst of the heat was gone from it as the afternoon eased towards a long summer's evening. He was also enjoying shocking the women who passed by and found him both disturbing and rather frightening, be they maids or matrons. On this afternoon few were young and none appealed to him. His hair was wet, and there were still droplets glistening on his skin. He had clearly emptied a bucket of water over himself to cool down after hours of labour treading the pelts. When Catchpoll approached him, his expression hardened, and he folded his arms in an attitude of belligerence.

'What do you want now, sheriff's man?' He did not sound keen to give any answer.

'I or, more importantly, the lord Undersheriff, wants to know what happened between you and your journeyman, Godfrid, this morning.' Catchpoll did not sound the least bit intimidated.

'Ha, he has come snivelling to you that I assaulted him, has he? Well, he is a liar as well as an interfering bastard, then. I threw him out, that's what I did, as would any man. I had the right. What is between a man and his wife is between the pair of them, them alone, and that self-righteous, meddling mongrel should have kept his ears closed and his nose out.'

'At what hour did you throw him out?'

'Just after the workday began. He came rampaging in, telling me, me, how I had to behave. Ha! Well, he can tell it from the gutter, which is where he will sleep tonight.' Fellman spat into the dust, narrowly avoiding Catchpoll's foot.

'And how was he when he departed? Cowed? Angry?'

'He ranted loud enough to have reached across Worcester to the castle itself, but no good would it do him. Nigh on finished his time as a journeyman he had too, and since there's none other of my trade in Worcester, he'll have to set his foot upon the road to Gloucester or even Oxford if he hopes to find work with another. He should have thought of that before interfering.' Fellman smiled at that, but it was not a pleasant smile.

'So, you did not brawl with him?'

'If I had he would not be walking,' growled Fellman.

'He says you gave him a bloody nose.'

'If I had fought him, I would have snapped his neck, so I did not. Last thing I want is the law sniffing about me again, trying to blame me for things I did not do. All I did was take him by scruff and belt and throw him out my door. I had the right, as I said. There is no law as says I cannot send a man in my employ about this business. I will not have him over my threshold, and there is an end to it.'

'And what will you do now, without a good journeyman?'

'I will get me an apprentice, a lad as knows his place. Until then, well, I can manage very well. Now, having taken my ease for a while in the sun, I need to see how my pelts are curing.' With which Fellman turned, pushed open his door and, having entered, shut it in Catchpoll's face.

'Fellman, my lord, denies doing more than throwing Godfrid out, but he lies. It is possible someone attacked the journeyman when he was in the tavern, but he was not so far gone in ale he would have forgotten it, nor so sober he could shift the blame to his former master. No, Fellman just likes the idea we know the truth but cannot do anything about it. He would no more confess it than take the cowl.' Catchpoll, returned to the castle and leaning against a wall in the shade, shook his head. 'What is more, if he set his fists to him out the back then there was none to see, and we have one man's word against another and nobody else to swear it. Howsoever, he did not actually deny giving the bloody nose, and for our purposes it is good enough for us to say Godfrid is not the killer.'

'I sent Walkelin to the taverns, and he came back saying at each they confirmed what he said. The only missing part was how long he was on the streets between them, but the first keeper said he was at the slightly muddled stage when he left.' Bradecote added the additional proof, as if they needed it, which they did not.

'And whoever killed Berta was not muddled, but very sure of his actions.'

'Indeed.'

The castellan, crossing the bailey towards the pair, stared at the sheriff's serjeant talking with the undersheriff without any appearance of deference and was both shocked and pleased. A man who did not command respect could not lead. He could not see respect was far more than a matter of obeisances and standing straight. He would have been even more shocked to know the respect was mutual. Serjeant Catchpoll knew the rules. He called the undersheriff 'my lord', especially before others, but it was far from subservient grovelling. A year of working together had changed antipathy and resentment, through grudging respect, to a relationship where each knew the strengths, and weaknesses, of the other, and both knew they made a team. There were times when they niggled each other, but it worked and worked well. Hugh Bradecote did not need Catchpoll to be stood rigid as a lance to show respect.

Bradecote, noticing Catchpoll stiffen, turned to see Simon Furnaux, lips pursed, approaching them and expected to be addressed. However, the castellan ignored him and looked at Catchpoll.

'While you were out, hunting killers to no avail, I have had a woman making complaint at the gate that she has suffered thievery. It is not the task of my men to look into such matters, but she was so persistent that she would not go away until threatened with incarceration. You will go and appease her, though I doubt you will find her goods.' Furnaux sounded annoyed but was secretly rather pleased. It meant he could order Serjeant Catchpoll about, over the head of Bradecote, and the undersheriff could not demur, since it was patently a minor law matter, fit for the attention of the serjeant, and had nothing to do with the killings.

'I shall attend to it, my lord. Where will I find her?'

'Find her? I have no idea. Ask at the guard chamber.' Furnaux looked down his nose, at serjeant and undersheriff both, and stalked away.

'I am not sure the lord Sheriff would not commend us both if we got rid of the lord Castellan,' muttered Catchpoll, looking at the receding figure with loathing.

'Well, since we are at a standstill with the killings, you might as well go and see what it is about, even if there is nothing to be done. Short of her saying she suspects her neighbour of stealing her kindling or her chickens, I doubt you can do more than say suitable words.' Bradecote gave a twisted smile. 'You need not make me a report upon return though, Catchpoll.'

Serjeant Catchpoll was able to find the name and vague direction of the old woman from a guard who had been present when she had come to make complaint, though he had not paid attention as to what had been stolen. The serjeant was muttering about the castellan, under his breath, all along to the Foregate, where he passed through and turned down to the riverside. He passed Fellman's dwelling and heard no raised voices. That might be a good sign, but it might as easily be bad. However, there was nothing he could do upon that matter and Oldmother Field had her complaint to make.

Within the house, Sibbe Fellman stirred the pottage with a hand that shook. She was a very frightened woman. The children were quiet, having learnt there were times when silence was safer. As long as her husband remained convinced the child she carried would be a boy, she would feel his hand the less, but if doubt as to his siring of the child entered his head but for a moment then her life was worthless. She had persuaded herself it was not a wicked act, presenting him as the likely killer of Ricolde the Whore. After all, it protected not only her own body, but the babe within, and also her daughter from violence, and was just restitution for all the bruises and beatings over the years. For one whole day she had felt freed from the fear of him and had looked to a rosy future. There was no hope of that now. Godfrid had been more than a source of care and love, he had been something, someone, at her back to make her feel there was some fixed point in her existence. Now he was gone, and she was left at the mercy of a man whom she felt would kill her by careless brutality if he did not do so by intent. The only small comfort was that her husband could not know about the babe, because both she and Godfrid still drew breath.

It had been a bad night. She had been uncomfortable, unable to settle and ease the ache in her back, and with the unborn child pressing on her bladder as the younger of the two boys thrashed in his sleep and kicked her from without. That he did so was 'her fault', said her husband, losing his own sleep and grumbling at her with increasing anger, blaming her even for the stuffy warmth of the chamber and the wriggling children in the bed. When she had risen to get water for him to cool his face and small beer for him to start the day, he had been in a foul mood. She was not fast enough; the children were too noisy; she was a burden to him, and fat. When she had sniffed and excused herself upon reason of her condition, he had turned and thrown the beaker at her, which hit her cheek and raised a weal, then he had come to her and taken her by the arms and shaken her, hard, shouting all the while. Godfrid, who slept in the lean-to at the back of the dwelling, had come in and added to the commotion, berating his master for his violence, and had been turned upon, and bundled out the back, where she had heard the sound she knew all too well, the sound of fist upon flesh. Godfrid was strong but gentle and unused to fighting. He must have been no match for Will Fellman. He had staggered out some short while later, near doubled up and with his face bloodied, cast her one despairing look and gone. Her husband had crowed his triumph before cowering wife and children and it had buoyed his mood all morning, leastways until she had gone out to buy bread and vegetables for the pottage. It would not last. It never did. Something would annoy him or he would take ale, and then . . . She shuddered and offered up a prayer for salvation.

Chapter Fourteen

Having worn his new boots for two days, Bradecote thought they and his feet might have reached 'an understanding'. However, most of that time he had been in the saddle or walking on grass, not the compacted earth and stony surfaces of Worcester's thoroughfares, and he had to admit the leather was not giving much ground as yet. His feet were hot and ached, and he was glad to remove his boots and lie upon his cot, arms behind his head, arranging and rearranging all that they knew into a pattern that might point them the way to the man who was doing the killing. The trouble was that every way he tried it, there were pieces missing and yet pieces left over that did not fit. It was mightily frustrating. In the end he tried to clear his mind of all of it and wondered about his wife, his son, his manor.

His son, Gilbert, was growing strongly, and he was

quite convinced that Christina's love and nurture were as responsible as how eager the baby was to feed. She showed love as great as if she had borne him, and he had even teasingly asked her if she preferred cradling Gilbert in her arms to lying in his own. His house was a place where happiness and contentment resided, and the manor, and even the smaller, outlying manors, prospered. The pease was bulging in the pod, where it would wait and dry for another five or six weeks, drying on the haulms, and the grain had seen a good growing season and was already achingly close to being ready to harvest. His steward thought it might even be a week early this year. A lot would depend upon whether the weather broke too soon. He wanted to be home. It was so close and yet so far, and until the killer of Ricolde and Berta had been taken, he could not return, at least not with a clear conscience. He sighed and wriggled his toes.

Since he had told Catchpoll that he need make no report, Bradecote was most surprised when the serjeant came to his chamber before the priory bell announced Compline.

'We has another piece of the shattered pot, my lord.' Catchpoll sounded buoyant.

'We do?' Bradecote sat up so fast his head spun.

'Yes. The complaining woman was Oldmother Field as lives outside the wall, down by the river.' Catchpoll could see this alone made the undersheriff look interested. 'She has been tending her husband as he ails and is heading for a shroud from what I saw of him. His years are many and his hours left are few. I would reckon she will be calling the priest to the cot side before the morrow. She had need to cut more kindling for the hearth, which her daughter's son did for her last week, though no hearth flames will warm the man to life and health, and he takes no food. When she went for the small axe to chop the branches, it was missing from behind the little shelter for the wood. She says as the lad promised her he put it back as always and her neighbours, who have helped over the last months, all say as they have not touched it, nor does she think any would steal from her. They live nearest to the riverbank, my lord, with the wood and axe kept down the side by the water. Only those who knew of it, upon the land, would know the placing of it, but anyone passing upon the river would see it, and it would not be difficult to row close and take it. My lord, we have the missing axe, or rather we know how and when Ricolde's killer got hold of one. I told Oldmother Field it was most likely in the river mud. She has been shut up close with her dying husband this week past and had not even heard of the death upon Bevere Island.'

'We are getting everything, everything except the man who did it, Catchpoll, and I would hate to fail in this one.'

'Aye, my lord, but we will come to the right end, I feels it.'

'Then let us hope the dawn brings us another step nearer.'

'Amen to that.'

Catchpoll did not lose sleep over the problem that faced them, even if his superior did. He stuck to the view it was no use worrying about things he could do nothing about and overnight he could achieve nothing, so he slept. He woke refreshed, though to another dawn that presaged a hot and dusty day. He doubted the lord Bradecote would be risen quite as early, and so did as he was sometimes wont to do, slipped from the cot and the sleeping form of his wife, dressed and went for a wander about 'his' streets, as though they spoke to him through the daub and wattle of the buildings and the ground beneath his feet. There were few folk about when he began his perambulations, and two of those slid back into the shadows and hoped he had not seen their faces, but by the time he was walking back towards the cathedral and castle, the craftsmen and vendors of Worcester were opening their shutters and laying out their goods, and the sounds of instructions, exchanges and imprecations were bringing the noise up to its daytime levels. Servants were being chivvied, apprentices berated and wives placated in a few cases. He turned the corner which would place the imposing bulk of the cathedral before him and almost bumped into a man coming the other way. The man had been looking down but raised his head as Catchpoll sidestepped. The serjeant found himself looking into a sombre face, a face framed by deep chestnut hair and a tidy beard just showing flecks of greying. It looked like their prayers had been answered.

'Sorry, friend,' he said, amicably. The other man gave nothing but a grunt in response. 'Don't I know you?' Catchpoll continued, lying shamelessly.

'No.' The man was not forthcoming and clearly had no wish to engage in idle chatter.

'Well, that is strange, because I know I have been a-searching for you since yesterday and the lord Undersheriff also. He will be mightily glad we have found you at last.'

At this the man stepped back, his look wary, but Catchpoll moved as swiftly forward, clapped a hand upon his shoulder and twisted his arm up behind him, in which position he pushed him in the direction of the castle. The man was not willing, but nor did he struggle, and he said nothing whatsoever. Catchpoll went to the Great Hall, but there found, most unfortunately, the castellan rather than the undersheriff. Simon Furnaux, feeling self-important, and also wishing to show Bradecote that he was at least as intelligent and decisive, decided that he should 'speak with the prisoner'. Catchpoll was almost inclined to release the man on the spot, but, with only the slightest grimace, duly placed the man before the castellan.

'Now, tell me what we want to know,' Furnaux commanded. The man stared at him, perplexed as well as worried. Whoever this man was he was powerful and not comfortable in good, decent English, which meant that he was dangerous.

'But I do not know what you want to know, my lord.' He made a belated obeisance.

Catchpoll could have helped, but it was so much more entertaining watching the castellan flounder.

'Well, er, did you kill them?' Furnaux decided the direct approach might be best.

'I have killed nobody, my lord.' The man's gloomy, rather surly demeanour had been replaced by a very lively fear for his life. His voice was still a monotone but pitched a little higher and rather more vehement.

'Easy to say.' Furnaux sneered. He was quite good at sneering. 'And truth upon oath, my lord.'

The castellan was now uncertain what to do or to say. He could challenge the denial, but he was not at all sure the man would give up and make the confession he wanted. He glared, not at the bearded man, but at Catchpoll, whose fault it clearly was that he found himself in this situation. The grizzled serjeant, however, seemed not to even notice and stared woodenly into space. It was fortunate for the castellan that at this point Hugh Bradecote entered the chamber, having been alerted by a man-at-arms that Serjeant Catchpoll had brought in a man under compulsion.

'Ah.' Bradecote's exclamation was a positive one, and he stepped forward, though to stand before the man, not to take a seat upon the dais next to the castellan. 'Our bearded friend with the chestnut hair. From what I have heard, Thurstan Shippmann is regretting letting you leave him. I wonder if you are going to feel the same way about leaving him. Give me your name.' The voice was confident, authoritative. It did not threaten but it did expect an answer, which came immediately.

'Robert the Steersman, my lord.'

'Tell me this, Robert the Steersman, if you are unknown to the rivermen of Worcester, why is it that your reason for leaving Thurstan was given as a family death here? Do your kin come to you in visions and wail about their passing?' He spoke lightly, but his eyes did not smile.

'No, my lord.' The man looked him at him, and his response was without hesitation. 'It was a sister of mine as died. I come from Tewkesbury, or rather was born there. My sister married a farrier who took over the forge out up on the road to Whittington. They know I works up and down the river, and my nephew came to the quay in case he saw me there or could at least pass the news to any of the boats as do the full length of Severn. My sister died in childbed with her eighth and the babe still trapped within her. It was simple chance that I was coming upriver just upon the day. I went with the lad to the forge, and she went into the earth the next day. Glad I am that I was there, whatever Thurstan Shippmann may say about taking me back.'

Hugh Bradecote said nothing, as a sick feeling churned his stomach. He was blissfully happy in his new marriage, but less than a year past he had watched life ebb from a woman at her travail, a woman who had been vibrant and happy the day before. He did at least have his son from the ordeal. It brought it all back for a moment.

'I have heard as there has been a killing in Worcester, or rather upriver, but it has nought to do with me, my lord.' Robert the Steersman felt the silence as doubt. 'I remain but to see Master Thurstan upon his return from Shrewsbury.'

'Then at least upon that I can give you some good tidings. From all reports, Thurstan Shippmann is cursing you, but because the man he took in your stead is poor at the work. He may swear at you, but I have little doubt he will give you charge of the steerboard when he gets back here.'

'You do not seek to blame me for the death?'

'I will send a man to confirm your words, but I doubt not he will return to tell me they are true. Whatever you may think of the law, it is here to take the guilty, not to blame the innocent just to look busy.' The last words were as much for the benefit of Simon Furnaux as the steersman. 'We want the man who killed not one woman but two, as of yesterday. You remain here within the castle gate only until the report is made and then you are free to go.' Bradecote looked at Catchpoll. 'Keep him in the guard room until whoever is sent returns from the forge, Serjeant Catchpoll.' He sounded very formal, not only because he wanted to show his authority over the steersman's release but to stress it to Simon Furnaux.

'Straight away, my lord.' Catchpoll was happy to play along, but rather regretted he would not hear what passed between the two after he had departed.

In fact, there was an inimical silence for some time as the two men stared at each other in open mutual dislike. Finally, Bradecote spoke, with chilling calm.

'Has William de Beauchamp replaced me without telling me so?' His mobile brows were raised.

'No, but you were not present and—'

'I was not in the chamber, but you knew I would be fetched.'

'I . . . was saving you time and trouble, Bradecote.'

'No, my lord Castellan, you were interfering, and to no good purpose either.' The steel sounded now.

'The man was brought to my castle . . . so I had the right. Besides, the Castellan of Worcester outranks an undersheriff.' Furnaux drew himself up to full height. He was still shorter than the tall, lean form of Hugh Bradecote.

'Not when it comes to the law, and it is "the Undersheriff of Worcestershire", if we are going to use formal titles. I do not dispose your men upon their watches, and you will not interrogate my prisoners. It is a fairly clear divide between

215

the two and does not require much understanding.'

'But you are letting this prisoner go, like you did the last ones.'

'Yes, because it will be shown that he is not involved, like the man yesterday, and the first one was taken upon false information. If it did not matter who was arraigned for a crime, all Catchpoll would have to do every time is drag in a person from the streets of Worcester. Only a fool would think that sense.' The implication was obvious.

'I shall report this to William de Beauchamp as soon as he returns,' declared the castellan, petulantly.

'Please do,' Bradecote threw over his shoulder as he strode out. 'I look forward to hearing his response.'

Serjeant Catchpoll did not let his expression give anything away when his superior arrived in the guard chamber, halfway between raging and laughing. Walkelin had turned up just in time to about turn and head off to the forge on the Whittington road, and had taken to four iron-shod feet to expedite his journey, not wanting to slog up the hill on a morning already feeling the heat of the sun.

'I don't reckon as he will be long, my lord,' offered Catchpoll.

'No, but I am wondering what we do when he gets back to us. Looking for the axe would be pointless, and if we found it all we could do would be to return it to the old woman. We may have a good idea it is one of two men, and in truth the son rather than the father, but we do not know what they look like, or even when they came into Worcester or why, after all this time, and we do know it is not the steersman, who was our best chance.'

'But if Berta died by the same hand he has not left, my lord. We has at least that.'

'Yes, but that makes me wonder also. If it was Ricolde's brother, surely he would have done the deed and departed, for that way our chances of ever discovering him would be non-existent. Staying in Worcester increases his risk of capture.'

'So perhaps, after the killing, he is one of the sort who is caught between wanting to be taken and avoiding our clutches, turn and turnabout. The simple repentant goes to a priest and then makes it easy to find them. This one is not quite like that but—' Catchpoll stopped. Bradecote was shaking his head.

'No, it is not that. Do not ask me why, but I feel it, strongly. Ricolde's death was planned, though we do not know how long in advance, be that hours or days. The man kills as intended, but then snaps. Berta was killed most likely because he saw an opportunity.'

'But he might have planned, all the same, my lord, and the plan was not set upon her, just the first of her sort he came across in a place where he could kill her without being seen.'

'True enough. Yet if we stick to Ricolde's kin, then he has no cause to kill again, bar as a distraction, and that is a risk.'

'He has developed a taste for it?' Catchpoll did not sound convinced. 'Killing is easier once you have done it the once. Or it is as you suggested, he simply thought that killing another would have us seeking a man with a different reason for the deeds. It did risk discovery, but in that he was at least part right, since we have had to consider it.'

Bradecote rubbed his hand across his chin and looked thoughtful but glum.

217

'And we are right to discount it? Two men, I mean? Yes, I know' – he saw the serjeant's expression – 'you will say we have tried everything to make it work and found nothing. It is just the fear that he might strike yet again.'

'If we worried ourselves over every killing that "might" happen we would be witless in a week, my lord. I don't say as we have anything to say this ends today, but we have to take all the pieces of our broken pot of the crime and keep trying. One way will work.'

Walkelin returned and with the news they had expected. The blacksmith at the forge had buried his wife but a few days since, and the place was one where he laboured whilst his children huddled in varying degrees of grief or incomprehension under the aegis of the eldest, a lad of eleven, who confirmed he had been sent to the Worcester quayside to give word to the riverboats and had found his uncle.

Robert the Steersman was set free to await the return of Thurstan Shippmann on his way down to Gloucester and the Forest of Dean, and if he did not depart happy, then he at least went with relief.

'We are not giving up, are we, my lord?' Walkelin's expression was a mixture of eagerness and worry.

'No, Walkelin, we are not, and in part because we dare not. With Berta not yet even in the earth we cannot simply say "The trail is too cold", even if we think that there is no trail at all. Did Serjeant Catchpoll tell you that at least we can say how Ricolde's killer found an axe?'

'No. We have found it?'

'Not exactly, lad. More a case we know whose axe it was and

how it was taken without anyone raising a hue and cry over it.'
Catchpoll explained about Oldmother Field.

'I have known her from my childhood. She lives across from
my Aunt Hedger. Sorry I am her husband is dying, though he
is a man of many years.'

'Well, she is also now an old woman without an axe to chop
her firewood. It was kept alongside the branches for kindling
upon the river side of their home, and when she went to use it
today it was gone and was last used a week past. That was the
weapon used to kill Ricolde, and anyone upon the river would
have been able to see it.'

'But wait,' Bradecote frowned, 'that would mean the man
took Ricolde, presumably insensible and wrapped in the
bedcover, and only as he was already rowing upstream did he
hit upon the axe as the way to kill her.'

'My guess is he first thought to use a knife, as he did with
Berta, but the axe . . . As you said before, my lord, it makes it
more an execution.'

'Which means he was saying she committed a crime. Now,
was the crime being a whore? Would that warrant such a death?'
Walkelin was keeping up with the undersheriff's line of thought.

'Jesu,' Bradecote paled, 'what if . . . and if he then realised
who she was, and they had . . .'

'You speak in ri—' Catchpoll suddenly realised what
Bradecote was thinking. 'Ah.'

'Ah?' Walkelin looked from one to the other, his face all
innocent perplexity.

'Does I tell him or you, my lord?' Catchpoll asked, slowly.

'Er, Walkelin. If her brother had simply paid for a night with

219

her and then found out who she really was . . . ?' Bradecote pulled a face and halted.

'You mean . . . Oh! Oh!' Walkelin went scarlet.

'As a reason to kill her, it stands up well, and taking her to where her mother was killed for sinning too, yes, it makes perfect sense.' Catchpoll nodded.

'So we have "where", and "how", and even "why", but "who" eludes us, and "who" is the most vital part.' Bradecote ran his hand through his hair. 'Except we do know "who", but not his name or what he looks like, so we are as lost as before.'

'But his name is Wilferth, my lord,' Walkelin pointed out.

'And how many of that name in Worcester do you know, Catchpoll?'

'A half-dozen, but none are close in age, or if they are I have known their fathers and mothers also. If your guess is true, my lord, then surely Wilferth son of Wilferth the Wife-Drowner came to Worcester to buy and sell, and discovered his sister by her mischance.'

'But that falls, Catchpoll, because he made the decision to row her upstream to kill her. A man who has not been to Worcester in years, likely tens of years, is he going to think up such a plan when in a state of horrified surprise? I think not.'

Catchpoll grimaced.

'And not only did the people of Claines say that he and his father did not come to Worcester, but if he had, then he would surely have seen his sister at some point when she still looked familiar to him, childlike enough.' Walkelin's offering was not in any way encouraging.

'So once again we say what fits cannot fit. I cannot see how this could be a worse hole.'

The sound of hooves clattered under the gateway arch and a loud voice was heard.

'Spoke too soon there, my lord. It did just get worse. The lord Sheriff is back.'

Chapter Fifteen

William de Beauchamp was not in the best of moods, although he had not ridden far since the day had begun to heat up. He had spent the last ten days dealing with arguments over the boundaries of two of his outlying manors with the Church, and they had a nasty habit of winning because, as one smug monastic had whispered to him, they had God on their side. They were also masters of the written word, and documents were a curse. He was sure they had 'written' some just in time to present them as 'since the time of your father'. There was no countering the combination.

His feet had barely touched the ground as he dismounted, when Simon Furnaux emerged from the hall and with hot words eager to be given voice.

'My lord Sheriff, at last. With you to take control of this, finally something will be done!' It sounded very dramatic, but dramatic was another thing the castellan did well, though it was not appreciated.

'By all the saints in Heaven, Furnaux, have you not the wit to wait until I have slaked my thirst and got into shade before you bleat at me?'

'How can it wait, my lord, when women are being brutally killed all over Worcester?'

'They are?' William de Beauchamp looked understandably astonished. 'Are there corpses littering the streets?'

'Two thus far, and nothing, nothing at all done about it.'

'Are both serjeant and undersheriff away upon another matter?' The sheriff frowned.

'No, my lord, we are here.' Bradecote crossed the now sun-drenched cobbles in barely a dozen of his long strides, with Catchpoll half a step behind him and Walkelin to the rear. 'And unlike the lord Castellan, I think we can wait until you are ready to hear all.' His voice was calm, even confident.

'All you do is wait,' complained Furnaux, bitterly, glancing at him sideways. 'You no sooner bring a man in than you let him loose. It gives the wrong impression, or perhaps the right one, that you do not know what you are doing.'

De Beauchamp looked from one to the other. There was clearly a very active animosity crackling between them like summer lightning, and he was quite surprised, because Bradecote was the sort to keep himself on a tight rein, even if Furnaux babbled like an old crone beside her hearth. He was an irritation but could be swatted away and forgotten.

'Inside, before I bake to death,' the sheriff commanded, leading them into the cool gloom of the hall and from the cross passage into the Great Hall itself. He took his seat and would have asked Bradecote to start at the beginning, but the castellan was determined to put his view first. Bradecote folded his arms and looked bored.

'My lord, I have had half of Worcester banging upon the gates, reporting corpses and thefts of weapons and the Holy Virgin knows what else, and your men, my lord, the visible sign of shrieval authority in your absence, have achieved nothing.'

'Really? Is that because many people reported the same two bodies? Or is there some rebellion planned that has Worcester full of weapons, now stolen by forces unknown? Tell me, Furnaux.' De Beauchamp looked at his subordinate and smiled, but it was one of those smiles that boded ill for the recipient. He disliked being taken for a fool, and Furnaux's exaggeration was asking him to be one to believe the man.

'I cannot give true numbers, my lord, for they did not see me, of course, but disrupted my men from their tasks. My serjeant of the guard has several times been—'

'Ah, so "half of Worcester" is now "several". Yes, I see.'

'My lord, the point is that your undersheriff has brought in three men, and all three has he set free thereafter.' Furnaux either ignored the irony or did not notice it. Bradecote did and hid a smile. Catchpoll did and smiled broadly, and Walkelin turned his face to the wall and bit his lip.

'Perhaps he had cause.'

'Then why were they questioned? A man may not be condemned upon evidence alone. He must confess it. He must have oathswearers swear upon his behalf. I doubt any of the three could muster the oathswearers. One man was not even of Worcester. So, all that is needed is the confession. From one surely he could have got that?'

'You, Furnaux, are the castellan, since I made you so. Bradecote is my undersheriff, since I made him so. I do not wish him to be castellan and am even more certain that I do not want you as undersheriff. Your understanding of the law is, shall we say, rather lacking in one important aspect. You see, if we hang the innocent, the guilty continue to break the law, and good men will not trust nor bad men refrain from misdeeds. Have I deliberately laid blame upon men who are innocent of crime, Serjeant Catchpoll?'

'No, my lord.' Catchpoll did not say that there had been a few cases where a man, one they knew had committed many crimes but not been caught, was 'guilty' of one where his involvement was less certain. The man was guilty of crime, just perhaps not of that one particular crime.

'Have we made the people of Worcester sleep easy by blaming a crime upon one now gone, or a stranger?'

'We have, my lord, but mostly when it was true enough, or the man disappears knowing we knows him should he return.'

'That, Furnaux, is how it is done. Taking up those who are worthy of being asked questions, and deciding they might as well confess and hang, is not how it is done. Stick to what you know. Now, find something to do in this castle of "yours" while I speak with my men.' It was a slightly polite way of telling him to get out, but only slightly. Furnaux swallowed hard, nodded his head in respect and left, his face pale with anger. Being berated by William de Beauchamp was unpleasant, but suffering it before a man he now loathed, and two jumped-up peasants, was an insult. He cast one glance only at Bradecote, but that said all he wanted.

'Tell me the tale and without adornment,' sighed De Beauchamp, accepting a goblet of wine from a nervous servant, who reported the lord sheriff had returned 'in one of his tempers'. 'I am interested in the men you spoke with but released, and you will tell me who and why. We start with two corpses since I went away.'

'Two, my lord, yes. They were women who sold themselves.' Bradecote wondered, even as the words left his lips, why he called them thus.

'So, they were whores.' De Beauchamp sounded slightly relieved and took a mouthful of wine.

'One was just a street whore, my lord,' agreed Catchpoll, 'but the first death, which was bloody and upon Bevere Island, was of Ricolde, The—'

'The Whore of Worcester.' De Beauchamp had obviously heard of her, if no more. He paled and crossed himself, which Bradecote took to mean he had known her, personally, as well as by repute. His expression became grim, and all relief was gone from him. He set his goblet aside. 'Then we find him, and he hangs. We do not fail in this.'

'No, my lord.' Catchpoll was equally grim, but less certain.

'We have nearly all, my lord, except the last bit that will give us the man in our grasp.' Bradecote wanted it to be clear they had in fact achieved a lot from poor prospects.

'Then commence at the beginning. She was no fool, Ricolde. How came she to be upon Bevere Island with a man who took her life?'

Undersheriff and serjeant between them provided the full story. At several points de Beauchamp raised a hand and sought clarification, although it did not appear to enlighten him much. In fact, by the end his frown of displeasure was more of confusion.

'Aye, my lord. It has had us knotted also. Just when it all fits, there is one part which breaks it all asunder again.' Catchpoll pulled a face.

'It has to be her brother. All sense points to that, my lord.' Bradecote tried to sound certain.

'But without a name to him, or his looks, we cannot discover him.' De Beauchamp thumped his fist in frustration upon the carved arm of the chair.

'That is our problem, my lord, and as yet we do not know our way out of it. The second killing does at least make it look as though he has not left Worcester.' Catchpoll knew it was small comfort.

'And you are convinced it is one man, Catchpoll?' De Beauchamp knew that Catchpoll's eye for detail with corpses could find links others would miss.

'Yes, my lord, and I did not come to it easy. We looked at it being one man copying another as best he could, but for all that this might be, I still feels it is but one.'

'That is feeling, Catchpoll, and I know yours is often right, but you cannot say, for sure, that it is not the case that Ricolde was killed by her brother who then left again and that this second killing is not just a man thinking to try his hand at murder in the shadow of another.'

'No, my lord, I cannot be sure,' admitted Catchpoll.

'What are you doing today?'

'We had only just released the steersman when you arrived, my lord.' Bradecote did not want it to sound an excuse, but it did so, nevertheless. 'Do you wish to take control of this yourself?' It was William de Beauchamp's right, but Bradecote hoped he would not avail himself of it.

'No, though I want to be kept informed. Greater events press upon us. De Mandeville is still causing the king trouble, and though I think the man a godless bastard, if matters fell perfectly, for me that is, he might yet make all simple. Robert of Gloucester has a wary eye upon us, but since I favour the Empress for all that I am Stephen's sheriff, he holds off. He is busy in Oxfordshire, but he could turn back upon us here. Do I trust that he will leave us be? No. I need to play a bigger game than hunting local killers.' He noted the relief on Bradecote's face. All to the good that the man wanted to keep it 'his' problem, though how it could be solved, William de Beauchamp could not say. 'And do not leave Furnaux in a pool of blood, however much he ires you. He has his uses.' The sheriff nodded, which was a dismissal.

'What exactly do we do now, my lord?' asked Walkelin, as they left the hall.

'I have been trying to think of something, but so far the best I can come up with is combing the streets of Worcester for men in their late thirties whom Serjeant Catchpoll does not recognise, which, I admit, is not much of a plan.'

'Hmm.' Catchpoll clearly agreed with him.

'Any better ideas, Catchpoll?'

'Wish I did, my lord. The lord Sheriff will not expect us to sit about waiting for signs from Heaven.'

'In that case, though my old boots are falling apart, if I am going to wander the streets on a hot day I am loth to do it in these new boots that are as yet unyielding. I am caught between those I have not worn in and those so worn they may cease to exist at all by eventide. I will go and put on the failing ones, say a prayer for them and meet you in the bailey.'

He turned and went up the narrow stair to his chamber.

He was thinking only of his feet as he entered but came up short and stood stock-still as if staring at a vision.

'Christina! What brings you into Worcester?'

'My horse, my lord. You were closeted with the lord Sheriff when I arrived but a short while since.' She dimpled and then laughed and came to him, hands outstretched. He blinked and took the offered hands without thinking. When he had left her but a week past she had seemed preoccupied, with a permanent small frown on her brow. He had even wondered if she was ailing, for her appetite was mediocre and she was pale of cheek. The Christina before him was a new woman.

'That is not what I—' He began, but she offered him her lips and pressed close, which silenced him for some moments. 'I am glad you obviously missed me,' he murmured, as he pulled back to look into her face, 'but—'

'The Sainted Edith has interceded for us. We are blessed,' she whispered, her eyes shining.

He stared at her, as realisation dawned, and his own eyes widened, not so much with pleasure as horror.

'Sweet Jesu,' he breathed. 'You mean . . . You are with child? You are sure?' He went white. It was not intended, but it was not the reception Christina had wanted or expected.

'Yes. I thought you would be pleased.' Her voice cracked. 'Our child, my lord. Do you begrudge me our child?' Tears, angry, hurt tears, sprang to her eyes.

'No! No, of course not, but—'

'But you are not pleased.' Her hands formed two little clenched fists against his chest.

'I . . .' He swallowed, hard, and the words came out with difficulty. 'I cannot bear the thought I might lose you, Christina. It unmans me.'

'But you will not lose me.'

'I had not thought to lose Ela. It never occurred to me until . . . She was there one day and the next she was gone. We have had so little time, my love, and—'

'Stop it. Stop it, Hugh.' She grabbed him by the arms and almost shook him. 'You are no coward. You cannot go through life in fear, you know that.'

'I am no coward for myself, but . . . There was nothing I could do, and . . . I would lay down my life for you, but that would not help.'

'Then it is your helplessness you fear as much as death. Listen to me and listen well. I have carried and given birth, aye, and lost too. This, of all babes, is blessed, because St Edith heard my prayers, saw our devotion. I am not afraid, and you must not be afraid.' There were tears running down her face. 'I never conceived a child out of love before, Hugh, and no child of my bearing has lived more than a dozen years. This child, I feel it, will be strong and wondrous, and St Edith will watch over it. I have never been more happy, my lord. Be happy with me, for me. Our child, conceived in love. Oh, Hugh.'

She wept into his chest, and he held her, trying desperately to do what she wanted and conquer his fear with her delight. It was not easy. She was perfectly right. He feared being able to do nothing to protect her, almost as he feared losing her. He pressed kisses into her hair.

'I love you. I will be strong for you, but give me time, Christina, to master my surprise.' He led her to the seat in the chamber and sat, with her pulled close upon his lap. 'Why did you ride to Worcester and not wait until I returned?'

'Because I did not know when that would be, and I have been, these last few days as the feeling of sickness faded, so full of joy. When the sickness fades then is there no doubt and much less risk of loss.'

'But you must take great care.'

'And I shall. You would laugh to see that I rode at but a walk, the short miles into Worcester, and with Tosti at my horse's head, so that even if it took fright, I would be safe. He looked very puzzled. Are you close to some end with the killing that has kept you? I would remain and have you beside me as added protection upon the return home.'

'More than one killing now, alas.'

'Oh no! How horrible. But surely, the more killings the easier to find the killer?'

'Easier, yes, but not yet a clear path. I would not imprison you in this castle, my love, but if you go about the streets, take Tosti with you.'

'You fear this person will kill again, and someone unknown to them?'

'Not really. I would have you have an arm to lean upon, lest you stumble on the cobbles, and I cannot give you my own.'

'My thoughtful, if over-cautious, husband. I promise that I shall do nothing in haste or without escort. Does that ease you?' She ran a finger across his brow.

He sighed. 'A little.'

'Well,' she purred, 'unless you prowl the streets of Worcester in the darkness also, my lord, I may offer you greater ease tonight. I have been poor bed company these last weeks.'

If it did not entirely quash his worry over her, it did give him something far better to contemplate, and it was an undersheriff barely concealing a secretive smile who, despite being told off for 'creeping back' to his worn-out boots, rejoined Catchpoll and Walkelin, and set off on what they all realised was a pretty pointless search about Worcester in the heat of the summer sun's glare.

Sibbe Fellman gripped the frame of the door, wondering yet again how the mind could obliterate the all-enveloping pangs of childbirth until the day came when the next babe was born. She had not even had warnings for this one, but then she felt it came a little ahead of its appointed time because of the fall, if you could call being shoved to the ground and kicked a fall. He had only kicked her the once, Holy Mary be thanked, and then stopped suddenly, as if realisation of the harm he might do hit him. He had reached a hand to help her up, but she had screamed at him, and he had shrugged and gone back out to his work. She had been trying to protect Golde, her eldest, from his wrath, and he had lashed out. Now Golde, still shaking from the beating she had received, was in tears at the sight of her mother's pain.

'Golde, go and fetch Widow Hedger. Tell her the baby is coming.'

The child dithered, caught between relief at being sent upon a task and the feeling that she ought to be there at her mother's side. Then she turned and ran, limping a little, to the neighbour her mother trusted. Panic seized her when the woman was not there, but she took a deep breath and knocked upon the doors beyond, asking for her, and at the third found her gossiping with a woman gutting fish. Widow Hedger did not need the child grabbing at her hand to speed her on her way.

She did not fuss over the woman in travail, for she had been there often enough before, but having another woman present eased Sibbe's mind, if not her pains. The widow rubbed her back and encouraged her, and calmed the children.

Will Fellman, in a morose humour, came in a couple of hours later and stood in the doorway.

'Like that, is it? Well, what about the meal this evening? The hearth is cold. Will it be over soon?'

'It will take as long as it takes, you knows that as well as I, and if you go without a hot meal for an evening, so be it. It would not be today if you had not been a thoughtless oaf.' Widow Hedger rounded on him. 'In her state, what possessed you?'

He was not a man who took well to reprimand.

'You have no place in my house. Get out, hag.'

'Don't be a fool. My place is here now and yours is not, though your house it is. What do you know of birthing a babe?' She was scornful and stood her ground. He wavered. As much as he wanted to be in command, he knew this was beyond his control, whatever he did. He growled, shouted at his wife 'to get on with it and not make a fuss', though it sounded stupid even to his own ears, and stormed out of the front door, loudly decrying all women and interfering old women in particular.

Sibbe had ignored him. She was in a private world that contained only her body and the force of nature and pain. Time and place had no meaning, though time certainly passed. It was as the evening cooled that she bore down, and Widow Hedger, holding new life in her hands, looked at Sibbe's strain-blotched face and said gently, 'It is a girl-child, small but lusty enough.' The baby cried in proof of this fact. Widow Hedger did not know whether to commiserate, or feel it served Will Fellman right that there would be a girl replacing the dead child in the cradle. She wiped its face and wrapped it.

'Will you do something for me?' Sibbe was exhausted.

'Yes, child, of course.'

'When all is finished here, try and find Godfrid. I would have him know, and I doubt he has left Worcester yet.'

'I will try, but if there is nowhere you know he may be—'

'I do not.' Sibbe took her daughter in her arms, and in the newborn she saw the features of the child she had shrouded but a week past. Her silent tears were not just for the dead and buried flesh, but the dead and buried hopes for the future.

Her good neighbour saw the older children settled, the mess tidied and mead warmed with herbs that her oldmother had sworn aided a woman's milk come in the better, and then the Widow Hedger drew her shawl about her shoulders and went out into what was near to gloaming. There were bats flitting down towards the river, and the sound of swallows taking the last flies of the day and drinking as they dipped to the river's idle flow. She had said she would look, but she would not look in the dark, for what decent woman would be about the streets then? She hurried within the walls of Worcester as the gatekeeper was preparing to shut the great gates. She asked after Godfrid, since at least here the man would be known. The gatekeeper shook his head and said he had not seen him recently. She gave him a sighed thanks and took the obvious course. With a man, seek first the tavern. Her own husband, long departed, had frequented them far too much. Her opinion of the male gender was not high, in consequence. She resolved to try the one by the gate, at the sign of The Goose, that of The Moon down by the quays and finish back at the one by the Foregate in case she had missed him. If he was not at any of these, then she might try speaking to her sister-son, Walkelin, in the morning. A sheriff's serjeanting apprentice ought to be better at seeking and it was more seemly than her asking everywhere for a man not kindred.

She did not enter any of the hostelries, but knocked and asked for the name of Godfrid the fellman's journeyman to be called. At the sign of The Goose and at The Moon she got shaking heads and no response. As she approached the tavern at the Foregate again, a man emerged, not quite steady upon

235

his feet. He swayed a little and looked owlishly at her as though recognition came slowly. She looked at him straight.

'You seek me?' The voice was a little slurred.

'I should have guessed. So typical of a man.' She shook her head and pursed her lips.

Chapter Sixteen

Hugh Bradecote lay feeling very satisfied with life in general, very relaxed and rather sleepy. His wife, whilst equally satisfied, was languid also of body but feeling very mentally awake. She laid her head upon his chest and her arm across him and posed her question.

'I know nothing about the killings here. Tell me about it, my lord.'

'Now?' He really would rather drift into sleep. 'Let it be until the morning.'

'No, for in the morning you will be eager to leave our bed and be about your duties.'

'Not too eager.' His hand stroked down her spine.

'Not too eager. That is good. But—'

'Oh, if you must.' He sighed. 'The main thing you must know is that the key is the first death, which was that of the finest whore in Worcester.'

'"Finest"? My lord, what do you know of—'

'Nothing, beyond Ricolde, that was her name, was hacked to death on Bevere Island, upriver. She was not, by every account, your ordinary sort of whore. Both Catchpoll and Father Anselm of All Saints held her in respect, and, in truth, I think I do too now.'

'Why?' He told her story and felt Christina tense. 'I am sorry, my love. It is not a happy tale.'

'No, and I doubt it is rare, though I have been as judgemental of such women, thinking them careless of their honour and person. What is rare was her courage in facing a life twisted when she was so young.'

'Yes, and it is something to do with her young life that touches this whole thing. If not, why was she killed so close to where she was born?' He sighed again and yawned. 'I would say her brother, Wilferth, would be my choice to be the killer, if he found his sister was living as she was, but then he would have known it for years if he lived in Worcester, so why be angry now? Besides, we know he did not come here when he and his father left Claines. What is more, all the men we have looked at were Worcester born and bred, bar a riverman from Tewkesbury and a fellman out of Gloucester, and none have the name Wilferth. He might be dead these twenty-five years or so.'

'What was the father's name?'

'He too was Wilferth.'

'Well, if they had the same name, it would be common for the son to go by a shortened name or nickname, to avoid confusion. Most like he was "Will" and could easily have kept it as man grown. You also know he was a youth when the mother was killed, a youth teetering towards manhood, but voice unbroken. Let us say he was thirteen. That means he is now in his late thirties, perhaps two score years. If the father drowned the mother and took the lad away with him, it was of course not likely he would simply move into Worcester where he would be seen by his old neighbours every time they came in to buy or sell, but the lad become man might return in later years. There is one thing more. A man who holds his son dear and close brings him up in his own image, as best he can. I say so with regret, if the father is bad. This father made his poor wife miserable and beat her, beat her so that even his neighbours felt he was unfair and long before he thought of her straying. Such a man would breed a son very like, a man who would treat his own wife poorly. So I say, tell me more of the men from Tewkesbury and Gloucester. Of what age and manner of man are they?'

Hugh was not feeling sleepy any more.

'Christina, you are a wonder, and do not be surprised if Catchpoll wants you to replace me as undersheriff in the morning. We have been blind! The fellman from Gloucester is a "Will", in his late thirties, and a surly man whose wife would dearly love to be rid of him.' He paused, his jubilation on hold. 'That, alone, is the thing that does not fit, alas.'

'What does not?'

'She came to us, his wife, after the first death was made known, and the manner of it, and showed us the cotte of her husband. He had just returned from upriver where he was collecting pelts from men who catch what animals they can. She came because there was blood upon the cotte, but the bloodstains . . . A man would not let that much blood dry on his clothing so that any who saw him would recognise it and question. But this had dried and then been simply dipped in water to wet it, and this was two days after the killing. She had smeared it on the cloth to make him look guilty. It was too clearly bloodstained, just not "right".'

'Blood may dry in a variety of ways, may be obvious or may fade, and does not always leap to the eye. If he had done a little to wash the marks when very fresh then may she not have thought her "evidence" needed to be more obvious, and have added to what was there and fading?'

'Jesu, she might at that! She had reason enough. Not only does he hit her – hit, not chastise – but she is carrying, and it is likely the child is not his. If she was afraid enough . . .'

'If she feared for her child, even a child not yet in the world, it would be enough to be the spur.' Christina spoke with the authority of one who had carried, had borne, had lost. It brought her back to the child within her now, and she offered up a silent prayer of thanks. There was silence between husband and wife as she prayed and he worked through all he knew, matching facts to this new theory. Her prayer finished the sooner, and she wriggled into a comfortable position for slumber.

'Now, since I have solved your problem and discovered your murderer, my husband, you can forget it all until sunrise.'

There was sense to it, he thought. Will Fellman would not be seeking admittance through the Foregate wicket in the hours of darkness to commit foul murder, with the gateman knowing he was within the walls. It even made more sense as to why Berta had been killed in daylight, not whilst touting for custom late of an evening. Hugh Bradecote, Undersheriff of Worcestershire, slept soundly.

He awoke to a loud banging upon the door and an urgent voice. His mind was clear in moments, even as Christina made vague noises and surfaced. The narrow window admitted the soft light of a summer dawn. He climbed from the bed, dragging his undershirt over his head. He opened the door, bare-legged and barefooted.

'There is a woman dead, my lord, and her body just found.'

Bradecote's blood ran cold. Last night he had been so sure, but was it a self-deception? Worse, might it be that his remaining in his bed had cost a life?

'Go to Serjeant Catchpoll's and wake him also. Tell him I will be with him shortly and have whoever reported the body kept at the gate. I have but to dress.'

'Yes, my lord.'

Bradecote scrambled into his clothes, bid his half-awake wife the briefest of farewells and went in haste to the gate, where he was taken aback to find Roger the Healer, his face grave, and with a slightly grey tinge.

'You found her?' His surprise was evident.

'Yes, my lord. I . . . I deal with the sick and afflicted, but nothing like this.' He crossed himself.

'You must show me the place, but how come you found her, Master Roger? It is very early.'

'Edwin the Turner's wife has a fever, and it worsened greatly overnight. He was banging at my door before the first hint of grey in the sky, and I was with her some time. When I left, well, I turned into an alley off Angers Lone, near to the Foregate to ease my bladder, and . . . she was there. I came straight away, my lord.'

'Yes.' They were now almost outside Catchpoll's dwelling, and the man-at-arms was gone but Catchpoll himself appeared at the door, hair tousled and hastily dressed, but very awake. He nodded at his superior.

'I sent Oswald on to Walkelin's mother's, so we can collect him on our way. Oswald said somewheres off the Foregate for the body.'

'Alley off Angers Lone, according to Master Roger here, who found her.' Bradecote noted the very slight change in Catchpoll's expression. 'We want to reach her before anyone else starts a panic in the streets.'

'We do that.' The three men, with Roger the Healer gripping the skirts of his long tunic and almost running, hastened north along the main thoroughfare of Worcester, with only the very first craftsman opening their shutters and yawning as they did so. Walkelin lived on Brudelwritte Strete, and Catchpoll went ahead and turned off to fetch him. The pair joined Bradecote and a panting Roger towards the far end of Bocherewe, and it was Catchpoll who led the way into Angers Lone and the alley, as Roger the Healer held back. The woman was lying face down, her coif askew and concealing her features, one arm flung out, the other somewhere beneath the body, but from her form and clothing this was no street whore. Catchpoll gazed at her for a moment, noting the position of her, and then turned her over. Walkelin let out a sharp cry and stepped back to sink against a wall, staring. Bradecote reached down a hand to grip his shoulder.

The Widow Hedger was 'cold dead', Catchpoll confirmed, as he closed the eyes. 'Reckon it was early in the night, and how else would it be, with a decent woman? But what was she doing inside the walls, even dusk late?' Catchpoll's question was to himself.

Bradecote looked nearly as stunned as Walkelin. At first a great weight of guilt descended upon him. Had he not kept to his warm bed, and warm wife, had he dressed and gone with Catchpoll and hammered upon Fellman's door, then Walkelin's kinswoman would be alive. Then he questioned. Why would he have killed her, and why on earth do so here, when they both lived outside the walls? She would not have arranged to meet a man she hated, and he could scarcely have dragged her through the gate and to her death here.

'I do not understand,' he said, quietly.

'It is a different death, but close enough. I would say the same man again, my lord. He took her through the throat, low, just above the collarbones, not a slash across the throat, so I am guessing he was facing her, and he grabbed her coif and hair, which is why it is so askew. That would silence her, though whether it killed her would depend how deep he went. If she was not dead the second wound did for her.'

'Master Roger,' Bradecote found his voice and called to the man at the alleyway entrance. 'What did you see when you came here?'

'I . . . I saw her lying, the arm out, not moving. I reached a hand to feel the heartbeat at the breast and there was none, and my hand came away bloodied, sticky.' The voice was quavering.

'Second wound was deep, right across and just below the ribs, my lord,' said Catchpoll, gravely, and then there was a short pause. 'He cut her like Berta too.'

Walkelin choked, and when he managed to speak his words were deliberate.

'My lord, you keep me off him when we catches him, or else they will hang a coddless corpse. I swear oath.'

'Catchpoll, my wife suggested last night that Will Fellman might well be Wilferth the son. He is of the right age, and perhaps he came to Worcester late and only discovered Ricolde was his sister the night he killed her. It makes good sense, even if we ignore the bloodstains his wife showed us. But this . . . Just when I was sure, this does not fit. The woman despised him, so she would not come to meet him, nor could he force her in the gate.'

'Why she is here is a mystery to me, my lord. But we can at least find when she came. Walkelin, go and speak with the man at the Foregate, lad, and find out who had the watch last eventide. He would recall her and when she came in. We will take her to your mother, tidied mind. Meet us there.' Walkelin, shaking slightly, nodded and departed. 'Better keep him busy, my lord,' advised Catchpoll, 'and he would not want to see his mother's first reaction either.'

'Agreed. The tavern keeper would have a handcart, would he not?'

'Most like, my lord, though at this rate we will have need to push one about with us. We can use the shawl to make her decent and cover her face.'

As Bradecote left the alley he sent Roger the Healer home. After all, he knew where to find him at need.

It was as they wheeled the corpse along the Bocherewe that it began, the susurration that would spread through Worcester in short hours. There was another body, another woman dead. Most assumed it one of the sorority of whores, and it was one of that number who begged to know the identity of the dead woman.

'You will not know her, for she was a widow woman from without the gates,' said Catchpoll.

'Have you a name to her?' Another voice, male and interested, spoke up.

'We do. It is the Widow Hedger.'

'Holy Virgin! I saw her outside the tavern of The Moon, yestereve.' The wheels of the cart ceased turning. Catchpoll and Bradecote both looked at the man, portly, with greying hair.

'Outside the tavern?' Bradecote frowned.

'Aye, my lord, she was asking after some man, but got no good answer. Not that he would get soft words from her if he met her, from her face. Poor woman, to end so.' The man crossed himself.

'So that was why she was within the walls, at least,' muttered Catchpoll. 'I can go back down to the quays when all is dealt with and see if the tavern keeper remembers what man she asked for. If it is Fellman, our prayers are answered.'

'But surely he would be the last man in Worcester, unless she came in, and late too, just to lash him with her tongue over some further mistreatment of his wife, and that sounds strange.'

'Let us not look at the problem that lingers, but what is good and new. The Widow Hedger came in of her own will, and once we know who she came to find, we most like have her killer. The end is coming, my lord, and with the name, it comes soon.'

They turned down Brudelwritte Strete, and Catchpoll stopped and indicated the door of a small dwelling. Bradecote knocked. When Walkelin's mother opened the door she saw the lord undersheriff, grave-faced, and a cart with a body upon it. That the body was gowned and a woman did not reach her brain.

'My son,' she cried and fell in a dead faint.

'That went well,' remarked Catchpoll.

'Shut up and help me revive her before Walkelin gets back and thinks his mother dead as well as his aunt.'

Bradecote bent to lift the not inconsiderable weight of Walkelin's parent from the floor and set her upon the bed in the rear of the chamber, next to a door that gave out onto a small yard. He opened the door to let in light and fresh air, and wafted his hand over her face ineffectually, then tried chafing her hand. He was not very good at reviving females. Had it been a man he would have emptied water over them, but he did not think he would be popular with Walkelin if he half drowned the woman and he returned to find her not only distraught, but wet and spluttering. Catchpoll, meanwhile, had brought in the body of Widow Hedger and laid it upon the floor, since the bed was out of the question. After a short while Walkelin's mother stirred.

'Be easy, mistress, your son is hale and hearty. In that at least I can give you good tidings.'

She looked up at the undersheriff, for a moment confused, then memory returned.

'He is not dead?'

'No, he is not. He is seeking information at the Foregate. Yet I do bring sad news, mistress, of your sister, the Widow Hedger. I cannot make it easier. She is dead, and by violence.'

The woman caught her breath upon a sob and put her hand to her cheek, and Walkelin filled the front doorway, his face implacable.

'By the violence of Godfrid the journeyman.'

'Godfrid?' Catchpoll's disbelief was patent, and Walkelin turned on him.

'Aye, the man we thought too gentle and decent to do more than tup his master's wife. We let him go, Serjeant. We let him go.' Walkelin's voice had risen to a cry, but he took himself in hand, breathed deeply and then continued. 'That was what I found from the gateman of the evening watch. My aunt asked him as she entered, just before the great gate was shut, if he had seen Godfrid, Fellman's journeyman. He told her no, and I checked again with the man who took over the gate. Godfrid has not left Worcester by the Foregate this day, so I shall find the bastard and woe betide him when I do.'

'We heard she asked after a man at The Moon tavern, but no man came out. Godfrid though? Why would she seek him, and can you see him killing any of the three women?' Catchpoll pulled a face.

'Even if we cannot, we need to find him. If he killed last night, then he cannot have left Worcester until the gates were opened, and not to the north. If he persuaded another gatekeeper to let him out by the wicket, then he would be remembered well enough. The trouble lies in that only at the Foregate would he be known beforehand. Walkelin, go to a neighbour and have them fetch your priest, and get a woman to sit with your mother. I will wait for the priest, since he will not be expecting a ripped corpse. Catchpoll, you try the east gate off Meal Cheaping, and Walkelin, you the Sutheberi gate. We meet at the castle, and if sighting has been made, we will catch him swiftly if on horseback. If nothing is known, warn the gate with the best description you can give, and we trawl through Worcester till we find him.'

Both men went without another word. A woman knocked and entered nervously, crossing herself as she saw the body upon the rush-strewn floor and bobbing an obeisance to the undersheriff. She said nothing to him but went to the bed to murmur over Walkelin's mother. The priest arrived shortly afterwards, and Bradecote set off for the castle.

Something was niggling him, and it was not the new boots squeezing his toes. Widow Hedger had come into Worcester, late of an evening, asking after Godfrid, who might, as far as she could have known, have already been on the road to Gloucester or Evesham and long gone. Why? His first thought was that he was in fact her son, but of course if that had been the case then Walkelin would have claimed him as such as soon as they had interest in him. Bradecote felt he knew the answer, but that it was just beyond him grasping it. Only as he set off back towards the castle did it surface, and when it did he stopped dead, and a woman behind him, bearing an armful of wood for

248

her hearth fire, berated him as she nearly cannoned into him and dropped half her load. He ignored her, spun on his heel and began to run. The only reason Widow Hedger would have sought Godfrid would be because of Will Fellman's wife and for something very important.

As he ran, Bradecote could think of only two reasons why Mistress Fellman would send another to find her lover. Either she had killed Fellman, in defence or because she had simply snapped, or she felt he was about to discover the sinful secret and her life was at risk. He thought the former unlikely. She would not run away, not in her condition, and not with small children to protect from him. What was more, the moment the news of Widow Hedger's killing reached outside the walls of Worcester, which would be swiftly with the gatekeeper full of news, Fellman would be more than suspicious. Ignoring his pinched toes, the undersheriff sped the faster. He was forced to slow at the Foregate, where a man with a cart and another bringing a pig in to sell were in an altercation in the gateway itself, but he edged past them and turned down past the archery butts and towards the river. He could see several people gathered outside Will Fellman's, and his heart, which was pounding, skipped a beat. Was he too late?

As he drew close it was clear that he was not, at least not quite. From within the house came a roaring anger and screaming. Those about the door, mostly women, stared at it as if it were solid stone. Bradecote, barging them out of the way, tried to lift the latch, but it was barred from within. The screaming was becoming even more frantic and was not from one person alone. He set his shoulder to the door, but it barely budged.

'Help me here,' he commanded, and a youth of about sixteen and an elderly man gave what strength they had. It was a good door, and, more importantly, must have had a heavy bar to it within. They charged it, several times, and Bradecote's shoulder ached as he thumped it into hard oak, but upon the fourth attempt there was a splintering sound as the keeper within tore from the frame, and all three tumbled into the doorway of the dwelling. Bradecote scrambled to his feet the fastest, his eyes adjusting to the low light. In a corner cowered the three children, the girl with a swaddled bundle in her arms. She was screaming, though the two small boys were mute. The room was in disarray, the cobbled-together pelts that covered the bed spilling off it and mostly on the floor, the palliasse itself with a rent across it and straw pushing up out of it like the insides of some eviscerated animal. Will Fellman was standing with his fleshing knife in his hand, his other hand a clenched fist, the knuckles white and bloodied. He was bellowing obscenities at his wife, who, white of face where it was not blood-smeared, held a stool before her as protection, the legs towards her assailant. Her gown was ripped from one shoulder and hung, half exposing a pale breast, marked with blood that dripped still from her nose. She was a cornered creature. As the sunlight flooded in through the doorway, she cried out to her daughter to escape. The terrified girl bolted for the door, but her father stepped sideways, thrust out his arm and grabbed her by the hair and turned, even as Bradecote drew his sword from its scabbard with a sound of sliding steel. Mother and daughter screamed as one.

Fellman was torn. He wanted to kill his wife, almost above all things, but self-preservation was the stronger instinct, and the girl and wailing infant were his guarantee of safety. The knife flashed at her throat.

'Stay your hand or her blood is upon you,' growled Fellman, eyes narrowed, teeth bared, feral, dangerous.

'You would not kill your own child,' said Bradecote, calmly, though he did not feel calm, nor did he believe what he said, for Fellman was beyond normal emotions.

'Who's to say she's even mine, or any of them my blood.' For a moment the knife blade was pointed at the two small boys. 'The bitch whored herself for the mewling scrap here, why not for every one of them? Bastards sired by bastards and born of that *firenhicge*. Welcome any man's pintle, excepting mine. She might as well take silver for it and be done. At least I would have good use of her then.' He spat in the direction of his wife, whose eyes were fixed upon the girl.

'See, I sheath my sword.' Bradecote knew he could not take the man before he killed the girl. 'Let her go and—'

'You take me for a fool, sheriff's man. She comes with me.' He yanked her hair, pulling her back with him as he edged to the doorway. His neighbours parted as clods before the ploughshare. The girl whimpered, looking at her mother, and as she half fell back, lowered her arms with the wrapped babe within them, and at his second tug, let it fall upon the rushes at her feet. It was not so far, and the child cried. Fellman snarled and would have kicked it, but the youth whose strength had helped little with the door had speed at least, and threw himself to grab the bundle and roll away, taking the blow to his back. Fellman was through the door, moving crabwise, with the girl off balance and crying out as her hair

251

pulled from her scalp. Bradecote followed, as close as he dared.

'Kill her and you are a dead man, Fellman, for there will be no cause for me to hold back, and whether upon my sword or at rope's end, you will die.' His voice held that promise.

'You want me dead anyways. This way she will not shame me as her mother did.' Fellman actually laughed. It was but sixty paces or so to the river's edge, and Bradecote's first thought was that Fellman would simply slit the girl's throat there and throw her body into the water. He felt powerless, though he was within a dozen feet of him. As the track dipped where coracles and small craft lay upturned upon the bank, the air moved suddenly beside his cheek, and an arrow found, if not its mark, then enough of Fellman's arm that held the knife for him to drop it as his flesh was split. He stumbled but kept hold of the girl and pushed her into the water, where she fell and went under even in the shallower depth. This gave him both hands to grab a coracle, step confidently into the flow and climb in with an action born of experience. Bradecote, caught for a moment between reaching for the girl and for the man, did neither well. He rushed into the water above his knees and pulled the girl's arm, as she spluttered to get her head above water, but let go before she had a foothold and she flailed once more. There were, however, others rushing to her aid, and so he launched himself forward to grab the rim of the coracle, hoping to tip Fellman from it. Unfortunately for him that extra step took him into deep water, and his grab became a desperate attempt to hold onto something to keep him afloat as he pitched forward. He missed, and Fellman brought down the paddle, hoping to hit him upon the head. As he went under at that moment the blow was inaccurate and caught him upon his shoulder.

Hugh Bradecote rode well, fought well, and swam not at all. He was burdened with boots and clothing and a sword at his hip that pulled him down. The water went over his head again, and he was scrabbling with his hands to find the gunwale of the coracle even as he surfaced, spluttering, trying desperately to get a lungful of air. He was no longer after a killer; he was doing his best to stay alive. The more he floundered the less often he saw sky and could take a breath, though his open mouth was gulping more water than air. He was drowning, and he did not want to die. He had a beloved wife, a child, another child unborn, and the Severn was taking him from them. He did not want to die. Dear God, he did not want to die.

Chapter Seventeen

Walkelin was neither naturally vindictive, nor prone to violent temper, being a young man of kindly disposition. His blood was up, however, as never before. His relationship with his aunt was not so close that her death broke his heart, but it shocked him, and he knew his mother would be very distressed. He also knew the manner of it, and he felt guilty, because he had taken Godfrid before the lord Bradecote, and he had been in agreement that he was an innocent man and should be freed again. He had let the man loose to kill his kin. It was shaming.

When the man at the Sutheberi gate said that a man of the age, size and colouring that were described to him had left Worcester an hour after sunrise he was not thinking like a sheriff's man, but as a sister-son. This was not the law's duty, it was kin right, and he would bring Godfrid back to Worcester through the dirt to hang and be glad of life's ending. He almost ran to the castle, saddled a horse and was very soon loping out of the Sutheberi gate and heading upon the road south the gateman had said Godfrid took a few hours past.

He had not lost all sense, however, and asked upon the way as he met folk coming towards Worcester, and at Kempsey where they pointed him on along the Gloucester road. At Stoke he was taken aback when a woman smilingly told him he would find the man he sought in the house next but one to the church. Walkelin thanked her but frowned. Why would Godfrid halt after but seven miles or so and at the dwelling of some villager? He dismounted and went to the door. Some argument was going on within, and a woman's voice berated. Walkelin knew that tone well; it was maternal disapproval.

The door opened, and a man stood before him, a man of the height, age and colouring of Godfrid. Yet Walkelin had never seen him before in his life.

'Yes?'

'I am Walkelin, sheriff's man. I need to know if it was you as left Worcester early this morning when the gate opened.'

'Aye.' The man reddened, and a woman who was undoubtedly his mother stepped forward.

'Getting ale-sodden is no offence to the law, howsoever it is foolish and sets his poor mother thinking he has been done to death in an alley.'

'No, mistress, it is not, but we seek a man of similar description, not your son, and we had to know if the man who left was him.' Walkelin felt deflated, defeated. What would Serjeant Catchpoll say when he returned, tail between his legs and from chasing an innocent man?

'You mean like the poor lad as is at the priest's house? Fair knocked me back when I saw him yester afternoon.'

Walkelin's jaw dropped, and his mind whirled like a dust devil.

'A "poor lad"?'

'Why yes. He had stepped aside from the track for his . . . needs and was bit by a snake. Fair poorly he was, but a strapping build, so the priest says as he will live, and indeed this morning when I went to offer prayers for my missing son' – she glared at the errant progeny pointedly – 'he said as he was no longer ailing in stomach and bowels, and was perfect of mind, which is more than yesterday, poor soul.'

'Thank you, mistress. I will speak with the priest before I return to Worcester.' Walkelin tried to sound official. He nodded and turned away, leading his horse to the house next to the church, which he reasonably assumed to be that of the incumbent. He knocked upon the door, and a habited figure opened it.

'Can I help you, my son?' The priest was of middle years, thin-faced but welcoming.

'Good Father, I am Walkelin, sheriff's man, out of Worcester. I would speak with the man you took in yesterday who was bitten by a snake.'

'He has done nothing wrong, surely?'

'I . . . It seems not, but he may know something important relating to a death.'

'Then come within. The leg is still swollen and painful, but he has taken food and drink today, and he is of sound mind.' The priest held the door wide.

Walkelin entered and saw, across the chamber and lying upon a narrow cot, Godfrid, the erstwhile journeyman of Will Fellman.

The hand that grabbed him did not let go, but it took what seemed a lifetime to get his head above water. He was semiconscious, everything vague and blurring. There was noise, shouting, a splash as rope hit the water just in front of his face, then more arms and he was being pulled, dragged and beaten upon the back.

The noise resolved itself into voices, words. He choked, coughed, spewed up water and lay upon good solid earth where the damped dust smelt glorious in his nostrils. He had no strength in arm or body to lift himself from the prone position, but someone rolled him over onto his back, and he was looking up into the concerned face of Walter of the Possessed Swans.

'Did the swans call you, my lord?' he asked.

Bradecote tried to shake his head, but it barely moved, and he closed his eyes again. If the river had not taken his life, then it had taken his strength. A beaker was pressed to his lips, and he swallowed. It was some form of mead flavoured with a herb that made it less pleasant, but presumably it was intended as medicinal. He choked a little, coughed, and as he tried to lift himself, other hands pushed him into a slumped sitting position. He tried to gather his thoughts when the only one that had meaning was that he was alive. He wanted to do nothing but breathe good air and be alive, but he knew he must think.

'Fellman,' he managed.

'You will not catch him, my lord, not as you are.' It was a woman's voice, motherly. 'Upriver he has gone, but be sure as any of us would send to the castle if he dared poke his nose back here.'

It was small consolation, in fact none at all. Bradecote focused. He placed his hands on his knees. It did at least stop the latter shaking.

'Best get up slowly, my lord, and take a good firm arm, just for a moment.' The new voice was solicitous but respectful.

'Shall we send a lad to the castle now, my lord, for a horse for you?'

'Serjeant Catchpoll.'

'I would like to see him carry you piggy-back,' chortled a wit from the back, and then fell silent as the undersheriff straightened his back. It took an effort, but he did it, and he looked round also. He was no longer the victim of an accident to be treated like a child; consoled, encouraged, lightly chivvied. He was the lord Bradecote, Undersheriff of Worcestershire, and 'power'. The wit shrank into anonymity.

'I can go to the castle if he is there, my lord.' The youth who had saved the baby, rather enjoying the brief period of being treated as a hero, offered himself as messenger and was sent off at a run. Bradecote was being practical. If he walked back himself, he presented a dismal sight, looking, accurately, half drowned and exhausted. Besides, since Catchpoll would likely bring two horses for speed, they could work up the east bank of the river faster on horseback than a man with a paddle in a coracle, which was not designed to get anywhere very fast. In fact, as long as Fellman kept to the river they would catch him.

'Mistress Fellman and the girl?'

'Don't be worrying over them, my lord, for they will do well enough now danger is past.'

'I would speak with her.' He walked, treading very deliberately, to the Fellman house, where the door was still open and an old woman was fussing over the little girl, wrapped in a blanket. Sibbe Fellman was on the ravaged bed, nursing her baby, who appeared little the worse for being dropped. She looked at the undersheriff, her face cleaned of blood but showing bruising, her eyes very serious.

'If he comes back, he will kill us,' she said, flatly.

'When he comes back, it will be with his wrists bound and to the castle, mistress.' Bradecote's voice held certainty. 'He is no threat to you or the children now. Tell me what happened, since yestereve.'

'The babe came and came early, since he shoved and kicked me. Widow Hedger, God rest her, came to my aid, for Golde is too young to help. She sent him, Will, packing. The child was born before sunset. I begged Widow Hedger to try and find Godfrid, who might yet be in Worcester, to let him know, if naught else, that he had a daughter. That would please him, just as the thought displeased my husband.' Sibbe Fellman blinked away tears and sniffed. 'Had I not sent her she would be living still. It is my fault, *mea culpa*.'

'No, it is not. It is no fault but that of your husband, and he has more than just her blood upon his hands.'

She only partially processed this information.

'This morning, it was along the street in no time at all that she was dead and report said Godfrid did it. He did not, my lord, I knew even before Will . . . Godfrid would not, could not kill. Will was out the back and heard the shouting. He came through, and when he heard, he came back in and shut the door, and he barred it. I knew then.' She paused, shut her eyes for a moment, then continued. 'He asked why Widow Hedger should want to find Godfrid, though he had guessed. I said nothing. That was when he dragged me off the bed, and he hit me first. Then he took up a knife and slashed at the palliasse, and what he did to the bed he said he would do to me, slow like. Golde took the baby from the cradle. He said she was next. I do not know if he meant Golde or the baby. I took the stool, tried to keep him away, but he would have . . .'

'Yes, he would. Did he say he killed Widow Hedger?'

She nodded. 'My lord, when you said more than just her blood . . . Did he kill the others?' She clearly did not know if he had done so.

'Yes.'

'But I . . . The cotte . . .'

'What you did, mistress, made us think him innocent, because we knew you lied.' He did not say more. Would they have taken him that day if she had not offered her proofs? If not that day, upon which? He could not be certain, but if they had been given Fellman's name upriver, and had not in part discounted him, they would have returned earlier and brought him in to question, quite possibly saving Berta from her fate. However, actively piling guilt onto this woman, one who had suffered so much, seemed cruel. He heard hooves outside, and then Catchpoll entered. Not by a flicker of emotion did he show just how glad he was that 'his' undersheriff was not floating face down in the river, and he ignored his wet clothing.

'I have two horses, my lord, and have sent a man after Walkelin.'

'After him?'

'Aye, my lord. Seems he got back to the castle before me, with news that a man of Godfrid's description left as soon as the gate was opened, and he has hared off on his own. God alone knows what he will do if he gets hold of him.'

'Let us hope he is saving most for under our eye, and by then we can give him the real killer. If Godfrid discovers that Mistress Fellman will be free of a husband in the near future, he might be persuaded to overlook sore ribs.'

'If that is all he is suffering. Well, we cannot help him or Walkelin. Head we up towards Bevere Island and looking for the coracle?'

'Yes, Catchpoll. He cannot carry that far even to conceal, for it is cumbersome when carried on the back. The danger is he takes it to the western bank, for beneath willows it could be disguised from distance. I wish he knew the river less well.'

'Nothing we can do about that, my lord.'

'No. Let us get going.' Bradecote looked again at Sibbe Fellman. 'We will catch him, mistress.'

Without waiting for any reply, he turned and followed Catchpoll into the sunshine. At least the heat would dry him fast enough, though not where it mattered most, where it would chafe. He grimaced as he mounted, and the pair picked their way along the bank where the last dwelling was close to the river and then set off a brisk trot, Bradecote scanning the far bank, Catchpoll the near one, and both with half an eye upon the Severn.

Bradecote was not fully concentrating upon the problem, and it dawned upon him too slowly that he ought to have sent Catchpoll back into Worcester to cross the bridge and work up the far bank. As they were, Fellman would be able to see them on one bank and head for the other, and there were places where the banks were too steep for a horse to get in or out of the water safely, let alone the beast having to swim across the breadth of river. The last thing he himself wanted today was to be back in the water, even clinging on to a beast that could keep itself afloat.

'I am a fool, Catchpoll, a damp fool. I think the river got into my wits as well as my lungs.' He voiced his concern.

'I can go back if you say so, my lord, but there's willow so thick in places you could not ride close to the bank on that section up to Hallow.'

'Which might be just where he goes ashore,' groaned Bradecote.

'That it might, my lord. Look.'

The river bend now revealed a coracle, empty, floating lazily downstream upon the river's summer indolence. Bradecote swore.

'We now know neither upon which bank nor where above us he came off the river.'

'But he cannot be that far ahead, my lord. A coracle is not built for speed. If you account the time between our parting from Walkelin to now, how much of it passed before you got yourself near drowned? Half? More?'

'About half, I should guess, though it seemed a lifetime in the water.'

'It was nearly all the lifetime you had left, had not our friend Walter come to your aid, as I hear.'

'True enough.'

'That being so, my lord, he cannot—' Catchpoll stopped abruptly and pointed. Ahead of them, where the river curved back and on the far bank, there was movement. It might perhaps be a roebuck that had come down to drink, but there was something quite large and alive among the willows.

'I can see, Catchpoll. It may be him. What is the bank like ahead, do you know?'

'It is near enough where we crossed when the river was frozen, my lord, and not too steep for horses there upon either bank.' He paused. 'Do you want me to cross, my lord?'

'You doubt my courage, Serjeant?' It flicked Bradecote on the raw, not least because he knew fear lay in his belly. 'I may not like it, in fact I swear oath I do not, but Fellman is almost certainly upon that bank, so my place is there. I shall go first, in case it is but a deer. Crossing once, yes, but please God not there and then back. Three times being wet is too much in one day. I will signal to you either way. Keep "him" in view as best you can, Catchpoll.' With which Bradecote swung his horse's head round and urged it down the bank into the water. It jibbed a little, as if questioning his sanity.

'Yes, mad it is, but in we go, my friend.' He patted the grey neck and set spur to flank. The horse entered the river cautiously, and thankfully the bed did not fall away too steeply. Nostrils flared, head raised, the animal began to swim, with Bradecote, his feet out of the stirrups, gripping on by rein and mane, and lying along its back, praying silently and giving thanks when he felt firm ground beneath the hooves. He was wet, yet again, but this time it mattered less.

The grey scrambled up the bank with ease, where it was not overgrown with vegetation, and Bradecote skirted the tangle of willow where they had seen movement. He noted his horse's ears moving, alert to sounds. It knew something was in the undergrowth and was suitably nervous. He scanned among the branches for movement. The trouble was that a roebuck might be as wise as a man and keep very still. He waited. The horse lifted his head, looking to the right, and Bradecote leant forward, peering between the ears. He did not think Fellman a patient man and pinned his hopes upon it. Be he never so cautious, if he moved he would be heard and seen.

It was not so much sound as a movement of branches and a flash of colour that was not a wild animal that gave the game away. That was human; that was Will Fellman. Bradecote yelled for Catchpoll, hoping that any urgent sound would bring him across, even as he heard snapping twigs and manhandled whipping branches. He wheeled his horse to the right and cantered to where he thought Fellman would break cover. Luck was against him, for a thick hedge came all the way to the willow thicket, and his quarry had the sense to be the far side of it. He thumped his pommel in frustration. He would do better to wait for Catchpoll, send him on foot through a patch of the willow and take both horses to where there was the first break in the hedge. That way Fellman could not easily double back, and if they could get him into a field proper it would be like dogs after a hare. He hoped it would not be a wheat field, for he could not bring himself to canter all over a crop near harvesting.

Hoofbeats sounded to his rear, and Catchpoll, very wet but surprisingly cheerful withal, arrived upon his still-dripping mount.

'He came out the far side of this, and no horse can get over or through, Catchpoll. Dismount and go into and out of the willow, and I will lead your horse to where there is a gap. Await me on the other side. He cannot turn about with you down here, and if we are lucky, the field will be open and we can catch him quickly.'

Catchpoll nodded, not questioning that the undersheriff would stay upon his horse and he, the older man, would be on foot. He kicked his feet from his stirrups and dismounted, grunting as his knees bent and muttering, for Bradecote's benefit, about how the wisdom of years ought to breed respect in the young. Bradecote shook his head and laughed as he took the reins and urged his own mount along the hedge line. It was some way before a break in the hedge gave him access at last to the land beyond, land that thankfully lay fallow. The opening was, however, obstructed with a hurdle, since sheep had been put into the field after the haymaking, and whilst Bradecote might have been tempted to see if he could get his horse to leap it and trust to his horsemanship to stick on its back, this was out of the question when leading another beast as well. He sighed, dismounted, moved the hurdle, led through both animals and closed the gap again. This all took valuable time. He looked down the hedge line but saw no sign of Catchpoll. He cursed him for an insubordinate old bastard, but then realised there was a slight crest to the field at the lower end, and he may simply have had cause to follow Fellman to keep him in view. He urged his horse into a canter, keeping his distance but working across. If Catchpoll was driving Fellman across the field and could not be seen, then Fellman in turn would not know that the undersheriff awaited him if he came up from the river.

There came an urgent shout, and that would not be Fellman. Seeing the far side of the field empty, Bradecote could safely turn towards the river. He kicked his horse faster, scattering bleating sheep, disturbed from their methodical chewing. A man was running, running towards him, head down, and only as he heard the beat of hoof upon turf did he look up and attempt to avoid horse and rider. He ran back across the field a short way, but then stopped. Had he realised that further effort was wasted and that he must surely now be caught? As Bradecote drew close enough to see the features he decided this was not the case. Fellman was standing his ground, no doubt hoping that the man with the sword would not draw it and strike him down or might give him some small chance to unhorse his opponent. He was a big man, a strong man, but he had no idea whether Bradecote was simply content to kill him and would draw his sword. The thought occurred to Hugh Bradecote. He could ride almost directly at Fellman to the last breath, swerve slightly and bring the blade up at the last moment to gut him. It would be easy, but it would not be the death this man deserved. So Bradecote kept his sword sheathed, and Fellman allowed himself a small smile, a smile that froze as the big grey thundered towards him to run him down. Bradecote flung the horse's head to the side and kicked his feet from the stirrups as he launched himself on top of the man. There was an element of surprise to it, and he had the added impetus of the horse's speed, but Fellman, though thrown flat on his back, did not have all the fight knocked from him. After the initial impact, he managed to roll Bradecote off him to one side and did what had had always done when angry and facing someone, he swung his fist. Bradecote was trying to get two hands about his throat, and so did not parry the blow which crashed down into the side of his head but too high to do more than crack against his skull. Fellman was not used to fighting when his opponent was fighting back, at least not effectually.

Brawling was not one of the knightly skills taught to squires, though Bradecote had learnt a thing or two from the adolescent scraps which gave an unofficial hierarchy among the youths. He had, however, fitness of body and wits, a strong sword arm and no illusions about fighting 'fair'. The blow stunned him enough to loosen his pressure on the man's throat, but before Fellman could pin him with his own weight he brought knee to meet groin, in sure and certain knowledge of who would suffer. Fellman's eyes widened, and he gave a grunting gasp as the pain took him. Pressing home his advantage, Bradecote rolled back so that he was uppermost, and sat high across the man's chest, pinning his arms with his knees, not that Fellman was resisting much at this point.

Hearing heavy breathing, Bradecote looked up and saw Catchpoll running towards them, though his pace slackened, and he grinned as he drew close.

'Glad to see you have the situation under control, my lord. I will get the rope from my horse.'

The word 'rope' clearly got through to Fellman's brain.

'You are going to hang me?' he managed, in a groaning whisper, his eyes still watering.

'Oh yes, you can be sure of that, but not here, not now. When you hang, Worcester will watch and spit upon your corpse when you stop twitching. Will they not, Serjeant Catchpoll?'

'Indeed yes, my lord. A fair treat for man, woman and child.' Catchpoll spoke with relish and as though he would be selling the right to get closest views.

Bradecote saw the flicker of fear at last pass over Fellman's visage and it pleased him. This man had filled others with fear for years: his wife, his children and now three women who had met death at his hands. It was right that he should know its clutches.

Catchpoll returned with the rope, yanked Fellman's hands above his head as Bradecote sat back and bound them. Bradecote got up from the ground, rubbed the side of his skull and looked at Catchpoll, where he saw his satisfaction mirrored.

'We got the bastard.'

'We got him, my lord.'

Chapter Eighteen

It was a pity, thought Bradecote, that they would enter Worcester across the bridge and not through the Foregate, since that would bring Fellman's neighbours out to stare. However, he made sure that he and Catchpoll hit the track that came from Powick to Hallow, and trotted much of the way to Worcester, which meant Fellman had to trot along as well, with dust rising from the horses going before him, and leaving him spent and dust dry.

Eyes followed them as they took their prisoner through the streets of Worcester. Knowing the chief crime of the moment was murder, few thought them to be bringing someone in for stealing eggs, and some women, relieved and angry, spat upon Fellman as he passed. Neither undersheriff nor sheriff's serjeant suggested they desist.

What Bradecote had not anticipated would be his

reception at the castle. The castellan, who was crossing the bailey, sneered and smiled also, having heard how close to drowning Bradecote had come.

'How long before you let this one go?' he mocked and then in feigned remembrance added, 'But of course you have let him go before, to kill more innocent women.' He made sure his voice was loud enough to be heard by all in possible range without resorting to shouting. Bradecote ignored him and strode past towards the hall, Catchpoll dragging Fellman behind him, and sent a servant to find the lord sheriff.

It was Christina who arrived first, however, looking pale and worried. She had eyes for nobody but her husband and came to him, controlling her voice with difficulty.

'You are unharmed, my lord?' She sought assurance, even though the sight of him upright and in command showed there could be little seriously wrong.

'Fear not, my lady, I am stoutly made.' He made light of it but saw her sway just a little and stepped to take her arm. Then he spoke softly and just to her. 'I am wet and a little sore in places, love, but no great harm has come to me. Be easy and have a care to yourself, especially now.' His hand touched her briefly below the girdle, and Catchpoll, who was studiously not listening, drew his own conclusions.

'I . . . I have tried, my lord. When news came and Serjeant Catchpoll left with your horse and another I told myself it was not as at first I dreaded, for why take your mount for—' She halted and bit her lip. 'And that you did not come straight back was a good sign, was it not, for you were upon your duties.' She trembled slightly.

271

'Beloved, go to our chamber, lie down and rest. When all is over, I shall come to you.' He wanted to hold her close, but this was not the time. William de Beauchamp's voice could be heard in the passage outside. 'I fear the greatest casualties are my new boots and still-wet feet.' He smiled at her. 'Go now.'

She smiled back, squeezed his hand and left, dipping a small obeisance to the lord sheriff as she passed him.

'So, you have him.' William de Beauchamp looked at Fellman, whose shoulders now slouched. He was tired, dusty, his arm hurt where the arrow had clipped it and he had no future. His expression was sullen, and William de Beauchamp did not like it. He came close to the man, but not too close, and struck him across the face, leaving his lip split.

'A man who kills women is not just a murderer, but a coward and a cur. I hope you hang slow.' He turned to Bradecote. 'I am glad you have disappointed Furnaux. He really hoped you might just be floating face down in the river.'

'We think equally well of each other, my lord.'

'Yes, you do, I have noticed. Get the confession and do not be gentle, that is a command.'

'Understood, my lord.' Bradecote was no sadist and before he had taken up the role of undersheriff would have stood firmly against any rough treatment, but these days he felt like de Beauchamp, and Catchpoll also, that sometimes hanging of itself was too easy. Berta probably died too quickly to be very afraid, and he hoped the widow was swift, but Ricolde must have known all the way up the river that her death was coming and not a good death either. Added to that was the violence he had wreaked upon wife and daughter, not just this day but upon many days. He had dealt in pain, in fear, and a little of his own would not be wrong. 'Take him to the cell, Serjeant.'

'Yes, my lord.' Catchpoll began to drag Fellman out.

'I will have the full tale later, Bradecote.' De Beauchamp nodded, part dismissal, part acknowledgement of a job done.

'Yes, my lord.'

As Bradecote emerged into the sunlight, Walkelin trotted into the bailey, with Godfrid, somewhat slumped, up on the horse behind him. When the journeyman dismounted his legs gave way. Bradecote wondered what Walkelin had done to him, for he looked pale and sickly, but his face bore no mark of violence.

'It was not him, Walkelin.'

'I knows that, my lord. He was down by Stoke yesterday and a snake bit him. He would return because he said that if my . . . Widow Hedger wanted to find him it must be about Mistress Fellman.'

'It was. You have a daughter, Godfrid, though you have no wife.'

'Already? But—'

'She will explain.' Bradecote looked about and called a man-at-arms, knowing he was Furnaux's. 'You, help this man to the fellman's house beyond the butts, and if any ask, tell them the killer of women was Will Fellman.' He turned back to Godfrid. 'You will have need of her from the looks of it, and

273

she of you. Make your confessions to a priest, and thereafter good luck to you both. Walkelin, come with me.'

Walkelin, not entirely sure if he was in trouble or not, since he had very definitely disobeyed instructions, followed his superior without huge enthusiasm. Serjeant Catchpoll would most certainly have his hide and for what? Failure. He sighed, but then frowned as the undersheriff led him to the cell. Catchpoll had replaced the binding rope about Fellman's wrists with shackles. Walkelin opened his mouth and then shut it.

'Nice of you to join us, Walkelin,' muttered Catchpoll. 'Does Godfrid still live?'

'He does, Serjeant.'

'Good. I was wondering how we would explain another corpse to the lord Sheriff.' He did not really sound terribly bothered.

Bradecote was looking at Fellman. Just looking at him made him feel angry, not for his trying to kill him in the river, but for all else he had done.

'The lord Sheriff was right. You are a cur and a coward.' The man shrugged. 'You killed innocent women.'

'"Innocent" women?' Fellman spat derisively upon the bare floor. 'Hah! Whores.'

Walkelin gave a low growl and hit him, full force, in the face. His head jerked at the contact, and he collapsed, unconscious at Walkelin's feet.

'My aunt was no whore, and even a whore would not deserve what you did,' Walkelin yelled, though the man could not hear him. He rubbed his throbbing fist with his left hand.

'We will ask the rest of our questions in a bit then,' remarked Catchpoll, as if Walkelin resorting to violence was an everyday occurrence, and walked out.

Walkelin, inadequately concealing his pain, looked at the undersheriff, expecting to be berated. 'I am sorry, my lord, but . . . he . . .'

'Serjeant Catchpoll was right, as he usually is, though do not tell him I said so, when he said we should keep "personal" out of it, Walkelin. However, you had justification.' Bradecote's voice was very even. 'We are flesh and blood, not stone.' He said nothing more.

Catchpoll returned with a bucket of water.

'Thrust your hand in that, Walkelin, and keep it there.' He dumped the bucket on the ground and looked at the inert form of William the Fellman. 'Some that goes to hanging is duty and some is pleasure. He will be a pleasure. Only thing that surprises me is he has lasted ten years in Worcester without me having cause to take him.' He sniffed. 'Made a good job of laying him flat, I will give you that, lad. Howsoever, I think we need that bucket.' The serjeant picked up the bucket as Walkelin withdrew his hand and cast the contents over the prisoner, who woke spluttering. Just to make sure he was awake, Catchpoll kicked him.

'Now, where were we? Oh yes, you were going to tell us why, just so we are quite sure about it.'

Fellman blinked, gathering his wits. 'I don't have to tell you anything. I did it, and there's an end.'

'No, you do not,' agreed Bradecote, 'but if you do not, I am walking out of that door, and all I will say is that when you hang you will be glad that your miserable life is ending, because Walkelin here really wants to hurt you, and Serjeant Catchpoll is only too happy to give him lessons in how to do so most effectively.'

The undersheriff's very calmness was unsettling and more frightening than bluster, and Fellman looked uncertain.

'I will enjoy that, my lord,' commented Catchpoll, with relish.

'So, you tell me. When did you decide to kill Ricolde, and why, and why on Bevere Island?'

'She was a whore.'

'Yes, but you knew that ages ago, and it meant nothing. When did you discover she was your sister? When you lay with her?' Bradecote was very matter-of-fact. 'Did you think killing her atoned for your sin?'

'Speak, you guilty bastard.' Catchpoll kicked him again.

'She was like her mother, a filthy whore. I wanted her to know that, when I did for her. That is why I took her to Bevere Island, and it was easier to—'

'Chop at her? Very brotherly. So, you rendered her insensible, wrapped her in her own coverlet and carried her to the river, took a boat to get you upstream to your own moored by Oldmother Field's and stole her axe.'

'If you know it all, why ask?'

'We like to know it is as we have thought. It makes the law happy.' Bradecote smiled, but not pleasantly.

'I do not care if the law is happy or not.'

'You really should.' Bradecote nodded at Catchpoll, who altered his balance to kick again.

'All right, so it was as you say,' cried Fellman, hurriedly.

'And when you got her to the island?'

'I told her, told her about her mother and how she died. She ought to have been afraid,' Fellman clearly felt he had been cheated that she had not been. 'The bitch actually laughed, at the end she laughed.'

'Good for Ricolde,' muttered Catchpoll to himself.

'I shut her up though. The blow was near clean through. After that . . . She had dare mock me, a man, when I held the axe, when she had to die. Is it a wonder I took it to her after that?' He tried to make his actions sound good and reasonable. 'When it was done, I carried on up the river, as I had planned. It was a hot day. I let the river clean my cotte and take the coverlet that was bloodied.'

'So why kill again? Berta was not your sister, and we had released you.'

'Was that her name?' He shrugged. 'One whore less, what would it matter? I reckoned as since you had been seen going north you would find out about her beginnings, ask questions. There was nothing that linked the two other than their "trade".' He paused. 'It felt good, too, almost as good as the first one.'

Bradecote was revolted.

'And why did you kill Widow Hedger?' Catchpoll had an eye on Walkelin as he spoke.

'Poking her nose in, the old witch. She it was, no doubt, who made you think of me in the first place. She threw me out of my own home when the child was coming, and when she saw me after, she laid into me, in the street where any might hear her shrillness, for acting within my right. If a wife is lazy, disobedient, lacking, then it is a husband's right to beat her. Had I known mine was betraying me I would have slit her before the others. They are all whores I tell you, faithless whores.'

Walkelin's fists were clenched, and he was breathing rather fast.

'She told you to your face what you were, and so you killed her and defiled her with the manner of it.' Walkelin shook his head. 'May God damn you to hell eternal, you miserable bastard. If you had committed rape they would take your codd before hanging. This is the next best thing.' Fellman was kneeling, and Walkelin kicked him, full force, between the legs. Fellman crumpled, curled up and was sick. Walkelin looked at his superiors, nodded and walked out. In the passage outside he leant against the wall and tears ran down his cheeks.

Catchpoll, impassive, watched the man writhe.

'Have we all we need, my lord?'

'We have enough, Catchpoll.'

They left him, and outside, Catchpoll clapped Walkelin on the shoulder.

'There's the law and there's justice. Sometimes the one needs a little help to make it the other, lad. That was by way of a little help, not that you can tell your mother exactly how.'

Hugh Bradecote wanted to go to his wife, but he felt he had something to do first. As he walked through Worcester, he did not have the expression of a man pleased to have attained his aim. The only people who might be the happier for all that had happened were Mistress Fellman and Godfrid the journeyman. He turned down the street where Roger the Healer resided. The man was in, busy shaving bark into a dish.

'I came to tell you, Master Healer, that Ricolde will have her justice. The man who killed her was her brother, Will Fellman.'

'Her brother? I thought she had no kin in Worcester.'

'I doubt she knew, until the last.'

'I am glad, my lord, that he is taken. I shall attend the hanging. I heard as how she was . . . disfigured. You do not think it was slow, her death?' His voice begged the answer to be 'no'.

'The first blow killed her, we are sure, for it almost severed head from body.' Bradecote did not permit a trace of doubt, although he knew it must exist. The likelihood was, from the blood pooling, that most of the wounds were upon her corpse, but all? He, and he thought Catchpoll also, did not wish to think too hard upon the alternative. Well, she was beyond pain and death now, and easing this man's mind cost nothing.

The Healer shut his eyes for a moment.

'Thank you, my lord. Thank you for telling me, in person.' As he opened his eyes, he noticed the undersheriff grimace. His shoulder, where the paddle had hit it, was seizing up.

'Have you any ointments for being hit with a paddle?' Bradecote gave a small smile. It was not a serious question, but the man nodded and went to among his jars, scooping a thick paste from one into a pot that he covered with cloth. He handed it to Bradecote.

'Rub that in, my lord and it will ease it, though a bruise takes its own good time. It is good for aching muscles also.' As Bradecote reached to his scrip he raised a hand. 'No, my lord, no charge. That is my gift, for what you have done . . . for her.' He nodded his obeisance and resumed his work.

Bradecote gave his thanks and went back to the castle, his mind at first on a woman he had never seen, a woman whose life had seen much misery and had ended in blood, yet who had touched people for the better and had striven to be herself. He offered up a silent prayer for her, and then thought, more happily, of his wife awaiting him. If she rubbed the ointment into his shoulder it was bound to feel the better for it. The morning was catching up with him, and he ached and felt tired. He did hope that she would not fuss too much.

He found her laid upon the cot, as he had suggested, and she did not fuss, but said nothing, opened her arms to him and smiled. He sat upon the edge of it, pulled off his boots and lay, with a groan, so that she could be close against him.

'I will be glad to get home,' he murmured.

'Would you wish to wait until the morrow, my lord?'

'No, for then I will be stiffer even than now. I will rest an hour, and if I do not fall sound asleep and wake too late, then I will give my report to de Beauchamp and we can be gone by early evening. It is cooler then, and before we go you can be a dutiful wife.'

'It is not a duty but a pleasure, Hugh, but are you not too sore for—'

'Not that, my love.' He chuckled and winced. 'Ouch. No, the Healer has given me a pot of salve for the bruise on my

280

shoulder, where it was hit when I was in the water.' He grinned. 'I wonder what it does for chafing?'

'Ah, well in that case, it will still be a pleasure, though I wish it were not needed. You will not be swinging Gilbert up in your arms for a few days.'

'I fear not. Quite a few days.' He closed his eyes.

In fact, it was several hours before Bradecote woke. He went to seek Catchpoll, since he thought he should also be before the lord sheriff when the report was made. He found him upon the step of the kitchen, with a beaker of ale in his hand. Catchpoll rose slowly.

'I stood Walkelin down for the day, my lord. His mother has the need of him. I told him how close he had come to really annoying me, going off as he did. He is mindful of his wrongdoing.'

'It will do him no harm to learn from it. I think you and I, if your beaker is empty, will go to the lord Sheriff and give him the complete story, then I can take my lady home. I would sleep in my own bed tonight.'

'None of this would ever have happened if another had taken the same course.'

'Which should be a sign to us all,' responded Bradecote, sounding pious but smiling.

Catchpoll drained his beaker, left it beside the step and got up with his accustomed complaints.

'Let us hope the lord Sheriff is content with what he hears.'

'Could we have taken Fellman earlier, Catchpoll? That is the one thing that does not rest easy upon me. For all that Furnaux hates me to the guts and I him, he was right in that we did let Fellman go the first time.'

'We did, but at that point could we have worked out he was Ricolde's brother? No. And the proofs we were given were false. The choice was no choice then, my lord. Until we knew about the past we could not make connection to the present, and by then Berta was dead and we had others to dismiss from our list before returning to Fellman. Whatever you do, do not let your conscience lash you before the lord Sheriff. He will neither agree nor like it.'

'Sound advice, Catchpoll. Let us speak with him.'

William de Beauchamp listened to them gravely. Taking Ricolde's killer was important to him, but her death could not have been foreseen or thus avoided. The other two women were but names to him, and he was glad more that it meant the inhabitants of Worcester would not be seeing murderers in every shadow for weeks to come and blaming the law, which meant blaming him. He disliked hearing their complaints. Burgesses were like churchmen, always wanting to take more, give less and complain.

As the bell rang for Compline in the priory, Hugh Bradecote helped his lady solicitously into the saddle, and, with Tosti at her other side, hand upon bridle, they walked their horses on a loose rein out through the castle gate, his knee almost touching hers. Catchpoll was by the gate, talking to the serjeant of the guard and broke off, to recommend the lady Bradecote have a care to herself and wish them a pleasant ride back to Bradecote.

'He cannot know,' whispered Christina, as they urged their horses forward.

'I sometimes think Serjeant Catchpoll knows everything, my love, but it would be a very bad thing if he ever knew that.'

She laughed, and Catchpoll heard it as he watched them ride away towards the Sutheberi gate.

SARAH HAWKSWOOD describes herself as a 'wordsmith' who is only really happy when writing. She read Modern History at Oxford and first published a non-fiction book on the Royal Marines in the First World War before moving on to mediaeval mysteries set in Worcestershire.

bradecoteandcatchpoll.com   *@bradecote*

To discover more great books and to
place an order visit our website at
allisonandbusby.com

Don't forget to sign up to our free newsletter at
allisonandbusby.com/newsletter
for latest releases, events and exclusive offers

Allison & Busby Books
@AllisonandBusby

You can also call us on
020 3950 7834
for orders, queries
and reading recommendations